A NOVEL OF SUSPENSE

I0590451

RICK CHESLER

Author of WIRED KINGDOM and kiDNApped

Printed in the USA.

ISBN-13: 978-0-615-92401-4

10 9 8 7 6 5 4 3 2 1

Visit Rick Chesler on the web at:
http://rickchesler.com

Acknowledgements

Special thanks to the following early supporters of this book: Marty Olver Archer, Jack Graham, CL Stegall, DL Fowler, Tony Eldridge, Tyler Van Dresar, Steven of LA, David Sakmyster, Solace Winter, Michael Nazarek Jr., Patricia North-Martino, Pat Cattigan, Barry Simiana

Very special thanks to the following early supporters of this book who had a part in the development of certain characters: Michael Sullivan, Sherry Wilson, Mattias Ek, Kelley L. O'Neill, Paul Wright, Heather Matwich, Henrik Kamstrup-Nielsen

Thanks to Stan Tremblay for his tremendous cover art!

Finally, I'd like to thank YOU—for purchasing this book, and all of the wonderful readers out there who take the time to interact with me via my website and social media sites.

-1-

MODEL CITIZEN

Matt Knox squinted at the morning sun invading his family's kitchen. He tipped back his glass to down the last of his orange juice and heard the front door slam as his two kids, Gavin, ten, and Caitlin, twelve, trounced outside to meet the school bus. Matt's wife, Summer, started the dishwasher and headed for the back door of their three bedroom townhouse. She called to him as she reached the door that led to the garage.

"Let's go, hon, you're dropping me off today, we need to leave a little earlier."

Matt slid his chair out from the table and stood, gazing out across the early morning glassy water of Sandy Cove Harbor. Their home was only a smallish townhouse, but it was on the water, which in California did not come cheap. The boat slip next to the weathered back porch gave it even more character.

"Right behind you, hot stuff." Even though she bore him two children and, as Matt was fond of reminding her, they'd done "pretty much everything a couple could do together" by now, he still couldn't keep from staring at her ass while she walked. With Sandy-blond hair halfway down her back, a subtle facelift and a not-so-subtle breast augmentation, she attracted almost more attention than Matt was comfortable with. He'd even heard his son's friends whispering the word *MILF* when they thought no one could hear.

He was a lucky man, Matt was thinking, as he heard Summer open the passenger-side door to his SUV. Then he spotted the pile of broken, colored plastic on the garage floor, saw the crushed taillight from whence it came. The waterfront garage was small, the SUV almost backed right up to the wall in order to fit inside.

"Summer? What happened to the taillight?"

She eased the door open just wide enough to sheepishly poke her head outside. "I'm sorry, honey. Last night when I took it to the store—to get that *Pino Grigio*—I backed it into the wall. This beast is too big for me. I meant to tell you, I just forgot."

Matt went to the driver side and turned the ignition, flipped on the turn signal. He walked back to the rear of the vehicle and shook his head. "Bulb's smashed."

He returned to the front of the SUV and turned off the engine, pocketing the keys.

"What are you doing?" Summer looked away from the visor mirror from where she was touching up her makeup to stare at him as if he'd sprouted a third eyeball.

"I can't drive it. Light's got to be fixed. I'll take care of it today."

"After you drop me off, right?"

"No, Summer, it's against the law to drive without working taillights. I won't do it. C'mon, get out."

Summer slammed her purse into her lap. "Matt, really!" She reflected for a moment. It wasn't an attempt to control her. After all, it was her fault that she'd ignored the check engine light in her sporty little BMW for so long. And Matt did hold himself to the same standards. She knew that even if she weren't around that he wouldn't use the car until it was fixed. That was his nature and she'd known that when she married him more than a decade ago.

"Would it kill you to break a damn law for once in your life?"

"Probably not. Might kill someone else, though."

A violent episode flashed through his skull.

"What are you talking about?"

He swallowed. "I just mean that if we can't signal, it might cause an accident. The laws are there for a reason."

"I'll drive it if you won't." She held her palm out of the open door for the keys. Matt shook his head.

"It's registered in my name. No vehicle of mine operates on the roadways unless it's one hundred percent street legal."

"Matt! You said while my car is in the shop, that you'd take me to work. What am I supposed to do?"

"I'll call a cab." Matt produced his cell-phone and pecked at its keys while his wife gave an exasperated sigh of defeat and exited the SUV.

"You'll have to call two cabs. I'm in the complete opposite direction, it would be stupid to share a cab."

"I can take the boat to work." Matt's job as a manager at the harbor's waterfront yacht brokerage meant that it was possible for him to get to work by boat, although he preferred driving.

"What about fixing the car?"

"At lunch I'll get a ride to Auto Zone, pick up a replacement tail light and swap it out myself tonight."

Summer slammed the SUV's door shut. "Sometimes I wish you'd be a little less perfect, Matthew Knox." She huffed out of the garage without kissing him goodbye.

-2-
ONE OF THOSE DAYS

Matt Knox stepped into his 14-foot Boston Whaler and steadied himself when he almost slipped on the deck, wet with morning dew. Friends who didn't live in the harbor had some romantic notion that it must be great to take a boat to work, but in reality, Matt rarely did it. A five minute drive in a warm car was much better than a twenty minute slog in an open boat on the wind, plus tying and untying the dock lines. He cursed when the outboard motor failed to start on the first pull. It cranked to life on the second, but he made a mental note to give it a tune-up this weekend.

Probably from lack of use, Matt suspected, eyeing the larger vessel that also occupied the dock in front of his home, a 42-foot sailboat. Courtesy of the yacht brokerage he worked for, he'd been taking potential buyers out on it lately, but it was far too large to be practical for the cross-harbor jaunt.

He cast off the lines of his Whaler and eased out of his slip into the small harbor channel. Matt waved to a retired neighbor jogging past with his dog on a walkway that paralleled the channel. It was a chilly morning despite it being mid June, not unusual for central California, and his breath fogged over his GPS display as he leaned over the unit to switch it on.

Matt didn't need the GPS for directions—he knew exactly where he was going, but a small boat like his didn't come with a speedometer, so he relied on the GPS to tell him how fast he was going through the harbor's posted five mph NO WAKE zones. It was hard to tell, after all, exactly how fast five mph was, especially with a breeze like there was today, and, like always, Matt wished to obey the law.

He reached the end of his small residential channel and made the turn into a wider harbor thoroughfare. A sleek speedboat, ignoring the no wake signs, caught up with him. Its pilot, another of the Knox's neighbors, called out to Matt. He easily recognized the European accent along with his long hair tied back in an auburn ponytail. He was from Sweden but here on some kind of sponsored visa working as a geologist for the state using some new Swedish technology to study one of the major fault lines that ran nearby Sandy Cove. When they first met at a neighborhood barbeque they had shared a laugh over the fact that they had basically the same name, and had been casual friends ever since.

"Sell your catamaran?" Mattias asked as he rolled up the sleeves on his seemingly ever-present green flannel shirt.

Matt nodded. His neighbors were used to seeing him with a different yacht every few weeks. He had the use of one from his brokerage to entertain potential clients until they sold. "Yeah, it went to a guy down in Santa Barbara, but now I've got a Hunter 42—barely fits at my dock, you've got to come by and see it!"

"I'll do that. Wine tasting at our place this Friday, hope you can make it."

"Sounds good, Mattias!" Matt said, as his friend's boat pulled away, leaving his little Whaler to bounce over its wake. Clearly, his neighbor wasn't worried about the speed limit, Matt thought, but then again most owners in Sandy Cove Harbor weren't. They lived here. Most paid property taxes and homeowner's association fees. Their taxes paid for the Harbormaster, after all, so why should they worry if they wanted to get where they're going a little faster? It was the rental boats they should be concerned with. It irked Matt that he was the only owner he knew of who regularly followed the "rules," as he heard Mattias and other neighbors refer to them—as if to diminish their importance.

But Matt knew that in fact they were real laws, and he intended to obey them.

He motored on through the harbor, now passing much nicer homes than his own—single family houses with true yards and large decks, still right on the water with even larger private boat docks than his own. There was no way he'd ever be able to afford one of these by working his brokerage job, that was for sure. Not that he was complaining. Many of the boats parked along these million-dollar-plus homes had been purchased through him. He made a good living and he and his family were lucky enough to live where they did.

Matt passed under a bridge to the harbor's commercial section where the waterway widened considerably. Sea lions basked on the swim steps of the larger boats, seagulls squawked overhead, and a Harbor Patrol boat passed by Matt heading under the bridge in the opposite direction.

The law enforcement officer merely smiled and waved at the pilot of the little Boston Whaler. He knew that Matt "the saint" Knox, as was his nickname in the harbor community, would have nothing worth writing up. As usual, he maintained a well running vessel, current registration stickers, life jacket on, no stray lines hanging over the side of his boat. Matt Knox's boat never slowed down immediately when a patrol boat came within sight, as almost all other boats routinely did. He didn't have to, because he was already within the speed limit. Everything was in perfect order.

The officer gave Matt a bored wave as he passed, making his rounds through the harbor. Matt returned the gesture with a smile before focusing on his destination ahead on the right.

Sandy Cove Yacht Brokers.

Should be an okay day at work, Matt thought, throttling down as he approached the expansive dock fronting the decades-old harbor business.

And then he saw one of his employees, John Samson, step outside the back door onto the walkway above the dock and point right at Matt's Whaler. A second man followed John out of the office. John retreated back into the building but the guest remained on the dock, his eyes closely tracking Matt's progress as he neared the brokerage.

Sal Jonason, Matt thought to himself as he cut power and glided up to the dock. *This isn't going to be such a good day after all.*

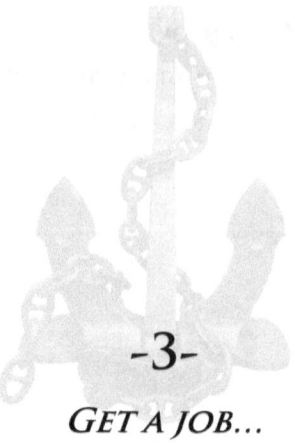

-3-
GET A JOB...

Jeremy Washington rubbed his temples while contemplating the pile of bills on his kitchen table. Eight A.M. Normally he'd be in his police cruiser by this time, making his rounds. Sitting alone at home just didn't feel right, but he had nowhere else to go. Wife at work, kids in daycare. He wasn't sure how much longer that daycare was going to last with him out of a job. He'd be watching the kids himself any day now.

The near subsonic bass of a rap track from a car stereo pounded through his thin walls. A knock sounded at the door of his shabby two-bedroom on the outskirts of town.

Wedged between agricultural fields on one side and a small but seedy commercial strip on the other, Jeremy was pressured in one direction by blowing dust, pesticides and migrant worker shanty-towns, and on the other by a stream of light but ever-present traffic to storage units, tattoo parlors, sports bars and a strip club. Sandy Cove in name only. To get to the beach meant a nearly thirty minute drive made longer by having to go the long way around the gated harbor and beachside enclaves.

"Come in," Jeremy said without looking up from his bills.

"I heard how it went down, man, how you doin'?" This from a Hispanic man about thirty years old. His jeans and T-shirt were covered in oily grease stains.

"Hey, Pablo," Jeremy acknowledged, still sorting through his bills. No matter how he did the math in his head, he couldn't see how he was going to be able to manage it all.

"Read about it in the papers," Pablo went on. "Shit! I'm sorry, Jer, man."

Jeremy looked up at his childhood friend, Pablo Sorocaba. "No worries," he mumbled.

Pablo looked around the living room, then toward the adjoining kitchen. "Alisa?"

"At work."

Pablo appeared to relax a bit and then took a seat on the couch next to Jeremy. "I just got off shift at the shop." He eyed the pile of paperwork on the table before reaching into his pocket.

"Here. Sal wants you to have this. It's from all of us." He tossed a roll of bills onto the table. Jeremy glared at his friend.

"What the fuck, you think I'm some kind of charity case?" It sat there on the household bills, at once the cause of and the solution to his problems.

Pablo averted his eyes while making some sort of shrugging motion. "We thought it would help out, you know, until you find another gig." He swept a hand toward the pile of bills.

Jeremy spoke slow and soft, his eyes still on the money. "You know I wouldn't need another gig in the first place if it wasn't for your money."

Pablo stood up from the couch immediately. "Hey man, you kept an eye out for us, and that's cool. We paid you for that. That was your prerogative, man. Not our fault you got busted. You were snitched from *your* side."

Jeremy looked up at Pablo and then hung his head, rubbing his temples again. "They said I'm not eligible for unemployment. Fired for cause."

Pablo eased back onto the couch. "We're setting something up right now. Something different. Not a gas station or a store. It's going down soon, but you could still get in on it. You know every cop in town, their schedules, how they operate..."

"Stop! Don't say another word, Pablo. I'm going to pretend I didn't hear that."

"But—"

"Don't! I'm lucky as it is that I only lost my job over this. They could have put me in jail. You know what happens to cops in jail?"

"Okay. I—we—thought that maybe if you would...if you would, take, you know..." Pablo stumbled over the words, digging his sneakered toe into the worn carpet.

"You thought that if I would take *bribes* to look the other way when I was on the job, that maybe now that I'm out of a job I'd help you guys actually rob something, join the gang for real after all this time, is that it?"

Pablo looked into his friend's eyes, gaze unwavering, but giving no verbal response.

"The answer is no, Pablo. I regret helping the gang like I did. I wanted the money to put my kid in a private school because Alisa says that's what he needs. But it's wrong."

Jeremy grabbed the roll of bills off the table and pressed the money into Pablo's chest, gripping his shoulder tightly.

"Tell Sal I said *No!*"

Pablo grabbed the cash, got up without another word and walked to the front door. Once there, he said, "Good luck, Jeremy." He opened the door and walked out.

"Don't do anything stupid, Pablo."

THE CUSTOMER IS ALWAYS RIGHT

Sal Jonason held out a hand as Matt's whaler glided up to the dock. Matt ignored his offer of help and instead tied the line to a cleat himself. Sal grabbed his bow line without being asked and pulled the front of the boat into the dock, securing that line.

"Something I can do for you, Mr. Jonason?" Matt asked as he stepped onto the dock.

"Yes sir, Mr. Knox, I'd like to test drive a boat."

Matt continued walking toward the entrance to his yacht brokerage.

"I said I'd like to test drive a boat!" Sal repeated, raising his voice this time. Matt turned back to Sal as he pulled the door open.

"When did you get out of jail?"

Sal Jonason tugged at his long, gray beard. He lifted his sunglasses from his eyes and parked them atop his shaved head. "I don't see how that's any of your business, Mr. Knox. Now listen here, I may not be a saint like you, but I have the same rights as any customer."

"You have to pass a credit check for a test drive, like any customer," Matt said as he entered the brokerage and let the door close after him. He was face-to-face with his employee John Samson as soon as he entered the business.

"He already passed the credit check," John said.

"Did you check his ID carefully?"

John nodded. "It checks out. We've sold boats to worse credit scores than his."

Matt frowned. He didn't think Sal would have been able to pass a credit check. A local boy gone bad, Sal Jonason was the town thug. A semi-professional thief in charge of a loose cadre of local hoodlums, he'd been in and out jail over the years. He sometimes held down a job as a commercial fisherman, but most of the locals suspected this was just to give the appearance that he had a legitimate income. But if he had passed the credit check, Matt knew they would have to give him the test drive.

John read his mind. "I can't do it. I'm already booked to take the Westons out on the Sea Ray. They're driving up from Montecito right now."

Matt exhaled slowly. "That's a solid lead, John, and I know you've been working hard to get them in here. You focus on that, I'll deal with Sal."

Just then the brokerage door opened and Sal stepped inside. "I'm looking for a cabin cruiser," he said.

Matt gave him the kind of look most people reserved for panhandlers before addressing John.

"Get me the keys to the Chris Craft."

-5-

HARD SELL

Matt Knox eased the forty-two foot cabin cruiser from its slip out into the harbor channel. From his peripheral vision he watched Sal Jonason take hasty little drags from his cigarette, glancing out at the harbor, then back to the dock, then to the sides. *Strange*, Matt thought. Most people thinking about buying a boat observed Matt like a hawk while he operated the craft.

Not this guy. Now Sal was speaking softly into one of those phone earpieces Matt always thought people wore to try to look important while they talked about the same stuff as everybody else. He saw him glance at his watch and turn away when he caught Matt's gaze.

This freeloader is probably just looking for a free harbor tour. But deep down this assessment didn't really sit well with Matt since Sal was at least sometimes a commercial fisherman. He'd been out on the harbor plenty of times. *He can probably handle a boat pretty well, too.* Still, he had requested a test drive and passed the credit check so it was Matt's job to show him the boat in action. He cleared his throat loudly to be heard over the din of the cruiser's engines.

"No bow thrusters, but we could retrofit some if that's important to you."

Sal flicked his butt into the water around turned around, apparently finished with his phone conversation. "Thrusters on a boat this size? It's not like this is a goddamn cruise ship. Fuck the thrusters."

Matt raised his eyebrows and let out a sigh. Thrusters were expensive little propulsion devices that allowed the boat to be controlled in tight spaces with a joystick as opposed to wrangling the wheel. It was an attitude he'd heard before from boating purists, especially commercial operators who really did know what they were doing.

But then why is this guy here? Commercial guys who know boats well usually do their own shopping without a dealer.

"I'm simply explaining the features of the boat to you, Mr. Jonason."

Sal stepped over to the wheel. "Let me drive."

Matt completed the turn out into the main channel and then stepped aside as Sal took his place. Once in control of the boat, Sal squinted ahead at the waterway, barely even glancing at the controls. Again, Matt thought, hardly the actions of someone considering a major purchase.

Matt told Sal some details about the controls, but the prospective customer merely listened without comment.

Then Sal bumped up the throttle, increasing their speed. They passed a smaller boat filled with tourists.

"Slow it back down until we're outside the harbor, please," Matt said. "No wake zone here."

Sal glared at Matt. It was the first thing Matt had said since getting into the boat that had elicited any real response from Sal. He maintained the speed.

"I don't want to go outside the harbor on this run. Wanna see how she handles in here."

"That's fine, Sal, but you'll need to slow it back down. We've got a good relationship with the harbormaster and need to keep it that way to do business here. Slow down."

Sal pulled another smoke from the pocket of his loose fitting sweatshirt and cupped his hand over it to shield it from the wind as he lit it. He looked Matt in the eye while he waited for the light to catch.

In his mind, Matt *rammed the heel of his right hand into Sal's face, shoving the newly lit cigarette all the way into his mouth...*

Sal pocketed his lighter and exhaled a cloud of smoke toward Matt as he calmly shifted the throttle back down. "Forgot I'm dealing with Matt the Saint," he smirked. Then he turned the boat abruptly, left into a smaller canal style waterway lined with private homes on either side, most with large yachts in front of them.

"Want to get a feel for how she handles in tight quarters, I guess?" Matt prompted.

"Something like that. Like to try docking too. Here looks like a good spot."

Up ahead on the right was an empty section of dock next to a huge, old wooden sailboat. Sal reduced speed and angled the boat toward the empty space.

"Whoa, Sal, what're you doing? That's a private dock. We can go to the public docks, or you can dock us back at the shop."

Sal ignored him while he continued to maneuver the boat. Matt could see that he was highly competent, his hands working the controls with practiced ease as the cruiser sidled easily up to the dock.

"Go ahead and tie a line for me, would you?" Sal said.

Matt's cheeks flushed crimson. "I will not! I just asked you not to dock here because this is private property." He looked up at the large house, hoping to see someone there getting ready to shoo them away, but it was clear from the way the deck furniture was covered that this was likely a second home for owners who hadn't yet taken up summer residence.

Matt looked away from the house and back to Sal, who pointed at the sailboat they were now docked next to.

"Matt, I need you to get me something out of that boat."

-6-

...YOU LAZY BUM

Jeremy Washington tossed the classified ads section of the newspaper down on the table. Job prospects were nil. Maybe he should check the Internet, he thought, and went to track down the laptop he shared with his wife. He didn't use it much. Never had time, what with being a cop, spending time with his family, and what little there was left for his friends after that.

He found the machine on the kitchen counter. His wife used it for recipes there and gabbing with her friends on social networks. Jeremy took it back over to the couch, where he flipped it open and brought up a well known classified ads site for the Sandy Cove region.

What the hell can I do besides be a cop, Jeremy thought, not knowing where to start looking. He'd been an officer for ten years, joining the police academy two years out of Sandy Cove high school. For those first two years, he'd sold used cars. He scanned the Sales section but found nothing about cars, just a bunch of marketing crap, MAKE $10,000 A MONTH WORKING FROM HOME b.s.

Just beneath Sales he saw it. Security guards. If he couldn't be a cop he could always be a rent-a-cop. That wasn't a step down, right? Nine bucks an hour. Jeremy felt the frustration begin to well up inside him and clicked away from the job ads. The silly uniform, lack of respect and not being licensed to carry a firearm he could handle. But nine bucks was not going to support his family even if he worked double shifts. He navigated to the weekend's basketball scores and looked at those instead to take his mind off his predicament.

He was still reading about the games a few minutes later when his wife walked in.

"Hey, Alisa. You're early." He didn't expect her back from her hair styling job for two more hours. She barely looked at him as she breezed into the kitchen and dropped her purse on the counter. "They cut my hours back a little at the salon. I'll have to see about picking up some more, maybe over at Stylez, but for right now we're going to have less coming in. How's your search going?" She opened the fridge, saw that it was mostly empty, closed the door again and looked over at Jeremy who was fixated on the screen.

"So far, not so good," he said.

Alisa frowned and walked over to the couch. She sat down next to her husband. "Well Jeremy, you're not going to find a job watching game highlights. How long have you been doing that? Did you even look for a job today?"

Jeremy sighed and got up from the couch, leaving the computer on the table. "I was looking until right before you came in. Believe me there's nothing great right now."

"Jer, I'm calling Lydia's daycare today to cancel for next month. If you get something..."

"That's fine. I'll watch her."

"Now what are you doing?"

"I was going to wash the car."

"Jeremy, come on!"

"What? It looks like crap."

"Who cares? We need money, Jeremy. Even on your police salary we were pretty much paycheck to paycheck. We can go maybe another month, if we cut out the daycare. Max. What are you going to do?"

In their five years of marriage, it was the first time Alisa had been confronted with a lack of money. Jeremy felt like he was letting her down, and what made that worse was knowing he'd screwed up his job all by himself. It's not like he got laid off due to budget cuts. He'd been straight-up fired (shit-canned, some of his buddies said), for crossing the line. A line Alisa had unknowingly pressed him to cross, in order to put their oldest child Octavier in a private school because the public ones had become gang central. And now their youngest wouldn't even be able to stay in pre-school.

"I really don't know. I'll find something. Every day I'll look."

"You can't just *look* every day, Jeremy, you have to *apply* for something every day."

"I don't see anything to apply for."

"Olivia says they're hiring security guards at the mall. Her son just got a job there."

"Shit." Alisa's coworker's son was nineteen, fresh out of high school. "Well?"

Jeremy walked to the door, throwing his hooded sweatshirt on.

"Where you going?"

"I'm going to do what you said. Apply for a job. But I'm going to pound the pavement, the old fashioned way, in person. I know some people. That online crap doesn't work for me."

"Where are you going to go? You're not just going to go out and drink with the boys are you?"

"No. I'm going to the yacht dealership over at the harbor."

"The *yacht* dealership? What do you know about yachts?"

"I used to sell cars, remember? So I have vehicle sales experience. Plus, my old high school buddy John Samson works there. If they do have anything, he'll hook me up."

Alisa perked up a bit, nodding. "Yeah, okay. That's what I'm talking about. Good luck, honey!"

-7-

THIS DOG DOESN'T FETCH

"That's Dallas Draper's boat," Matt said. "I sold it to him a couple of years ago."

Sal nodded. "He's got a ring of keys in there somewhere in the salon, I need you to go in there and get it for me."

The squawking call of a seagull broke the silence before Matt responded. "What for? You doing some work for him?"

"Something like that." Sal's cellular phone lit up and he scrutinized its screen before putting it back in his pocket without having spoke.

Matt looked at the boat. Its canvas wheelhouse cover was buttoned down tight liked it hadn't been used in a while. As usual, the beautiful teak decking was oiled and polished to a shine. Glancing up at Dallas' house, though, one over from the one they were docked at, he could see kids' toys in the yard and recent gardening projects in progress.

"The Drapers don't leave town for the winter. If you need something from Dallas, go ask him yourself. Not to mention, Sal, this is supposed to be a test drive, not a chance for you to run err–"

Matt forgot about whatever he was going to say as his mind processed the fact that Sal now pointed a pistol at his chest.

-8-

HE WHO HAS THE GUN

Matt slowly put his hands in the air. "Okay, okay. Calm down. I'll get the keys. I don't know what's going on, but I'll get you the keys."

What worried Matt even more than having a gun pointed at him was the fact that the holder of that gun seemed to be nervous. The barrel wavered while Sal's eyes darted about in their sockets like rats in a maze.

He's probably on crystal meth or something, Matt thought. Whatever it was, he was clearly not in his right mind.

"Good. Put your hands back down and start walking." Sal jerked the gun toward the dock.

In his mind, Matt *darted to Sal and grabbed the gun before he could aim it at him again. He jabbed the barrel up hard under Sal's shocked face, into the soft spot under his chin, and pulled the trigger...*

In actuality, Matt slowly made his way to the side of the boat while Sal tracked him with the shaky pistol. Matt reached the side and unlatched a section of rail that lifted out of the way on a hinge.

"Don't try anything. I ain't in the mood." Sal wobbled the gun in his hand as if to demonstrate his loose grasp on reality. He must have been barely holding it together at the brokerage, Matt thought, knowing he was going to go through with this crazy thing, and when he actually started doing it the stress took hold.

"I don't know what your problem is, Sal, but you must be pretty desperate to try something like this. Maybe I can help if you just put the gun down."

"Shut up. Get the keys. Anybody asks you what you're doing, you say you're just checking on a good customer's boat. Make some shit up, but make it believable. I'll be monitoring the radio, too, so don't get cute. You contact anybody and I shoot up that boat with you in it. Don't care what happens after that. I'd probably take myself out along with you. Clear?"

"Crystal." The guy was even more on the edge than Matt had suspected. He began to wonder if he would live through this.

"Give me your cell-phone. Real slow."

Matt did as he was told, tossing him the device from a safe distance.

"Now go. Be quick about it."

Matt stepped out onto the dock. There were no other boats operating in this quiet side channel, and he saw no people in the waterfront yards, which was not unusual for a Monday morning. He moved at a brisk walk down the short stretch of dock to Dallas Draper's yacht.

A floating yet functional antique, Matt had sold the one-of-a-kind yacht to Mr. Draper after an exhaustive multi-year search for an all-wooden vessel in good working order. Definitely the most unique boat he'd ever sold, it stood miles apart from the mass produced chrome-and-fiberglass jobs he dealt with every day. Dallas was head curator at the local maritime museum, a professional nautical buff, and he'd made it perfectly clear that only a "real wooden sailing vessel" would do, and nothing built after 1950. When Matt finally sold him the sailboat, Dallas had been so pleased that he gave Matt the equivalent of his annual Christmas bonus as a tip.

Matt shook aside the memories as he walked up to the yacht's rail. *Concentrate. Do what he wants. Stay alive.*

After casting a sideways glance at Sal, who gave him a friendly looking wave without showing the gun, Matt stepped aboard Dallas Draper's pride and joy.

-9-

HERE YOU GO

"Dallas? Hello, anybody onboard?"

Matt Knox's topsiders padded across the teak deck planks as he made his way toward the main cabin. Wood doors closed it off, but Matt could see that they were unlocked. He pulled the doors open and stepped down a short flight of stairs into the yacht's salon.

From in here Matt could see through the windows to the Chris Craft beyond and the figure of Sal Jonason standing at the wheel. Mounted on the wall at the bottom of the stairs was a marine radio. Matt eyed it longingly but continued past it deeper into what served as the "living room" of the yacht.

Curved beams overhead framed an elegant space, well lit by rows of brass portholes on either side in addition to a skylight hatch on the ceiling. A combination kitchen and wet bar occupied one corner while a dining booth was built in directly across from that. A couch and bookshelves lined much of the room's remaining wall space.

Matt's eyes were drawn to the wall over the sink, and there he saw it. *Almost too easy.* A keychain holder made from wood and bamboo matting in the shape of a dolphin. A single keychain hung from one of its posts. Matt went to it. It was a knot of rope about the size of a large gumball attached to a brass ring with several keys on it. Matt instantly recognized the knot as a common mariner's knot known as a monkey's fist, used to create a weighted line. And in the old days, Matt thought, larger ones were used as weapons.

He peered through a window and saw Sal peering right back at him. He noticed that he now wore a hat and sunglasses where before he only wore the glasses.

Hey, that's my hat! The bastard is wearing my hat! Matt had left his baseball cap on the dash of the Chris Craft last weekend when it was sunny out during another test drive. *If that's all he wants I'll consider myself lucky. If a guy with a gun wants my hat, he can have it, no problem.*

Matt snagged the keys off the rack and pocketed them. He exited the cabin, closing the doors behind him. Outside on deck Matt was startled to see a Harbor Patrol boat prowling out toward the main harbor from deeper inside the canal neighborhood, behind them. It was the same officer who had waved at Matt earlier in his Whaler.

Matt watched as the patrolman glanced over at the Chris Craft. *He probably knows it doesn't belong there.* Then Matt froze in shock as Sal gave a friendly wave to the patrolman from behind his hat and glasses. The officer returned the wave.

He probably thinks Sal is me!

Matt watched the patrol boat pass into the main harbor channel and turn left, toward the ocean. Then he hopped off the yacht onto the dock.

He walked back to the Chris Craft and stepped aboard.

-10-

I DIDN'T SIGN UP FOR THIS

Matt Knox plunked the monkey's fist into Sal Jonason's waiting palm, the one not wrapped around the pistol.

"Can I go now, Sal? You can take the boat if you want."

Sal waved the gun from Matt to the steering wheel. "Take us out to the main channel and make a right." He took a seat in the high chair opposite the captain's seat and let the gun dangle between his knees.

"Okay." Matt was pleased with that direction since it was back toward his dealership. Not that he supposed it mattered whether he was pleased with it or not, but he hoped it meant that his ordeal was almost over. He turned the boat around while Sal propped his feet up on the dash.

A few minutes later they were turning into the main channel, heading back deeper into the harbor. An electric powered pontoon boat passed them going the other way, its operator and sole passenger giving them an absent-minded wave.

"Go ahead and wave back," Sal said, waving himself at the pleasure craft. Matt gritted his teeth and did as he was told. He knew that Sal wanted them to blend right into the harbor scene, not to stand out in any way, and that included returning waves.

Out of habit Matt glanced at the instrument panel and noted their speed: exactly 5 mph. Then he laughed out loud at the absurdity of his practiced action. *I'm worried about being pulled over for a speeding ticket while I'm being boat-jacked—pirated—by a lunatic with gun! Getting stopped would be the best thing possible for me right now...*

"What's so funny?" Sal demanded.

It took Matt a second to realize that his laughter hadn't been only in his head. *Think fast.*

"Just nervous I guess."

Sal blew a cloud of smoke his way but said nothing. A few minutes later he pointed down a small side canal. "Go down there."

Matt turned into the small residential waterway.

"All the way down to the end and make a left."

Matt knew that there was no outlet from that passage. It was an aquatic cul-de-sac, a dead end except for the people who lived there. They reached the end of the canal and Matt made the left. He looked both ways but saw no other boats being used, only those tied at their home docks.

Up ahead on the right loomed a new home once under construction but put on indefinite hiatus since an economic downturn affected home sales in the area. Its bare cinderblock walls reached for the sky from a weedy lot. A realtor sign lay knocked over in the dirt.

"Pull up here," Sal said, pointing at the bare concrete wall beneath the construction site.

Matt put the boat in idle but made no move for the wheel. "There's no dock there."

"Put out your fenders and ease up against the wall."

By now Matt could see that arguing would only prolong his ordeal. He felt reasonably sure Sal didn't intend to kill him here—there were inhabited houses on either side and a busy road not far beyond. Matt concentrated on cajoling the large craft up to the concrete wall—where a dock would be placed if this home was ever completed.

He heard Sal jump down to the deck and walk back to the stern. When Matt looked up from his maneuvering he was surprised to see three other men walking toward the boat from out of the partially constructed dwelling. At first Matt thought they might be construction workers from the house, but although they looked like they could be dressed for that kind of job, they carried no tools. Sal waved them over.

As they neared, Matt recognized one of the men as being one of Sal's crime gang members from around town.

"C'mon Pablo," Sal said to the man, who had stopped to tie his shoe. He stood up and trotted to the boat.

"What's going on, Sal?" Matt demanded. Sal's trio of cohorts jumped onto the cruiser and then Sal pushed the boat away from the wall.

All three men filed into the main cabin, waving and saying a quick greeting to Matt and Sal before closing the door behind them.

"Who are you people?" Matt called after them. They ignored him.

"Sal?" Matt repeated the question.

Sal took his seat again opposite the captain's chair. "Take us back out to the main channel, turn right."

-11-

IF IT WALKS LIKE A DUCK

Flustered, Matt shifted his gaze from the closed cabin door–behind which three of Sal's associates were now doing who knows what–to Sal himself and then to the residential canal that led to the main harbor channel. "Sal," he said as he turned the yacht's wheel, "are you...are you..."

Sal glared at Matt while the yacht dealer grasped for the word. "Are you *pirating* me?"

Sal chuckled. "No, matey. Just taking a little test drive, see if she's right for me." He slapped the dashboard a couple of times.

"Well, Sal, I'd say your test drive's about up. You've seen how she handles in the harbor, like you asked. I've got to get her back to the brokerage—"

"We've got one more stop, matey, then I promise ye, you'll ride this old scow right back to the dealer, you will. Yarrrrrgh!" Sal threw his head back in a hearty laugh. Matt's eyes went to the pistol dangling ever so casually now from his right hand.

Matt called them "mind crimes." Crimes he committed only within the confines of the neural mass in his skull. For as long as he could remember, these mental enactments of crimes both large and small had kept something within at bay and had allowed him to live a one hundred percent law abiding life. He had long supposed they were some kind of stress relief mechanism cooked up by his brain in response to conforming so rigidly to life's pressures, but he had never told anyone about them, not even his wife.

And he never fought them. In fact, he usually welcomed them as a way of tuning out a boring situation, like stealing a pack of gum while waiting in a long store line, or perhaps robbing a bank while waiting to see a teller. Like a sort of daydream, he fell into a semi-functional trance during a mind crime, as he did now, while piloting a yacht through the harbor that he knew as well as his own back yard, which in fact it was...

Sal was turned sideways in the swivel seat, head thrown back, still laughing about being called a pirate, his gun dangling from one hand. Matt rammed the throttle to full speed ahead, the sudden acceleration knocking Sal from his perch. The pirate landed awkwardly on one of his kneecaps followed quickly by an elbow. Matt was sorry it wasn't his skull, but he sure wasn't sorry that the gun now lay by itself on the deck between him and Sal.

The pirate made a move for his pistol, but Matt hopped down from the captain's chair, getting to the weapon while Sal still crawled toward it. Sal put his hands up in a gesture of meek surrender.

"You win, man. It's cool."

Matt backed up to the cabin door and slipped a padlock through the door latch. Then he walked back over to Sal and said, "Bring me the gas can from the dinghy."

The cabin cruiser sported a small inflatable boat hanging off the back. Sal's face contorted into a mask of pain and anguish. "Look, man, that's crazy. You don't have to do that. It's over. I'll jump overboard right now if you want. So will my guys. Or call the cops."

"Too late for that. Do it or I'll shoot." Matt lowered the barrel to aim for one of Sal's kneecaps, the same one he smashed falling to the deck. Sal limped over to the dinghy and fetched the gas can. Matt kept the gun pointed at Sal while he grabbed the fuel can and backed up to the locked cabin door. He poured the gas around the bottom of the door. It was old wood and not an airtight seal.

"Mr. Knox! Please don't do that!"

"Give me a light."

Sal started to cry. "I—I ain't got one. What the f-"

"You've been blowing your fucking smoke in my face all goddamn morning. Give me a light."

Sal slowly reached into his pocket and removed a silver butane lighter decorated with a black skull and crossbones. Matt cackled upon seeing its design.

"See. A pirate, I told you! Now light it for me."

"Please, Mr.—"

"Do it. He cocked the pistol's hammer."

Sal produced a flame from the lighter that danced in the harbor breeze.

"Toss it." He indicated the pool of gasoline at the foot of the cabin door.

Pablo started to protest but Matt aimed the gun at his head. Sal tossed the lighter. The entire door was alight instantly. Sal looked like he was about to freak out and run for it.

"Close your eyes."

Sal looked confused. "What for?" Urgent yelling now emanated from within the cabin below.

"Do it or I shoot." Sal closed his eyes.

Matt kicked him as hard as he could in the face...

"Are you deaf? I said, right fucking *here!*" Sal's voice brought Matt back to reality as he snapped out of his reverie and took in their surroundings: Still in the harbor. Main channel. Not as far up as the turnoff for the yacht brokerage, but still in the main commercial section. There were on-the-water seafood restaurants here, jet-ski and kayak rentals. Being Monday morning, traffic of any kind was light.

"Lookit where I'm pointing at!" Sal demanded. Matt saw that he had in fact been pointing out a specific destination. He followed his finger to the shore on their right. The lettering on the sign of the weathered wooden building was faded but still legible, especially to Matt:

SANDY COVE MARITIME MUSEUM

A knot formed in Matt's stomach. He wished he had actually gone through with his mind crime. If it was self-defense it wasn't against the law, right? But it was too late now. He fought back with an obvious defense, but one he also recognized as being pitiful.

"Sal, the museum's closed today. It's closed every Monday."

As he had feared, Matt's suspicion that Sal was well aware of this fact became apparent when he fished the monkey's fist out of his pocket.

-12-

CULTURAL ENLIGHTENMENT

"Take the keys and open the museum front door. I'll be right behind you."

Matt hadn't thought much about what Dallas' keys opened, but the Sandy Cove Maritime Museum made perfect sense. Dallas was curator of this museum. That he kept a spare key on his yacht, which could take him to the museum on the water, should have been no surprise.

"I'm not going in there."

Sal looked at Matt as if he were a teacher confronted with the dumbest kid in class for the third time that day. He pointed the pistol at Matt through his sweatshirt pocket.

"It won't take long. Believe me when I say it's not worth fighting over. We go in, take care of a little business, we come back out and that's it. You take your boat back alone."

"I'm dropping you off here?" Matt was pleased at the prospect of being rid of them.

"Now you're gettin' it."

"Why do you need me to go in? You have the keys."

"Because we do. You want to stand around talking about it all day or just go do it?"

"Do *what*?"

Sal cocked his head to one side. "Dallas asked me to do a little inventory work for the museum."

"Yeah, right! That's why you have me at gunpoint?"

"I haven't slept in two days, man, I'm not thinking straight. I told you I'm really on edge. I could fucking snap at any second."

"I can see that, Sal, so why don't you go in with the keys I got you and do whatever you're going to do? What do you need me for in there?"

"'Cuz nobody will think twice about Matt the Saint Knox walkin' into the museum with a key, that's why. Now take the keys."

Matt gave Sal what he hoped was an evil look and took the monkey's fist that dangled from Matt's hand. He stepped off the boat onto an empty dock and walked up a gangway to the sidewalk fronting the museum. Matt was very close behind him, almost giving him a "flat tire," as Matt heard his kids say. Below in the boat, Matt could hear the three men coming up out of the cabin, laughing, joking. They sounded like they'd been drinking.

The museum was in an old Victorian style two-story house. Not a large building. A hand-carved but now faded sign reading, SANDY COVE MARITIME MUSEUM hung from ropes over an entrance alcove. Wooden double doors offered no glimpse as to what lay inside, but a wood etched sign framed by seashells and bearing the establishment's hours of operation hung from a chain on the door. Next to MONDAY it read CLOSED. Every other day had hours of 10-4.

Matt stepped up to the door and took a quick look around. He saw no one, nor could he hear anyone beyond the museum's closed doors. He tried the door anyway, to see if it might be open. It was not.

"Hurry it up," Sal rasped from behind him.

Matt examined the keys that hung from the monkey's fist. He'd never really taken a good look at them until now. About a dozen keys. One of them, Matt couldn't help but notice, was an iron skeleton key. It looked old. The rest appeared to be normal keys of various sizes. He picked the largest one excepting the skeleton key and tried it in the door.

It turned with a *click*, and Matt pushed the door open.

-13-

Taking Inventory

Sal shoved Matt over the threshold into the museum. Matt steadied himself and took a look around the entrance hall. He'd been here a couple of times before on family excursions, the last time about two years ago. As he recalled, his kids had been pretty bored, breezing through the place as quickly as possible so as to put the rest of a summer day to better use. Dimly lit from high above, Matt recognized the wall mural depicting the map of Earth known to sailors of the 1700s. Upon its stylized ocean waves, imaginatively rendered sea monsters destroyed ships and consumed men.

Sal's three accomplices rumbled through the door after him. The cavernous space darkened further with the closing of the door. Matt watched as Sal pulled on a pair of white latex gloves and the other three men did the same. A couple of them had flashlights and they flicked them on. The two without lights unfolded large, empty duffel bags.

"What's going on, Sal?" Matt asked, terrified now.

"Stay with me, Matt ole boy. You're the key man, as in, you've got the keys." Behind them one of Sal's men chortled loudly.

"Pablo! Shut it. Let's get to work."

At the center of the entrance hall was a glass display case on a pedestal, containing an antique brass diving helmet. Pablo raised a pipe wrench to it. He motioned to one of their associates, a stocky Mexican sporting tattoos of cursive writing on his neck.

"Juanito, put the bag over it, won't be so loud." The man lay his bag over the display cube. As was intended, the canvas muffled the sound of Pablo's wrench shattering the glass. Juan shook the glass off the bag while Pablo hefted his prize.

"This thing's *heavy*, man!" he said, easing it into the duffel.

Sal watched over the act before proclaiming, "Good work, boys. Let's fill 'er up and get 'er done!" He pointed his pistol at Matt, who had been standing silently, watching the theft-in-progress. "Move it, Saint. Stay with me." Sal waved the pistol deeper into the museum, where two long rows of display cases framed a central room featuring several standalone exhibit cases.

Matt walked over to one of the cases. He stood there as Sal pointed at the case and Pablo followed with his pipe wrench. Soon a lot of old seafaring tools found their way into Sal's duffel bags: sextants, telescopes, various brass and copper fittings. While his men loaded the bags, Sal flitted about the room appraising its wares. He seemed conscious of both time and the fact that they would only be able to carry so much.

Over the next few minutes, Sal would point, Pablo would smash, and the other two men, whose names Matt hadn't yet heard, would fill their bags. Navigation charts hundreds of years old, the bell from a slave trading ship, unopened nineteenth century rum bottles—all of these and more ended up in the bags. They progressed through the museum rapidly, but seemingly without fear of alarms or discovery.

And Matt knew why. The museum was old. Dallas Draper was old. He'd been running it since before electronic alarm systems were commonplace, and, like his taste in boats, Dallas was old-fashioned. He locked the display cases and when he left he locked the museum doors, but that was the extent of his security. It wasn't like he kept works by Da Vinci and Van Gogh or had the Hope Diamond in here. To him it was only a collection of old nautical curiosities that were just interesting and valuable enough to warrant its location on the town's harbor.

Matt was jarred from his unpleasant thoughts by the muffled sound of more glass breaking. Sal had found the section devoted to the whaling days. Harpoons, ivory scrimshaw, candles made from whale oil, 1800's flensing knives and the like were captured by Sal's cavernous duffels.

Sal moved to a section of the room devoted to the sea's natural wonders. Black pearls, large shark jaws, sea otter pelts and seal skins, giant clam shells and beautiful coral pieces were on display in a translucent case. But this one was different. Sal whistled sharply. "Saint! Get over here." Pablo and the other two were finishing up in the whaling area.

"Now!" Sal commanded, raising his pistol at Matt's chest. Matt walked over to Sal in front of the display. He could see it was of a different type than the smaller glass ones. "It's plexiglass, Saint. It's not going to shatter." At this Pablo appeared with his pipe wrench, nodding in agreement. "We need those pearls."

But near the end of the case was a metal lock. Sal waved Matt over to it with the tip of the gun. "Try the keys."

Matt fumbled through the smaller keys one at a time until one worked. He pulled two metal latches apart and then slid the case open. Sal's goons filled their bags like greedy kids on Halloween.

"Onward!" Sal said, pointing to the museum's other main room. They proceeded to make their way through the museum, plundering artifacts and destroying things to get at them as they went. Sal froze in front of a case with wall signage above it reading PIRATE TREASURE.

Gold and silver coins recovered from shipwrecks gleamed dully in the low light. Small piles of uncut rubies and emeralds once destined for the King of Spain also shared space in the display, as well as a few custom jewelry pieces.

"Saint!" Sal said to Matt, who stood next to him looking into the case. "Let's go, this one's Plexiglas—try the key." Matt glared at Sal as Pablo and the other two goons circled around. Matt tried the same key that had worked in the other lock. He shook his head and then cycled through a few more from the monkey's fist.

"Hurry it up!" Sal demanded as the lock finally gave with a *click* that caused the men to cheer in hushed whispers. "Let's go, let's go!" Sal urged as his men swept the coins and jewels into the bags. Matt watched as Sal scooped up a handful of rocks and looked down into his open palm, mesmerized. Matt was enraged watching these men pillage the museum, at being forced to aid them. Yet at the same time he could do nothing about it; he felt impotent.

In his mind, *Matt leapt on Sal and slammed the hand with the stones into his face. His mouth filled with the raw gems and Matt covered his mouth and tipped his head back. Sal's gang jumped him but Matt blocked out the pain of their pummeling and kept a deathgrip around Sal's head, closing off his mouth. He saw Sal struggling for air, his Adam's apple surging as he swallowed the pretty little pebbles...*

"Do they taste good, Sal! Do they? You wanted them so bad, make them a part of you."

"Sal, over here!" Pablo called from another display case. Sal looked over his shoulder and let the stones fall into a bag. "C'mon, Saint!" he said, waving his two bag handlers along with him. When they reached Pablo they found a collection of cutlasses.

"Pirate swords!" Pablo said. Accompanying signage told the men that the weapons were of French Naval origin. Their blades featured intricate ornamental designs.

"Glass case, smash it!" Sal said. Pablo tried to lay a bag across the glass to muffle it when it broke, but by now the bags were too full. He smashed the case anyway with the pipe wrench. The thieves' hands darted inside the shattered case and plucked out the old weapons. Sal's phone lit up in the semi-darkness and he glanced at it.

He whistled a two-tone, high-low–high-low rapid pattern that reminded Matt of some kind of forest bird to elicit everyone's attention. "CJ's around the corner with the van. Says he saw a cop two blocks away."

-14-

YOU FORGOT SOMETHING

Pablo pointed at a display case in a corner where they had not yet had time to look. "What about that one?"

Sal was already on the move. "No time. We're good enough, let's go." Sal and company ran toward the back of the museum, where apparently they already knew there would be an exit. Out of recent habit, Matt ran after Sal, but a part of him really wanted to see what they were going to do next.

They reached the back of the first large room they had plundered. A velvet rope with a sign proclaiming, STAFF ONLY BEYOND THIS POINT blocked off a narrow hallway. Sal and company stepped over the barricade and jogged down the hall carrying their laden bags. Along the way they passed a narrow staircase leading up, but ignored it in favor of a red EXIT sign that beckoned over a door with a panic bar.

Sal calmly pushed the door open and stepped outside, peering quickly in both directions. Seemingly satisfied with what he saw, he held the door open for his associates and then stepped into the doorway before Matt could walk through.

"This is where we part ways, Matt the Saint. Go back through the museum and out the front door the way we came, get back into your boat and go on about your business. You keep your mouth shut about what happened here or you'll be sorry. Understand?"

Matt nodded. Out of his peripheral vision he saw a white Ford Econoline van pull up in the alley behind the museum, its side door already open. Sal's men flung their bags into it and jumped inside. Sal pointed inside the museum. "It's been nice working with you. Now go!"

Sal waited to move until Matt had retreated back into the museum with the door closed behind him. Didn't want him to see the van's license plate, or the driver, Matt guessed. Through the closed door, Matt heard the van door slide shut and the getaway vehicle accelerate down the alley.

He turned and walked into the museum in a daze, a trance, a stupor, struggling to believe what had just happened to him. *What the hell was that? I was...*He searched for the right word as he stepped back over the velvet rope. *Not really kidnapped, not mugged or assaulted...I was...forced to help rob a museum?*

Matt almost laughed out loud at the absurdity of it, but, as he looked around the room of shattered display cases and ravaged exhibits, he came to terms with the reality. *I better get the hell out of here.* Then something caught his eye as he began moving deeper into the room.

A display case stood in the corner, unmolested. He moved to it, drawn by curiosity as strong as though it were a tangible force of physics, like gravity or a magnetic field. In their haste to abscond with the booty, Sal's gang had been forced to leave it untouched. The nearest case to it was that containing the swords.

Matt reached the display case and peered inside. Without the flashlights, and with the track lighting above the exhibit off, Matt found it difficult to see. Instinctively he reached into his pocket for his cellphone—it would provide some light—only to remember that Sal had taken it from him and not given it back. *So I was robbed.*

He began to tremble with anger at the knowledge that the person who did this to him, who had technically caused him to break laws—to rob a museum—now had his phone. But then for a moment he saw clearly into the case.

Guns.

They were old, like everything else in this museum, but they looked real enough. There were a few long barreled weapons that looked to Matt's untrained eye like rifles, and, positioned in the center of the case, two shorter barreled guns. A sign mounted above the case bore a photograph of the smaller guns, which looked like what Matt thought of as antique pistols.

He leaned close to the wall in order to read the sign in the dim light:

MUSKETS: The Flintlock Blunderbuss

Adaptable in that almost anything handy would fit in its barrel, pirates utilized muskets to spray bits of glass, nails and even small stones in order to commandeer a vessel. These muskets were fairly small and portable, and had a way of commanding undivided attention. The pair in this collection date from 1795, and remain in firing condition with all original parts.

Matt looked down from the sign to the actual muskets. They certainly looked authentic, with ornate flourishes on a wood and metal body. The copper barrels flared at the opening. Then his eyes adjusted their focal point until he saw his own reflection staring back at him for a moment in the case.

You've broken laws! Sal forced you to do it, but still, you did it. You're still in here, aren't you? Isn't that against the law? Shouldn't you have run out the back door screaming for the cops the second you heard the van drive off? What are you doing?

Almost as though he had an itch, his fingers scratched inside his pants pocket where the monkey's fist waited.

-15-

SOUVENIRS

"Matt, where've you been?" John Samson's face revealed some concern as he quizzed his boss, but he didn't wait for an answer. "There's somebody I'd like you to meet."

Matt Knox froze in the doorway to his private office. The average test drive was less than an hour, and he'd been gone far longer than that. It was nearly lunchtime now, and he'd hoped John might be already out to the Grog N Grub trying to hit on that blonde bartender he liked. But in fact, there was a man standing next to John.

After leaving the museum, Matt had taken the yacht back over to Dallas Draper's sailboat and returned the monkey's fist without incident. Then he'd taken the dealership's boat straight back here, also without attracting any attention. During that trip, Matt had wrestled with what to tell people about his...*experience.* That's what he thought of it as. Like he'd been sucked up into a spaceship, experimented on by aliens and beamed back down to Earth, still in one piece, but somehow *different.* And then there was Sal's threat.

Matt turned around, a backpack hanging off one shoulder. "Oh, hey John. Listen, I'm real sorry about that. I should have let you know I'd be out longer than usual." Matt fidgeted in the doorway to his office.

"I called your cell."

My cell! Now in the possession of one Sal Jonason.

"Anyway, Matt, this is Jeremy Washington, he's an old friend of mine. He's looking for a job..."

Matt heard John's words but wasn't listening to them as he thought about how Sal now had access to a treasure trove of information about him—numbers for his wife, kids, colleagues, friends, photos of his wife in a bikini, and did he remember to delete that one he'd taken of her in the shower?!... He tried to stop thinking about all the ways his phone could now be used against him as he focused on John's visitor.

"Yeah, look John, the test drive went fine. Mr. Washington, nice to meet you." He shook hands with the guy in a daze while his mind went on attempting to calculate the potential damage done to him by Sal's Three Hour tour. *My online bank account!...*

John, seeing his boss was lost in thought, intervened. "Matt, Jeremy here is looking for a sales job. I told him that maybe you could talk with him about any opportunities we might have. Do you think you might have a minute to discuss that right now?"

Matt shifted the backpack uneasily on his shoulder. He stepped into his office while giving John an easy smile and a slow nod. "Uh, sure. Come on in. Jeremy is it?" The guest nodded.

John motioned for Jeremy to walk into the office. "Thanks, Matt. I'll be at the front desk when you're done, Jeremy."

Matt motioned to one of two chairs positioned in front of his desk. "Have a seat." Jeremy did as he was told while Matt placed his backpack on his desk and sat down facing Jeremy, tenting his hands.

"So as John was saying, I'm interested in any sales positions you might have here," Jeremy led off. "I do have some experience with—"

"We don't really have any openings right now," Matt cut in. He knew it was rude, but then again the guy had pretty much invited himself in for an interview, hadn't he? *I've got a lotta shit going on right now and don't exactly have time for this community service crap. I need to get back to thinking about this Sal situation...*

Jeremy's eyes widened. Matt continued. "Economy's tough and boats are a luxury item. The real high end stuff still sells—wealthy people are still spending—but it's not like we need to take on someone new to handle that. It's an elite market, anyway, and we can only have highly experienced yacht brokers handling those kind of accounts."

"John mentioned that maybe you could use somebody part time, working on commission only, who brings in their own leads. So I would cost you nothing out of pocket, I only make money if you make money directly as a result of one of my leads."

Matt stopped drumming his fingers on the desk and really looked at the person in front of him for the first time. Jeremy noticed the shift in attention, relieved that his interviewer was finally seeming to notice him. He had seemed mentally occupied, Jeremy thought, attributing it to the tough business climate.

"Say, you look familiar to me," Matt declared at length.

"Oh?" Jeremy said, sounding less confident now.

"Yeah, do I know you from somewhere?"

"No sir, I don't believe—"

"Wait a minute! I know. I saw your picture in the newspaper. And on the local news!" Jeremy sighed and lowered his eyes.

"You were that cop who got kicked off the force for corruption, weren't you? Is that you?" *What if he's still a cop and this is some kind of setup because I helped rob the museum?* Matt was fully alert now, eyeing Jeremy while awaiting his response.

"Yes sir, that was me, but I'm looking to go in a completely new direction now, and I—"

"I *knew* it!"

"Sir?"

The revelation had temporarily interested Matt, but the news stories hadn't mentioned Jeremy's connection to Sal's gang by name, only a vague "corruption" charge and in the newspaper for those who read deep and carefully, the charges of "taking bribes."

"Look, Jeremiah, we don't really need another sales guy here, okay?" *I need to call my cell company and cancel my account before Sal does something with my phone!* He stood, hoping to signal a firm ending to the meeting.

Jeremy looked flabbergasted. "It's Jeremy. Mr. Knox, if this is about my police work, let me assure you—"

In his mind, Matt...*gripped his desk from the bottom edges and flipped it over fast so that it landed on Jeremy's lap as he sat there in the chair. Jeremy started to stand, but wasn't fast enough, so unexpected was the assault, and the heavy furniture piece caught him across the knees. Matt jumped on top of the desk, adding his weight to the pressure causing Jeremy to howl in agony...*

"It's not about your getting fired from the police, although that doesn't exactly make you a frontrunner for a position if we did have one. We just don't have any jobs right now. Good day, sir, please show yourself out now." He pointed at the door.

Jeremy uttered a half syllable in surprise, but said nothing. Then he managed, "Thank you for your time, Mr. Knox," and turned and went to the door. He opened it, glared ever so slightly at Matt, whose lips looked suspiciously like they were turned up in the beginnings of a smile, and then closed it behind him.

Alone in his office, Matt leaned against the locked door and exhaled all the air in his lungs. *Crazy guy.* He made a mental note to tell John that they were absolutely not hiring right now so don't bring in anymore nut jobs. *Now get to work!*

The view from the office was impressive, looking right out on the harbor, but Matt went to his picture window and closed the blinds. He picked up his work phone. He dialed his cellular company and told them he left his phone in a public place by mistake and needed his service cancelled until they could send him a replacement.

Then he leaned his head on his desk and let loose a flood of emotions and jumbled thoughts he'd been trying to hold inside during that stupid job interview. *I just robbed a museum!* At first he trembled with rage while he relived it, like one of his mind crimes in reverse, where he was the victim. He had been forced at gunpoint to break the law!

Matt picked up the phone to call the police, then returned it to its cradle without having dialed. His thoughts were a maelstrom of conflicting feelings: He should report his forced burglary. But Sal could target him and his family if he told police about the crime. He could potentially even be held accountable for the theft and destruction, couldn't he? Stranger things, and all that. There was that woman bank manager supposedly forced to rob her own bank with a bomb strapped to her, but later it turned out she was in on the entire heist and arrested. Sure, he was Matt 'The Saint' Knox, he'd be cleared eventually, but who needed that hassle, even for a little bit?

And then something else, coming from deeper within, made its message heard, faint of voice but laden with import.

It was fun, though, wasn't it?

-16-

HONEY, I'M HOME

Matt Knox docked his Boston Whaler in back of his house and walked up the steps to his backyard gate. He opened it and strode up to the sliding glass door. He pulled it open and stepped into his kitchen, where Summer was preparing dinner. He could hear Gavin and Caitlin fighting over a video game controller in the living room.

"Hey, hon, how's work?" Summer asked while chopping some asparagus.

Matt slid the backpack off his shoulder and let it dangle from a hand by the strap. The rest of the day after the job interview had been on the slow side, and he'd had time to think further about what he'd done that morning. For some reason the prospect of telling Summer he'd been forced at gunpoint to rob the local museum embarrassed him, as if he'd done some dirty thing. Also, he knew she'd insist he go to the police, yet at the same time would be absolutely terrified that Sal might make good on his threat to make him sorry.

"Not bad. Kinda slow. Smells good," he said, referencing the salmon she had on the stove.

"Ready in about fifteen."

"I'll go change," Matt said, heading for the living room and the stairs to their second floor.

"Hey, Matt—did you get that light for the car?"

Matt stopped dead in his tracks. *The tail light bulb!* With all he'd been through he'd completely forgotten about getting the light.

He slapped the hand not holding the backpack on his forehead in an exaggerated motion of forgetfulness. "Oh, wow. I'm sorry! Totally forgot. It was pretty busy at work, and I just didn't remember."

Summer looked up from her chopping. "I thought you said it was slow at work today, hon?"

"What?"

Summer let her knife rest on the cutting board while she turned to look at him. "Just now when I asked you how work was you said it was kind of slow." She smiled at him when Matt looked confused. "I'm not picking on you, silly, I'm just saying. That's what you said."

"Right. Well, what I meant was that it was slow in the sense that we didn't have a lot of customers, but we did some internal organizational stuff—I'm training John on our new database system—and that kept me occupied."

"So how am I going to get to work tomorrow. My car won't be ready until Friday. They have to wait for a part they ordered. You want me to take a cab to work all week while you take the boat?"

Hell no. The thought of being seen boating around the marina all week made him nervous. Passing by the museum in a boat, by Dallas Draper's yacht...he needed to distance himself from it, emotionally, physically.

"No, that's not really practical. Tell you what, Summer. I'll get the light tomorrow for sure and put it on tomorrow night."

"Okay but how will I get to work tomorrow? You don't want me to drive it with a broken light, remember?"

Matt looked at his wife. That problem now seemed beyond trivial to him. "I'll go ahead and drive it anyway and take you to work, pick you up. It'll only be for one day."

Summer raised her eyebrows and smiled. "Wow. Matt the Saint Knox is relaxing his standards? I'm proud of you, honey."

-17-

FIVE FINGER DISCOUNT

The next day at lunch Matt Knox pulled up to the Auto Zone. In the store, Matt found the replacement tail light cover and bulb and stood in line to pay for them. He was surprised at how long the line was.

Ten minutes later he was still two customers away from the check-out stand. He stood next to a kiosk display that held an assortment of pseudo-automotive knick-knacks: multi-tools, small funnels, hanging air fresheners, bungee cords, cigarette lighter power adapters, and trailer hitch covers. *Bunch of useless cheap crap from China*, Matt thought. He looked around him and saw only overworked, underpaid employees busily trying to placate customers who had thirty minutes before their lunch break ended.

The person now at the counter was yapping to the clerk about some desert dune buggy race he was in last weekend (that's why he needs new shocks), the clerk nodding, uttering the most appropriate monosyllables he could without pausing to slow down the transaction. Matt plucked a keychain light from the rack and looked at the price: $3.99. He held it underneath the light bulb box as the dune buggy guy left and Matt was one up from the counter.

If I was going to just take this stupid keychain without paying, how would I do it? Just stand here in line I guess, holding it out of sight, but still holding it because they must have cameras in here on the ceiling or whatnot.

Matt felt strangely alert, like he was in a mind crime but this time it was real. He hadn't done anything wrong—he was just holding an item while he approached the counter, but the thrill in knowing that this is exactly how he *would* steal the item if he were to go through with it was almost exhilarating.

In fact it reminded him of the feeling he got when he was in the museum.

Matt examined the box for the bulb while the woman in front of him at the counter fished around in her purse for her wallet. It was a boxy cardboard package with the bulb itself held in place on a cardboard insert near the front. The box was much bigger than was actually needed for the little bulb inside, but Matt supposed it provided cushioning while making it harder to steal. The box itself was not shrink wrapped. Matt's eyes darted around surreptitiously, looking for signs anyone was watching him. No one seemed to be.

Without looking down at the package, Matt pulled back one of the edges of the box just a bit and slipped the keychain light into the light box. He looked down at the box quickly and could not see any noticeable damage to it. He tipped the box in his hands but couldn't feel anything moving inside.

It'll work.

Then it was Matt's turn to step up to the counter. He smiled at the clerk and handed him the two boxes and a twenty dollar bill at the same time. If they did have anything on camera, he didn't want them to be able to look up his credit card information. Also, immediately handing the money to the clerk gave him less time to look at the items. Matt had figured this much from his many mind crimes.

Matt's stomach felt like it did at the top of a rollercoaster drop while the clerk scanned the two boxes and put them in a bag. But then the cash register was open and he was giving Matt a few ones and some coins, thanking him for his business.

Matt told the clerk to have a nice day and walked out of the store. In his car, he attached his new keychain light to his key ring and started the engine.

-18-

NEWS AT 11

Matt sailed through the rest of his work day, spirits buoyed by his shoplifting rush. He was beginning to see a budding pattern in his actions: the driving with a broken light, the keychain theft–they were just an attempt to continue the excitement he felt after leaving the museum. The petty crimes brought back the intense feelings he experienced the day before like some kind of perverse high. He tried to justify it. *My whole life I've never broken a single law, don't I deserve some kind of leeway?*

That night after dinner Matt finished installing his new tail light. He walked back into the house, where the kids were already in their rooms and Summer sat on the couch in the living room watching the nighttime local news.

"Light's fixed," he declared.

"That's good, babe. I'm sorry I broke it."

"Just don't let it happen again or I might have to punish you." He swatted her playfully on the butt. She grabbed his hand and said, "Honey, look at this, have you seen this?"

Matt looked up at the TV, where a reporter was setting up a new story. "What?"

"The maritime museum on the harbor was robbed, they think yesterday. You didn't hear anything?"

"No, I haven't heard about it. Shhh, let me listen." Matt watched the TV as a blonde female reporter stood with a microphone in front of the museum entrance.

"Bad news today for fans of the Sandy Cove Maritime museum. The long-time local attraction has been robbed of many of its exhibit items, with damages being estimated at close to $100,000. The museum is closed on Monday, yesterday, which is when Sandy Cove police say they believe the crime occurred. Employees who reported for work at the museum this morning told police that while there were no signs of forced entry, some of the exhibit display cases had been smashed, the valuable items inside removed, while others appear to have been unlocked with a key. Police are asking anyone with information about the crime to call this hotline number."

"That's terrible!" Summer commented. "We had such a good time there with the kids last summer, remember?"

"Yeah," Matt said, noticing it now read $25,000 REWARD above the hotline number.

"That's like stealing from the whole community. I mean, it's not like a bank or something where it's just insured money. The stuff in that museum is really unique."

Matt nodded in agreement. "It sure is."

-19-
PRIVACY POLICY

The next day at work found Matt walking into the yacht brokerage where John Samson was pretending to organize the brochures on a waiting area table. Matt always thought that the waiting area was pretentious bullcrap—as if there were so many people clamoring to buy huge boats that they needed a waiting area for them—but upper management said they needed it, god forbid someone ready to purchase a mega-yacht did happen to walk in without an appointment and everyone was busy. John looked at Matt expectantly as he walked past. Matt merely said "Good morning," as he barreled toward his office.

"Hey, Matt, you got a second?" John called.

Matt stopped and turned around. "What's up?"

John cleared his throat a couple of times as he walked over to him. "Jeremy told me you were sort of rude to him yesterday in your office."

For a split second, Matt couldn't figure out who the hell Jeremy was or why John would be upset, but then he remembered the job interview with that fired cop desperate for work. *Jesus.* He had been so preoccupied ever since he saw that newscast the night before, thinking about the reward offered—*twenty-five grand, that's enough to start a lot of people snooping around*—that the interview had slipped his mind completely.

"Jeremy? Oh yeah, right. I'm sorry, Matt, but we don't have any positions open right now. You saw our quarterly numbers in that conference call last week. The business just isn't there. Even on a commission–John waved him down. "It's not the fact that you said there's no work. It's the way he said you acted toward him. He was insulted, John. You really offended him."

Matt had only half his brain on the conversation while the other half tried to analyze if it was possible for Sal and his gang to frame him for the robbery and collect the reward on him. *Holy shit! How screwed would I be...these guys use me to take the stuff out of the museum, and now they could point cops to me while collecting the reward from Dallas Draper! I didn't wear gloves in there and they all did!*

"Matt? Do you have a response? I know you're my boss, but I still feel like you owe me an explanation for what happened yesterday."

That snapped Matt back to the conversation, but it also brought him back angrier after his less than comforting realization. "Well, you know what, John? Tough shit. Let the guy find his own goddamn job, this isn't some community service we're running here. Not to mention he was just all over the news for being tossed off the police force! I don't need some sorry-ass troublemaker representing me. Now get back to work on that follow-up list and stop pretending like you're doing something useful."

John's mouth dropped open for a second but he regained his composure quickly. He walked away without another word and went to his desk in an open area of the main room. Matt retreated to his private office and closed the door.

He stayed there until John left to go out for lunch, probably at the Grog N Grub again, but Matt wouldn't know because John hadn't asked him if he wanted to go. *No surprise there, but it works out for the better.*

Matt stepped out of his office and went to John's desk and woke up his computer. The Sal situation had been steadily gnawing away at his peace of mind all morning. He couldn't stop thinking about how royally they'd screwed him. Matt browsed through John's digital file directory until he found what he was looking for—TEST DRIVE APPLICANTS.

He opened that folder. Every potential customer who wanted to test drive a yacht had to pass a credit check, and Matt remembered being surprised that Sal had, although John assured him that his info was legit.

He scanned a long list of files organized by last name: when he saw *Jonason, Sal*, he clicked it. An application opened. Matt didn't even look at the bottom half of the form where it asked for annual income and other questions aimed at painting a financial picture of potential yacht buyers. What he needed was right at the top, second line.

Home address: *Sandy Cove, 23442 23rd Street, #317.*

-20-

BE YOUR OWN BOSS

That same morning, Jeremy Washington was having breakfast at home with his wife, who was already dressed for work and about to leave. Last night he had told her how terribly the job interview had gone at the yacht brokerage and she had done her best to make him feel better. Today was a new day, though, and Alisa reminded her husband that they needed income, and soon.

"You gotta get back out there, babe," she said, sliding her chair back from the table as she took a final bite of bagel and cream cheese. "Don't let that jerk at the yacht place get to you. Consider it a practice interview and know that you'll go into the next one that much more polished. I have to go."

On their small TV on the kitchen counter, the morning news played a rehashing of the museum robbery piece that had first aired last night. Jeremy and Alisa had seen it while laying in bed then, and it didn't seem as though any new information had been added. Nevertheless, as Alisa headed out the door, squeezing one last promise out of him to find a job today, Jeremy perked up at a thought bubbling up from his subconscious.

This thought coalesced at the same time he saw the overlay appear on the screen: REWARD: $25,000.

I can find out who did this! If this had happened three weeks ago I would be responsible for finding out who did it, as a cop. But I still know

*where a lot of this town's dirty laundry is aired, and in the law enforce-
ment community I still have a few connections who might give me more
than the time of day. Hell, Sal probably knows who did it. I could always
ask him.*

Right now, it seemed to Jeremy like he had a better chance at earning that $25,000 than he did of finding a real job. And who knows, he
thought, watching the news segment conclude with a close-up of shattered display case glass on the museum floor—maybe if he was suc-
cessful on this case alone, he could start a private consulting
firm...*Jeremy Washington, Private Investigator!* It had a nice ring to it.

He picked up the morning edition of the Sandy Cove Gazette, but
instead of looking at the job ads he'd circled earlier, he flipped back to
the front page and carefully read the piece on the museum theft, pausing occasionally to take a few notes.

When he was done, Jeremy grabbed the keys to his old Bronco and
headed for the door.

-21-
NETWORKING

Jeremy pulled onto the road in front of his house and switched on the radio. Not his Bronco's car stereo, but a two-way police radio he'd installed years ago as a way to keep up with what was going on even while off duty. Never know when he might need to call in a favor. His wife had scolded him for it, saying it was no different than a Wall Street guy taking his smartphone with him on vacation. But scanning through its frequencies, Jeremy was glad he had it now.

There was a traffic stop going down on Main Street, an aggressive panhandling complaint from the Starbucks over on 34th, and a shoplifting call at the WalMart. Pretty typical day, Jeremy reflected with a pang of sadness. He'd almost forgotten that he wasn't in his patrol car. He smiled as he visualized the person attached to the dispatcher's voice. *Miss ya already, Linda.* Jeremy knew Alisa wouldn't miss her, though. There had never been an affair, but the Latina was a childhood friend of Jeremy's and Alisa told him she didn't like the way the two looked at one another at the annual parties, especially at the last summer beach barbeque.

Jeremy had tried to tell Alisa it was the working relationship he had with Linda that he valued, not her looks. When he was on the road, hers was the voice of Home Base. Backup. Safety. Her voice gave him the same feeling now. Especially when she 10-4'd his partner—correction, former partner–that he'd be taking a break at the airport lot.

Jeremy knew the spot, and the man, well enough. He turned toward the airport. Ten minutes later he rolled past the main parking lot, then the heliport and the cargo planes, and finally past empty runway until he could see the tall weeds that grew on the other side of the chain link fence.

Just on the other side of this fence, Jeremy knew, was a small patch of dirt carved out of the weeds. He didn't know how it got there, but for years cops on duty had been using it as a quiet place to pull over and get some rest.

Tommy would be having his Dunkin Donuts and coffee while he monitored the radio, Jeremy knew, and as he rolled into the lot he had to laugh as he saw Tommy drop his bearclaw in surprise. He wasn't used to cars creeping up on him here. Pulling up fast would be dangerous in any other vehicle besides a marked police cruiser or Jeremy's old Bronco, which he had no doubt Tommy would recognize.

Jeremy parked and stepped out, throwing his hands up in a mock gesture. "Don't shoot, Tommy!"

Jeremy watched his ex-partner scoop up his dropped breakfast from the seat. He heard a few curses emanate from inside the cruiser, and then the front door swung open and Tommy stepped out.

"Damn, Jeremy, you're lucky I recognized your ride, man. What's up?" Then, in a softer tone, "Hey, how you doing, man?"

Jeremy walked over and slapped him on the shoulder. "I'm alright. They haven't assigned you a partner yet?"

"Guess they figure you're the only one who could handle me." Jeremy laughed at this before Tommy continued. "Nah, they tell me end of this week I'll have somebody."

Tommy was about Jeremy's age, but he looked a few years older. He'd worked construction for ten years before joining the force, and the outdoor work had imparted a weathered look to his skin. Jeremy knew that the cop's mustache he sported covered a scar he'd received in an off-duty bar fight many years ago. Jeremy removed his sunglasses as he took a step back to look at his friend.

"You working anywhere yet?" Tommy asked.

"Not yet."

"Listen, if you need a loan, just say the word."

Jeremy shrunk back at the suggestion. "That's not why I'm here."

"Okay, so why are you here then? You miss this beautiful spot so much?" Tommy joked, casting a glance around the weedy, trash-strewn lot.

"What can you tell me about the museum job?"

Tommy cocked his head to one side, a gesture of surprise. "Museum? Not much, man. As you can see, I'm here and the detectives they assigned to solve that case are there, at the museum. And I wasn't even on duty when the call came in from the employees."

"Yeah, I know. But what have you heard? Is there a suspect?"

A seagull flew overhead, cawing in the silence that followed the question.

"No. Last I heard it was pretty cold. They did lift some prints, is what I heard, but they're still in the lab."

"Who's the lead detective—Flannery?"

"Fuckin' A Flannery. Who else? Just between you and me, lotta the younger detectives are hoping that this case will be Flannery's swan song. It's big enough that it would give him something respectable to go out on."

"One last hurrah and then sail into the sunset?"

"That's what they hope, so he gives someone else a chance at a promotion in this small-ass town. Hey, what's it to you, anyway—the museum case? You come all the way out here to ask me about that?"

Jeremy scuffed at the ground with his shoe. "Well, like I said, I'm not working right now. I'm looking, but it's not easy, and I saw they're putting up a twenty-five grand reward for—"

Tommy's faced changed at the mention of the reward, his eyes narrowing. "Whoa, Jeremy, I don't think that's such a good idea, man. I mean, what, you're gonna ride around town in your Bronco, playing Sherlock fucking Holmes? You need to find some steady work, dude."

"I'm looking. While I look I need something else to do. It might as well be this. All I need is for you to help me out a little. Like you just did."

"Jeremy. Didn't you just learn your lesson? You were let go for doing shit you're not supposed to do. Now here you are, asking me to do shit I'm not supposed to do. Fuck's wrong with you?"

"I'll split the money with you. I'll do all the work. You just give me some intel now and then, I'll give you half. We can do this, man. Old Flannery doesn't give a rat's ass about solving cases as long as it looks like they're trying. He'll arrest some gang bangers and say they did it, they'll be found innocent in trial, but that'll be a year later and the town will have forgotten about it. We can be partners again, man!"

Tommy's squad car radio squawked, and he turned and strode toward it. "I guess I can do it for half."

"Thanks. How about the stolen goods report?" Jeremy knew that for an unsolved case like this a list of stolen items would sometimes be circulated throughout the force with an alert to watch for them as a way of generating leads in the case.

"I'll try to bring it tomorrow."

Jeremy nodded. "Thanks, Tommy."

"Don't raise me on your scanner," Tommy said, pointing back at the Bronco. "Just meet me here same time tomorrow. The lab results should be in by then. Don't call my cell either."

Jeremy slunk back to his truck. The last part of his ex-partner's message was clear: you're poisoned goods, I don't want anything to do with you publicly. But a smile materialized on Jeremy's lips as he backed out of the lot.

He was back on a case.

-22-

HOW THE OTHER HALF LIVES

Twenty-third street was on the edge of Sandy Cove, out by the agriculture fields. Matt Knox slowed his SUV while he scanned the apartment complexes for street numbers. His heart palpitated; his breathing was rapid and shallow. Three minutes ago he'd seen a red light at an intersection that was not busy but which carried traffic in a fifty mph zone. He saw the light, saw that no one was coming, as far as he could tell, and plowed through the red doing fifty-five.

At 23442 he slowed to a stop and double parked. The building was a three story walkup, probably built in the 1970s. Nothing special, though not decrepit either. Clothes and towels hung out to dry on some of the balconies. It was a working class place, and most people who lived here held down some kind of job, many more than one. Matt saw that a driveway led around to the back of the building.

He turned in and followed it back. This time of day most of the tenants were either at work or sleeping after getting home from a graveyard shift. Matt parked under a carport next to an old pickup and shut his engine off. He looked for it but did not see the white van Sal had used as a getaway vehicle. He didn't know what kind of vehicle Sal drove, if any, but he knew he didn't have a job which meant there was a good chance he was home.

#317, third floor. Matt listened out the window of his SUV for signs of life. The place was quiet. No TVs, no music, no barking dogs. His heart rate was returning to normal, the high of his daredevil traffic stunt wearing off.

He reached underneath his seat and pulled out the backpack. He stepped from the vehicle and eased the door closed without slamming it. Pleased to see another stairway at the back of the complex, Matt walked to it and began to climb, his anger rising with each step. The museum heist had somehow changed who he'd become, Matt thought. His lifetime attitude of law abiding now felt like an old piece of clothing that didn't quite fit him anymore.

He found #317 almost directly at the top of the stairs. The door had a peephole. Matt opened his backpack, removed the blunderbuss from it and tossed the empty pack over the railing to the parking lot below. He'd already loaded the antique weapon with powder and ammunition, but he packed it down one last time before tucking it into his waistband, beneath his shirt and behind his back.

What are you doing here? He asked himself as he brought his hand up to knock on the wooden door painted yellow. *Get an explanation from Sal. Why me? What was he supposed to do now? Maybe ask Sal if he could do another job with him, just for the rush, he wouldn't even need to be paid...*

Matt's face flushed red, like a mood ring for his conflicted mind. Then his right fist was repeatedly coming into contact with the front door. He stepped back a little from the peephole.

"Minute," he heard a male voice call out from inside.

Matt reached back and felt for the musket. Right where it should be.

He heard a hand on the doorknob.

-23-

CUSTOMER RELATIONS

Sal Jonason's voice snaked through the crack of the open door held back by a security chain. "Get the fuck outta here right now, Saint."

Matt took a step back, holding both hands out in front of him. "Customer satisfaction follow-up, Mr. Jonason. We do them all the time. I'd like to discuss your recent test-drive experience." Matt figured this would ease Sal's mind in case neighbors were listening.

Silence, followed at length by the tinkling of light chain. "I know where you live, too, you know." Sal's beard seemed to protrude through the opening first as he pulled his door open wider. Clad only in a pair of black shorts, his face looked he hadn't shaved in a couple of days. Matt smelled the pungent odor of marijuana.

"This will only take a few minutes, Sal. I just want to make sure that you get the most out of your visit with us the other day."

Sal shot him a look of disgust. "You wearing a wire?"

The question caught Matt by surprise. He hesitated just long enough to further arouse Sal's suspicions before replying in the negative. Then Matt added, whispering for effect as if the neighbors might be listening and might even care, "Why would I want the cops involved? I helped you guys rob the place!" Then Matt raised his voice, his body seeming to act on its own. He hadn't known he was going to do it even a minute earlier, but he yelled at Sal, full voice, "I

ROBBED A FUCKING MUSEUM, MAN! IT WAS FUCKING AWESOME! CHANGED MY WHOLE BORING GODDAMN LIFE!"

A dog began to bark somewhere on the next block, but otherwise all was quiet until Sal spoke again.

"You sure about that, Matt the Saint Knox? Doesn't sound like something you'd do." From behind the door, Sal shook the hand that was holding his pistol.

"Oh, I did it, alright. I even got a little souvenir, would you like to see it?"

"Yeah."

"Let me in and I'll show you." A car turned into the driveway and started toward the back.

Sal stepped back and pulled the door open, pistol raised at Matt. "Get in."

Matt stepped into Sal's living room. There was a couch, a coffee table supporting several Tecate beer cans and an ashtray. Matt couldn't see or hear anyone else besides Sal.

"Pull the door shut and lock it," Sal commanded. Matt obeyed.

"Turn around and take your shirt off," Sal said.

Matt slowly turned from the door until he faced Sal. He unbuttoned his collared work shirt and held it apart. "I'm not wearing a wire, Sal."

"What you got to show me?"

"I need to pull it out of my pocket. Don't freak out," he said, nodding at the pistol in Sal's hand.

"Slow."

Matt eased his hand into the front right pocket of his slacks. He removed a small object and turned his hand over, uncurling his fingers. The black metal skeleton key lay across his palm.

"You got that from the museum?" Sal asked.

"Yes."

"From where?"

"From Dallas' keyring."

Sal gave a condescending smirk. "*That's* your souvenir? That's not a museum piece, it's just some key."

"But what does it open, Sal?"

"How the fuck should I know? We got everything good outta that place anyway."

"We didn't get everything. There's an inscription on the key. Read it," Matt said. He tossed the key onto the coffee table where it bounced once and came to rest with a clatter. Sal glared at Matt once and then moved to the table. He took a seat on his couch and slid the key toward him.

Matt forced himself to slow his breathing. The barrel of the blunderbuss itched the small of his back beneath his open dress shirt. Sal was holding the key now, flipping it back and forth in his left hand while he looked at it, the pistol held loosely in his right hand.

Sal held the key up to a ceiling light and squinted at it, saying, "I'll be goddamned."

Matt's right hand reached back inside his shirt. He whipped out the old musket and pointed it at Sal's head. Sal registered the motion, raising his own weapon far too late.

The blunderbuss cracked with an acrid gunpowder blast. Sal's head snapped back and his handgun bounced off the couch onto the table. The window curtain fluttered as it danced to the beat of stray shrapnel. Sal flopped face forward onto the coffee table, half slumped to the floor.

Matt jumped over to the couch and kicked Sal's gun a safe distance away. He looked at the spreading sheet of blood under Sal's face, at the smoking blunderbuss, then back to Sal again.

"Sal?" No answer.

For the first few seconds Matt could see ripples in the pool of blood underneath Sal's face caused by his breathing. Then the ripples stopped.

Matt sucked in his breath as he comprehended what he'd just done. He saw the skeleton key on the table a few inches from the blood, where it had fallen from Sal's hand. He picked it up, careful to avoid the bits of crushed glass that he'd used to pack the blunderbuss covering the table, and then took a quick look around the room.

Two cell-phones lay on the kitchen counter. He recognized one of them as his own. Careful not to leave any prints, Matt plucked both phones from the counter and dropped them into his pocket.

Then he went to the front door and looked out the peephole. No one stood waiting outside, drawn by the gunshot.

"Later Sal," Matt said. With his shirt over his hand to avoid leaving fingerprints, Matt pulled the apartment the door open and left.

-24-

Business as usual

Matt Knox pushed open the door of the yacht brokerage. He let John Samson's glare bounce off of him. He could hardly feel anything through the foggy afterglow of the first serious criminal act he'd ever committed in his life. He was pretty sure he was smiling. He vaguely registered that there were half a dozen prospective boat buyers crowded around John's desk, a huge crowd for their laid back operation.

"Matt, glad you're here. There's someone I want you to meet!" one of the customers called. There always was, when you were getting ready to buy a yacht. John shooed a couple of the guys Matt's way. Matt greeted them enthusiastically. He felt like he'd just jogged around the block and knocked back a triple espresso. He pointed at the chest of one of the men.

"You. Megayacht. Cayman Islands. Every winter. Can you picture it? Let's go over some figures in my office, gentlemen." The customers laughed excitedly and Matt ushered them into his private domain. Matt looked back at John to find him staring at him, a smile on his face while he shook his head. Matt gave him a thumbs up sign and shut the door.

Inside his office, Matt Knox didn't think about what he'd done at Sal's, but he leveraged the thrill of it to propel him through his high stakes sales meeting and the rest of his work day.

-25-

DEAD MEN TELL NO TALES

Jeremy glanced at his Bronco's radio clock. He had a lot of time to kill before his meeting with Tommy tomorrow. The lab results on the prints lifted from the museum would be useful, but in the meantime there had to be more he could do.

He recalled that one of his first thoughts was to ask Sal what he knew. Then he shivered as he pulled up to a red light. *Pablo. What'd he say when he came over?* Jeremy scanned his memory, rolling his window up to block out the distraction of classic rock blasting from the car one lane over. Something about a big job, not a store or a gas station...

Have to get to Sal's! Even if he wasn't involved, odds were he knew someone who was. Sal lived in the same section of town as he did. But it was Sal who had gotten him into so much trouble in the first place...The blare of the horn from the car behind him ripped him from his thoughts. The light was green. He shifted into gear and sped through.

Fifteen minutes later Jeremy pulled his Bronco into the driveway of Sal's apartment. He wasn't sure what Sal's ride was these days, but as he rolled into the parking lot, he didn't see any of the classic muscle cars the crime ring leader favored.

He parked in one of the empty stalls and headed for the back stairs. *Place is pretty quiet*, Jeremy thought as he made his way up. He figured

Sal would think he'd come to take him up on the offer relayed by Pablo. He turned over various phrases in his head...*I didn't come here to join your gang, Sal...Sal, thanks for the cash Pablo brought over, but I'm good. Sal—*

Sal's front door was ajar. Jeremy had been here not all that long ago, to set up the deal that had ultimately gotten him fired. He hoped that maybe Pablo was here. The prospect of talking to Sal alone made him a little nervous. He wasn't afraid of him, but a one-on-one meeting was uncomfortable for Jeremy, maybe because they had once been much closer friends, back in high school.

Sal and he had parted ways a few years after graduation, when Jeremy signed on for the police academy and Sal supported himself with ever escalating illegal enterprises. For a while they still saw one another at local parties and church, but then as Jeremy married and became a father, he stopped socializing with his old circles. They drifted apart as friends, although as residents of the same small town, they couldn't help but see each other now and then. Enough so that when Jeremy had fallen on tough times and sought to boost his income, Sal felt comfortable suggesting a "business proposition:" cash for information on police schedules and for looking the other way during his own beat.

While that arrangement had proven modestly profitable for Sal and his cohorts, it left Jeremy in his current circumstances, and he didn't relish needing to go to Sal to ameliorate his situation.

He didn't think Sal would leave his front door open for too long, either. Like all career criminals, Sal possessed a healthy though not incapacitating dose of paranoia.

"Sal?" Jeremy called out. He certainly didn't want to startle him by walking in unannounced. He knew Sal was never far from his hand-gun-of-the-month. It could be a 9mm or a .45 or maybe a .38. At one time or another Jeremy had seen him with all of those and then some.

"Sal, it's Jeremy. Can I come in?"

Jeremy had still not received a reply by the time he walked to the threshold. One more time: *"Sal?"*

Weird. He didn't hear a shower running or a radio playing or the sounds of sex.

Jeremy pushed the door back with a single finger. It creaked loudly on its hinges. "Hey, Sal, is—"

He cut himself off as the door swung open a little more and he took in the scene in the living room. Instinctively, Jeremy brushed his hand against his hip, but there was no gun there. His head swiveled as his gaze roved around what he could see of the apartment from the doorstep.

Sal—at least he was pretty sure it was Sal—lay slumped over on the table, the lower half of his body somehow still supported by the couch. The face had a lot of blood on it, but the beard was recognizable. As a cop, Jeremy knew it wasn't safe to go into the apartment. What if whoever had done this to Sal was still inside, in one of the back rooms?

But Sal was once a good friend, and he had come here for information from him. He ran to the unmoving Sal and placed two fingers on his carotid. It was definitely Sal, he could see now. But his fingertips felt no pressure kicking back at them.

Lifeless. Jeremy removed his cell-phone and used it to take a picture of Sal's bloody head before he turned and bolted for the door.

What in God's name had done that to his face?

-26-

IN FOR A PENNY

Jeremy sped away from Sal's apartment complex. *Sal's dead!* He had trouble believing it even though he'd seen it with his own eyes. Who had done that to him? Sal had always been a criminal as long as Jeremy knew him, but he'd never known him to actually hurt anyone. Had he gotten in over his head and been unable to pay back a drug dealer?

Strawberry fields gave way to gas stations and auto repair shops as Jeremy drove on in a daze. He thought of calling his ex-partner but decided against it. Tommy wouldn't like the fact that Jeremy had gone over to Sal's at all, not to mention he'd told him not to call. Better to wait until their meeting tomorrow to bring it up.

Jeremy actually looked at what was on the side of the road and saw Cove Collision Repair coming up on the right. Pablo worked there, although he hadn't been thinking of Pablo. Had he subconsciously drove this way because he wanted to see him? Pablo had told him that Sal was about to start a big job. *Jesus, he'd even asked me if I wanted in on it. What did they do?* He had to find out.

Jeremy pulled into the shop and parked off to the side. He got out and walked past the office building directly over to the cavernous work garage. Not terribly busy. Jeremy counted three technicians working even though there was space for about a dozen. Pablo was one of the three, pulling out a side panel dent on a Range Rover with a suction cup tool.

He looked up in surprise at Jeremy's approach, leaving the suction cup to hang from the vehicle he'd been working on. He gave him a fist bump and made a show of looking around the shop in all directions, as if to remind Jeremy that they could possibly be overheard. Pablo shook his head.

"You're too late, Jer."

Jeremy's gaze bored into his friend's eyes. *He knew already? Don't assume anything. Make him tell you.*

"Too late for what, man? To watch you make that little dent even bigger with all your suction things?"

Pablo laughed. "Hey, I know what I'm doin', man. You shoulda seen this thing yesterday."

"I still think you guys go out and sideswipe parked cars to bring in more business."

"That's not a bad idea. I meant you were too late for the job I told you about the other day. You want a job denting cars for us instead?" Pablo gave him a crazy grin.

Jeremy laughed. If anyone was watching or listening he felt like he'd put on a sufficient show of normalcy. Time for the bombshell. He lowered his voice a little but forced himself to keep a half smile on his face while he delivered the news.

"Pablo, what was that job you and Sal were working on?"

The auto tech looked up from his job. He gave Jeremy a quizzical look. "I asked you if you wanted in on it, man. You said no. It's too late now."

"So you did it—the job—whatever it was?"

Pablo nodded and repositioned the dent puller.

"It's done."

"Already?"

"Yeah. I told you it was coming up."

"Well how'd it go?"

"Good. It's done."

Jeremy watched Pablo start to pull out the dent. "Sal's done, too, Pablo. I mean he's dead."

Pablo looked up from his work. "Say what?"

"I just went to his apartment and found him...here, look." Jeremy flipped open his phone and called up the photo he'd taken of Sal in his apartment. He handed it to Pablo, whose features assumed an intense look of incredulity. Pablo looked up from the image and turned his head quickly this way and that. He lowered his voice to a raspy whisper.

"What the fuck is this? Is this for real, man?"

Jeremy's eyes bored into Pablo's as he nodded. "What happened? What was that job you told me about?"

Pablo set his dent tool down, his gaze fixed on the garage floor. "The maritime museum," he whispered.

Jeremy felt his skin crawl. He'd sort of suspected Sal was involved, but he wasn't expecting it to be so easy to confirm. But as he stared into his friend's eyes, he also gazed into a choice. The reward was for information leading to a conviction. With Sal dead, the heat would come down even harder on Pablo, who, in his misguided way, had tried to help Jeremy.

"Jeremy? What's the matter? You okay?"

Jeremy nodded as he shook himself from his thoughts. He'd have to come to terms with that later. "Yeah, I just...I can't believe it. I went to Sal's to ask him if he might have heard anything, and..." He trailed off, picturing Sal's massacred face.

"Did you call the cops?"

Jeremy shook his head emphatically. "Stay out of it, man. One of his neighbors will call before too long."

"What did you go to Sal's for?"

The question caught Jeremy off guard. "What?" Some kind of power tool started up on the other side of the garage, and both of them were glad for the noise cover.

"You heard me."

Jeremy turned his hands palms up, a gesture of surrender. "I told you, I wanted to talk to him."

Pablo got up from the car, stood eye to eye with Jeremy. "Yeah I heard you. What I mean is," Pablo said, scraping the floor with one foot, "why do you care so much about Sal all of a sudden? You're not a cop anymore." Pablo let that sink in just long enough to make sure Jeremy felt the pain, before continuing without giving him a chance to speak. "And you already knew there was a decent chance Sal was involved. I told you something was going down."

"I wanted to hear it from him."

Pablo's eyes narrowed, "You're after that fucking reward, aren't you?" He kicked the car he'd been working on, hard, denting it.

"Chill out. Where's all the loot now, Pablo?"

Pablo looked around the shop, stooping to pick up his dent tool after regaining his composure. "I don't know what you're talking about, snitch." He went to work on the car again, positioning his dent puller over the newly created damage.

Jeremy turned and walked away.

-27-

WALKING THE DOG

The Knox family filed out to the sidewalk through their front yard. "Yard," was a bit of a stretch, Matt supposed, closing the picket fence gate behind them. The token patch of grass wasn't large enough to do anything with. The real value of the house lay in the canal front dockage that was essentially their backyard.

"When's the last time we went for one of our after-dinner walks?" Summer asked her family.

"Three weeks ago, Mom," Caitlin said, skipping ahead on the sidewalk. The walks were Summer's idea. They started out as Monday-Wednesday-Friday, then gradually decreased in frequency as the novelty wore off and competing demands on their time interfered.

"Definitely time to get back to it," Summer said, before calling, "Come on, Gavin." Their ten-year old was practicing a skateboard move a half a block behind them. He flipped his board right side up with a foot and skated over to them, easily catching up to his sister while his parents walked side by side behind.

"If we hurry we might catch the sunset," Matt said, glancing up at the June sky. "Let's go," Summer said, grabbing him by the hand and pulling him forward. Quite a few people were out and about, and Matt waved to various neighbors putting out the trash, walking their dogs, or driving slowly past. When they reached the end of their block they turned onto a walkway that led along the harbor's edge.

"Thanks for being so understanding about the car, Matt," Summer said as they strolled along the water, a waist-high railing along their left side. "I'm sorry I broke the light."

"Don't worry about it. It's fixed now," Matt said, looking out at the boats lining their slips in the harbor.

"So how was your day today?"

Matt looked over at her, reading her expression carefully, but she was already on to shooing the kids away from the rail.

"It was good," he said, correct in his assumption that she'd barely registered his response.

"Gavin! Stop that right now!"

"I told him to stop too, Mom, but he wouldn't," Caitlin said, twirling her hair with one hand and pointing at her brother with the other.

"It's just a rail stand," Gavin said, standing on his board balanced precariously over the railing's lower bar. "Not like I'm going for a backside reemo whip into a rail-slide combo or anything like that."

"Gavin, get down before you end up in the water!"

"Water's better than concrete, Mom," Gavin said, bouncing off the rail and landing confidently on the sidewalk, feet still firmly planted on the board. "Saltwater would really screw up my trucks, though."

"That's right, and we wouldn't be getting you another board, either," Summer said, seizing at any kind of motivating factor to keep him off the railing.

"No worries, I'll work on my freestyle," Gavin said, executing a 360 spin before skating smoothly off on the walkway ahead.

Summer shook her head. "Where does he get that attitude from? I don't know how many times I've told him not to do that. I wasn't like that when I was a kid. I was very obedient. And you're not like that. You've never broken a law in your entire life!"

"He's not breaking the law by skating here."

Summer rolled her eyes. "I know, Matt, but the recalcitrance, the urge to just do whatever the heck he wants. Where does it come from?"

Before Matt could answer, they heard a dog barking and a man calling after it, out of sight past a hedge row along a walkway leading from the residential street to intersect the one they followed. But the animal wouldn't stay out of sight for long.

"Oh, shit—Matt! That's the Sullivans' dog." Then she cupped her hands to her mouth and shouted, "Caitlin, Gavin! Back here, now!"

The animal that bounded out onto the walkway was so large that had they been closer to the mountains it would be routinely mistaken for a bear. It was a dog, however, just an extremely large one. The dog's owner, Jim Sullivan, ran out on to the walkway. A retractable leash, collar still attached to one end, dangled uselessly from one hand while a bevy of plastic bags to accommodate the dog's appreciable waste protruded from his pants pocket.

The Sullivans lived on the next street over from the Knox's, one further back from the water, Matt liked to remind them. A few years ago their long-time pet, a golden retriever, had to be put to sleep after a drawn-out battle with cancer, and the Sullivans had reacted by getting another dog. This one, though, was not a retriever but a Caucasian Mountain Dog, special ordered straight from Russia with the paperwork to prove it, as if buying the largest possible canine would make it that much easier to forget the pain of losing their last one. The dog had a habit of getting loose from its owner and bolting, though, and even when it was on a leash it seemed to Matt like it was barely under control. The beast had to weigh the same as Jim Sullivan, if not a little more.

"Alex!" Jim yelled. "Sit, Alex, sit!" That he gave the dog a decidedly human name like Alex somehow only served to infuriate Matt even more.

"Aaaaaaalex!" crowed Jim's wife, Cathy Sullivan. Small in stature, she nevertheless possessed a commanding presence. Cathy walked casually out to the waterfront, looking on while her husband went after the animal. She walked over to Summer and Matt, an apologetic expression on her oval face with wide set blue eyes and a straight nose over a set of perfect teeth. A spray of tight blonde curls flowed past her shoulders.

Summer ignored her approach as she welcomed Caitlin into her arms, relieved that at least one of her kids was safe. "Gavin, look out!" Matt shouted.

The dog was accelerating down the walkway, apparently excited by the boy's skateboarding.

"Don't worry, he's big but he's gentle as a lamb!" Cathy said, flashing a pretty smile. The Knox's ignored her.

"GAVIN!" Matt bellowed.

His son finally stopped trying to nail his fronstide 720 or whatever the hell he called it, and looked up in time to see Alex barreling in his direction. Jim Sullivan ran behind him, much slower than what Matt thought of as his ridiculous mid-life crisis of a pet. Some guys went for sports cars, others for fast boats or young women, but not Jim Sullivan, oh no–he was into dogs. Big fucking dogs. And this one was the largest Matt had ever seen. Its head was level with Jim's chest when it stood on all fours.

Gavin could see that there was no way he'd be able to just skate past the creature, which moved surprisingly fast for its massive bulk. Summer shrieked as it became apparent the Caucasian Mountain Dog wasn't going to stop. Cathy's expression changed from one of amusement to that of mild puzzlement. "Alex!" she called, as if her thin cry could halt 175 pounds of marauding animal on a dime.

Gavin pushed off on his board toward the rail, Alex almost to him. Jim still ran toward the dog, while the rest of the Knox clan and Cathy looked on in frozen horror. When Gavin reached the rail he executed a hop maneuver where he jumped the board onto the upper rail and then balanced there in one place—the "rail stand" he'd practiced just minutes earlier.

Alex now turned, a playful expression on his face, tongue lolling, as he easily sidestepped his owner to head for the rail. Gavin leapt from his perch in the direction of his family, board held in one hand. He landed on the skate deck and kicked off to gain more speed. His move confused the dog for a moment, but the animal quickly recovered and sprinted after his quarry.

"Jim, get your damn dog!" Matt yelled.

"Alex, stop! Sit!" Jim's yelling became more frantic as the massive pet increased his speed toward the boy, who jumped off his board upon reaching his family, hoping that being in the group would keep him safe. Gavin came to stop in a grinding slide behind Matt and Summer, who clutched Caitlin tightly. Cathy Sullivan now shied back from her dog, who ran around the group in a circle, as if herding them.

Jim Sullivan walked up to the group, both hands in the air. "Calm down, everyone, just calm down. Alex!" But the oversized canine ignored his owner and charged at Gavin, gripping the skateboard in its mouth and tearing it from Gavin's hand. The dog shook his head in a flurry and let go of the board, arcing it through the air to drop at Matt's feet.

The dog remained crouched at Gavin's feet, barking up at him in an excited frenzy. Gavin's eyes were wide in terror as he shrunk back from the beast. Jim caught up to the dog, patting it on the backside, saying, "It's okay, Alex—buddy–it's okay." But that did nothing to calm the animal. Caitlin cried, burying her face against Summer's shoulder. Cathy's curls bobbed up and down as she began trying to pull the Knox's away from the dog. "Give him some space," she yelled.

In the commotion, none of them noticed Matt picking up the skateboard. He raised it above his head with two hands. Took two steps until he stood just behind the giant mountain dog. Then Matt brought the skateboard down with his full force onto the back of the animal's head. A sickening *clunk* sounded when the edge of the board connected with Alex's skull. The big dog squealed and rolled to one side pawing frantically at the ground as if trying to get up.

Summer took Caitlin and Gavin by the hands and ran down the walkway. The dog started to get up and Matt swung the board, baseball bat style, into the side of the pet's humongous head, severing one of its massive ears.

"That's enough!" Jim yelled, putting a hand on Matt's shoulder. "Don't hurt my baby!" Cathy shrieked. Unbelievably, the dog wobbled up and started to walk toward the rail, away from the people. "It's okay, Alex. Take it easy, boy. Cathy, go get the car and call the vet, we're going in."

Matt walked up to Jim. "Your stupid animal almost killed my son! The law says it has to be on a leash. Who the hell do you think you are!"

Jim's face was a mixture of rage and bewilderment. "I *had* him on a leash, you asshole," he said, shaking the empty collar in Matt's face.

"This isn't the first time this has happened. I read the neighborhood association newsletter. Your damn dog is always free-ranging around the neighborhood terrorizing people."

"Forget it," Jim said, turning away from Matt and running to the aid his pet, who had collapsed in a heap by the rail. Blood drooled from its mouth to puddle on the concrete, some of it sliding over the side into the water. Summer and the kids, as well as Cathy had all disappeared back into the neighborhood.

"It'll be easier for me to forget when this menace is gone," Matt said. And he began shoving the dog toward the walkway edge, legs dug into the concrete, hands on the dogs haunches, like a defensive lineman practicing a block.

"What's going on!" Cathy Sullivan called, running back out onto the walkway. "Jim, the car's right up there, let's go."

The mammoth dog barely fit under the rail, but Matt forced it through with one last shove, even with Jim Sullivan tackling him at the last minute. They heard a loud splash as Alex fell into the harbor fifteen feet below.

"Jim, get him!" Cathy Sullivan said, pulling her husband off of Matt. A few people had noticed the commotion and were starting to approach from some distance away, others observing from their backyards or windows. Matt looked down and saw Alex struggling in the water. There was no easy access down there, no ramp, no ladder, nothing.

"Jump in there, asshole. That's your dog down there!" Matt said to Jim. "I guess you just let him go wherever he wants, no leash, right? That's what happens."

Jim Sullivan leaned over the railing, a mortified look on his face, but balking at the fifteen foot drop along a barnacle-studded concrete wall into the putrid looking marina water with its mysterious layer of billowing, yellow foam. Alex was down there, straining to hold his gigantic, fractured head above the foamy weird stuff. Jim took off his jacket and handed it to his wife, but the action was slow and tentative, as if to buy him more time to make a go-no-go decision, not the automatic reflex of someone stripping off clothing on their way down because it would hinder them once in the water.

Matt began to walk away, calling back as he went, "Oh, so you won't even get wet to save your own dog? You let your last dog die, too, had it put to sleep. I guess you never should have owned a dog to begin with."

Jim stood there with tears rolling down his face as Alex was lost from sight beneath the piss colored froth.

"You're a monster, Mr. Knox!" Cathy called after Matt as he left the walkway for the street.

"*Monster!*"

-28-

YOU SHOULD SEE THE OTHER GUY

Matt Knox stripped off his blood-soaked T-shirt as he emerged from the walkway out onto his home street. He balled it up and tossed it into a trash can meant for dog waste disposal. He didn't need to call any more attention to himself. Then, realizing it was an odd hour to be standing around with no shirt on, Matt started to jog, tossing his son's blood-caked skateboard into a neighbor's trash bin as he passed. He'd gotten carried away with the dog but what was done was done.

And he felt pretty good.

Matt passed by a few houses, lights on inside, people having dinner, watching movies, arguing, wondering how to save a few bucks, living their normal lives. He was just out for a jog. No big deal, do it all the time. A young guy passed him, running the opposite way on his side of the street. He was a real jogger as evidenced by his outfit, an mp3 player tucked into a sweatband, and his overall physical condition. The guy gave Matt a polite wave but his stare lingered on Matt's shoes. Topsiders. Boating shoes, not running shoes. Oh well. It wasn't against the law to run in boating shoes.

Matt reached his house. Summer greeted him as soon as he was inside.

"How are the kids?" He pre-empted her.

"Oh, Matt, they're fine. That was great how you stood up to that brute of a dog. Are you okay? There's blood on your face."

"It's not mine."

"Let's get you washed up. What happened to your shirt?"

"The gentle giant tore it up. I threw it out."

The kids came running out from the living room.

"Dad, that was awesome!" Gavin said. I saw you nail the dog with my board. Where is it, anyways—my board?"

Matt flashed on thick tufts of hair matted to the edge of bloody wood. "Sorry, kiddo, it accidentally did a radical aerial all the way into the harbor. Don't worry, though, we'll pick you up a new board."

"Awesome! Thanks, Dad!"

Summer led Matt to the downstairs bathroom and turned on the hot water. She tenderly applied a washcloth to Matt's face and neck, as if she couldn't believe he could be completely uninjured with that much blood. But Matt's skin was intact.

"How are the Sullivans? Did you talk to them? How's the dog?"

"Beats me. I got the hell out of there as soon as I could."

-29-

WHO ARE YOU?

"So what's your game plan for today?" Jeremy's wife asked him at the breakfast table. *Meaning, what are you doing to find a job.*

"I've got some leads to follow up on."

"Sounds good. Good luck." She pecked him on the cheek and left for work, again leaving him with only the morning news for company. Jeremy stared into the small screen, not seeing it. He had been unable to tell Alisa about discovering Sal's body because it meant explaining what he was doing there. He was supposed to be finding steady work, not running around--how did Tommy put it?—playing Sherlock Holmes. That reminded him: his meeting with Tommy was later today. He needed to pick up a pair of TracPhones beforehand. He wanted to be able to call Tommy if needed but contract accounts linked to their names were off limits. The Tracs were pre-paid with a set number of talk minutes, and would protect their identities.

He wasn't sure exactly when it happened but at some point Jeremy realized he was actually watching the TV. The same blond reporter who had covered the museum robbery was there on screen, only this time she was talking about Sal. Sal Jonason's dead body, discovered early this morning by a friend sent to check on him when he hadn't shown up for his part-time job at a fish packing plant. External shots of Sal's apartment building played out across the screen.

Jeremy gripped the edge of his counter tighter. *Will they say if they suspect anyone had entered the apartment recently? Maybe I shouldn't have gone in there...*

But by the time he finished this thought the piece was over already, and a different newscaster was saying something about the body of a dog that had to be fished out of the harbor.

Jeremy spotted Tommy's patrol car in the airport lot and pulled his Bronco alongside. He exited his own vehicle and got in on the patrol car's passenger side.

"You know that when they assign me a partner someone'll be sitting there and we won't be able to meet like this."

"That's why I brought these," Jeremy said, holding up two TracPhones and handing one over to Tommy.

"Good idea," Tommy said, taking the device.

"Stolen item list?" Jeremy prompted, getting right down to business. He had no time to waste and with the phones he was already spending money he didn't have. He either needed to earn that reward or else find a damn job.

"Got it," Tommy said, consulting his patrol car's computer. He pressed a few buttons and squinted at the screen until he took his hands away. "Here it is. This is some weird shit, not your typical stolen goods."

Jeremy leaned in closer while Tommy recited from the list. "Whaling harpoons, black and white pearls, animal pelts, whale ivory art pieces, Japanese glass floats, maritime art including paintings, sculptures and drawings, ships' logs, antique brass fixtures, two 1800s muskets or revolvers, cutlasses, swords or machetes, historical maps and charts, various seafaring articles." Tommy looked over at Jeremy and handed him a piece of paper.

"Here's a printout of the initial police and lab reports, you can read it later."

Jeremy nodded his thanks. "A lot of those antiquities are certainly identifiable," he said, folding the paper into his pocket.

"The department already contacted local pawn shops as well as the major museum brokers listed online. Craigslist and eBay also have flags. If someone tries to hock one of these things without going person-to-person in the real world, we'll know about it."

Then Tommy frowned and looked over at Jeremy. "I know that doesn't really help you—us, that is—in terms of capturing that reward. But hey, every now and then the Sandy Cove PD does actually manage to solve a crime, there's nothing I can do about it," he finished with a smile.

"Even a blind squirrel runs across a nut once in a while, is that it?"

Tommy laughed and Jeremy went on. "That's okay, we need as much info as we can get, no matter how you slice it." Jeremy said.

Tommy adjusted the controls on his police band.

Jeremy considered using this break in the conversation to tell Tommy about Sal, but checked the impulse. Their new partnership was still in its infancy. Doubtless he would have already heard by now, anyway, it being on the news and all. Maybe Tommy would mention it to him. If so, Jeremy thought, maybe then I'll tell him I was there, and about his conversations with Pablo. For now though, he wanted the flow of information coming his way.

"So how 'bout the lab report?—anything?"

Tommy raised his eyebrows. "They did get something. Not much, but something. Coupla latent prints lifted from a piece of shattered display case glass. They already ran 'em through IAFIS as well as the local databases and came up with no matches, though."

"Hmmm." To Jeremy, that was odd. He wouldn't expect anyone on Sal's gang not to already have a criminal record.

"Probably a staff print, or a visitor," Tommy said. "They found staff prints in the rest of the museum—in the second floor office. Thing is, they wiped everything pretty clean in the public display areas. There should be a bunch of prints just from the employees and visitors, but it was clean."

"Are they interviewing the employees? Making sure it wasn't an inside job?"

"They are. And they'll be comparing what they did find to the mess of staff prints in the employee only spaces. Don't have the results on those yet. But I'll try to get that next."

Jeremy stared at the image of the two fingerprints Tommy had called up on his patrol car's computer screen. A thumb and forefinger, not already in the databases.

Must be an employee print they missed.

-30-

FOOD FOR THOUGHT

Not ready to brave the confines of his own apartment alone when he should be working, Jeremy drove toward the harbor. The June gloom was finally starting to lift, the sun peeking through remnants of foggy clouds. He made his way from the airport toward the waterfront, visualizing Sal's brutalized face at a yellow light here or during a left turn there. What would the coroner's report list as the official cause of death?

He knew that for a homicide the coroner's report would be thorough, meaning it would take a while to produce, and tightly guarded, meaning that unless you were a fly on the wall when the detectives talked to the coroner during their initial assessment, you'd have to wait for the official report. But he had a report of his own. When he pulled up to a red light, Jeremy flipped open his cell-phone and brought up the snapshot he'd taken in Sal's apartment.

There was Sal's bloody head. Jeremy's stomach shriveled at the site of it. He could barely make out Sal's facial features for all the blood. Thick smears extended from where his face had come to rest on the coffee table, mingling with...something else, was that a black smudge? Difficult to say for sure with the low quality phone-cam shot.

The horn from the car behind him jarred his attention back to the road. Jeremy snapped his phone shut and tossed it on the passenger seat. *Who would have done something like that to Sal?* A dispute with his gang over the stolen museum loot? But why such a weird, over-the-top death? Jeremy was intimately familiar with gangs, both from growing up in the area and as a result of his professional exposure as a cop. No ordinary handgun did that. Didn't look like knife wounds, either, not that he had ever seen, and he'd seen a lot. A sawed-off shotgun? Maybe, but too close and a shotgun wouldn't have even left that much of Sal's face. Maybe someone poked the barrel just inside the door and blasted him from there?

Reaching the waterfront and turning left along Harbor Boulevard, Jeremy wished he'd taken a few more snapshots inside Sal's apartment. He doubted any shells or casings were left behind, but he might have picked up on a few more details. The grisly nature of Sal's demise had rattled him so much, though, that even his veteran police officer self had not fought the urge to get the hell out of there.

Jeremy came to the parking lot of his favorite fish and chips place and pulled in. It wasn't a fancy joint, and the lord knew he didn't have money to burn, but he needed to eat and he needed to think, which was hard to do in his place with all the bills lying around. The fact that Fisherman's Catch was directly across the harbor's main channel from the Sandy Cove Maritime museum didn't hurt either. It was barely 11:00 A.M., but The Catch, as locals called it, was open for business, both lunch and fresh caught fish filets by the pound to go. In fact, Jeremy could see as he approached that the establishment fairly bustled, mostly with fisherman already back for the day before the wind picked up too much outside the harbor.

Jeremy pulled open the weathered, wooden door, its ship's bell chime clanging as he stepped inside. A chalkboard displayed the fresh catches and specials of the day. He walked up to the counter and placed an order for beer battered halibut from a nineteen year old he'd busted a year earlier for tagging graffiti on a bridge.

"Hey," the kid said as he rang up Jeremy's order.

"Staying out of trouble, I hope, Donovan?"

"Yes sir. I hope you are, too," he said, preparing to give Jeremy change. *Ouch.* He was about to tell the kid to mind his own when a portly gentlemen Jeremy knew to be the owner of The Catch stepped up to the register.

"Donovan, watch the grill for a minute, will you? I've got this." The kid walked back into the kitchen and the owner handed Jeremy his twenty back. "It's on the house."

Jeremy averted his eyes and lowered his voice. "Come on, Mark, I can pay. Take it."

But the big man encircled Jeremy's hand with his own massive paw until Jeremy felt the crumpled bill tickle his palm. "Nonsense. Your money's no good here today. I reserve the right to refuse service...and money," he finished, releasing Jeremy's hand from his monster grip.

It embarrassed Jeremy to take what he thought of as a form of charity, but he knew it was because Mark was thankful for the time a few months ago when Jeremy and Tommy had responded to a call about suspicious activity inside The Catch after hours. They'd caught a burglar red-handed, sneaking out through a window with a week's worth of register cash and some computer equipment. A few minutes later and the guy would have been long gone.

"I have a new catch coming in on the back dock—enjoy your lunch, Jeremy!" Mark, who moved surprisingly fast for someone of his enormous bulk, turned and headed for the kitchen.

"Thanks," Jeremy called after him. He picked up his food at another section of counter and took his tray to the outside seating area. He had his pick of the wooden picnic tables on the patio overlooking the water. Nice and quiet out here, too, Jeremy thought, setting his tray down on a bench, if a bit windy. The boisterous conversation between the fishermen inside was now muted, replaced with the clanging of sailboat rigging coming from the boats in the slips below.

Jeremy took a bite of his fish as he looked at the businesses across the harbor. A row of tightly spaced wooden buildings crowded against one another. Pirate Willie's bar, not yet open for the day, a boat and jet-ski rental operation, a ticket booth for watersports activities–whale watching, parasailing, fishing, etc.–and the Saltwater Sweets Shoppe with its taffy machines twirling away in the window—all of these together took up about as much space as did the Sandy Cove Maritime Museum, which sat off to the left of the other buildings from Jeremy's vantage point.

Jeremy had been there a couple of times, a long time ago, on school field trips. Busloads of excited kids still filed through its doors, and hundreds of families visited every summer during peak season. He racked his memory but couldn't think of ever making a response call there as a cop. It was just a quiet, long-time local landmark. Until a couple of days ago.

Even from here, Jeremy could see the yellow police tape that criss-crossed the entrance alcove: CRIME SCENE DO NOT CROSS. A CLOSED sign hung in the admissions window, but Jeremy figured there might be employees inside assessing the damage. Smoothing out the printed police report on the table, he considered trying to enter the museum but quickly decided against it. There could also be police detectives in there, and it would be trouble were he to be seen by them. Trespassing, possibly even impersonating an officer, it wouldn't be good. And what could he hope to find, anyway? The CSI guys have had 48 hours to comb the scene for evidence, Jeremy thought.

What did he really need to know? Jeremy mulled this over, forking some coleslaw. Pablo already told him that Sal's gang was responsible. He knew Sal was dead. He knew who the core players in Sal's gang were. But the reward wasn't for information leading to the capture of those responsible, it was for return of the stolen items. Pablo wouldn't tell him what they had done with the loot, and Sal was certainly not in a position to tell him anything.

Jeremy began reading through the police report, glancing up occasionally to look at the museum itself. The report was surprisingly brief. Most of the investigative content was a thorough accounting of all of the missing items.

Other than that it stated only that the first two employees on duty Monday morning called in to report the burglary. Their names were given. They said they saw no sign of a break-in from the outside—no door locks had been tampered with, no windows broken, nothing. But inside, some of the glass display cases had been smashed, while others appeared to have been opened with a key. Two latent fingerprints were found on a glass fragment. Jeremy frowned as he finished reading the report. Nothing new here compared to what Tommy already told him.

It wouldn't be long before the department sent a few marked units to interview the remaining members of Sal's gang. But officially, they didn't have anything. They'd hope to scare a confession out of them by their mere presence, but they also knew that Sal's gang wouldn't scare easily. To leave almost no evidence behind indicated serious planning. They'd know the report would be anemic.

Jeremy looked up from his plate in time to see a figure in shorts, sandals and a Hawaiian style shirt duck the police tape and enter the museum.

-31-

I SPY

Jeremy took the last bite of his fish and stood. The guy who entered the museum still hadn't come back out yet. He set the empty basket on top of the trash can and left Fresh Catch through the patio door.

A footbridge spanned the harbor's main channel not far from where he was. Curiosity drew him across. *Who is that guy?* The museum was closed, but he still managed to get inside. If cops were also inside, they must have let him in. Or else, Jeremy thought, walking past a mother with a stroller on the bridge, he had a key. Either way, it really made Jeremy wonder who this person was.

He made it to the other side of the bridge and stepped off onto the sidewalk fronting the museum. A few people strolled by on the water-front walkway, one or two turning to look at the museum as they passed, but no one was stopping. Jeremy turned into the open alcove entrance when he reached it and walked toward the door.

What are you doing? He'd just told himself he wouldn't come here, but his desire to know what was going on overwhelmed his better judgment.

If it's locked, I walk away.

Seeing no one coming for a fair distance in either direction on the walkway, Jeremy moved quickly to the shadowy rear of the alcove, out of reach of direct sunlight. He looked, but the door was closed flush against its frame, not open even a crack. It was fixed with an older style brass door handle set with a matching brass knocker in the shape of an anchor mounted above it. Looking high above him, Jeremy could see two gargoyle figurines carved into the ceiling molding, peering down. He wondered what they'd seen the day (or was it night?) of the burglary.

He leaned his head in close to the door but could hear no voices coming from within. He thought fast. *What will I say if someone sees me? If it's cops, I could say I just wanted to shoot the shit with some of the guys, I really miss 'em and all and knew a bunch of them would be here...* Jeremy stifled a laugh as he put his hand on the handle's lever and applied pressure. It wasn't locked. Pulling slowly, he got the door open a crack and peeped through.

No one in sight.

With a glance back to be sure he wasn't being observed, Jeremy entered the museum.

-32-

PRIMARY KEY

Matt Knox sat at his desk in the yacht brokerage, turning over the black skeleton key in his hands. He held it up over his head so that it caught the light coming in from his window. He read the inscription again: *Davey Jones' locker.*

He flashed on Sal's last words: *I'll be goddamned.*

Matt doubted if Sal's utterance was meant to be prophetic, though he supposed it may well be true in that context, so it must have indicated that he was surprised. And if he was surprised by the inscription, then it must mean something to him. *Right?*

Swiveling in his chair to adjust the way the light hit the key, he wished now that he could have waited a few more seconds to shoot him so that he could have asked him what he meant. But with Sal reaching for his weapon, that had of course not been an option.

He wondered what it opened. *Davey Jones' locker.* He was aware of its meaning as a nautical superstition for when sailors die at sea, when they are sent to the ocean bottom, to Davey Jones' locker. But to have a literal key for it...could it be a local business—a bar or pub, perhaps? Sandy Cove wasn't a big town, though, and there weren't any establishments with that name that Matt had ever heard of.

He let the key drop to the desk with a *clink.* The metal itself was quite heavy, likely pewter, Matt decided, but possibly brass, painted black. Could be a boat name, Matt mused. He'd certainly seen more than his share of off-color nautical monikers. But this was a weird key for a boat. Certainly not an engine key. It didn't look all that secure, either, almost four inches long with only four teeth. Maybe it was to a boat's wooden cabin door, Matt thought. If so, it would be difficult to find. He thought back to Dallas' yacht. Its cabin door had been unlocked, but Matt recalled seeing an ordinary door lock fixed into the handle. No way this key would fit it.

He turned to his computer and called up a database he had of all the boat names his business had ever dealt with. While waiting for the program to open, he heard the noise of hammering coming from outside.

Turning around to look, he saw a couple of city workers atop a light pole hanging a banner reading, 4th OF JULY: FIREWORKS FROM THE BARGE, COVE BEACH, 7PM. Only a couple weeks away, Matt thought, turning back to his PC. He made a mental note to confirm with Summer that they were going this year, as they did almost every year. It was a town tradition going back a long ways. The fireworks were detonated from a floating platform just offshore, and the people watched from the beach with picnic dinners and barbeques. Usually the mayor gave a patriotic speech invoking Sandy Cove's relatively short history.

Matt went back to his computer. He typed in *Davey Jones Locker* and submitted his search.

-33-

AFTERMATH

Jeremy closed the door softly behind him and stood in the museum's entrance hall. Two now empty glass display cases graced either side of the entrance way. No one was in sight, but he could hear the sound of footsteps on crushed glass in the next room. It occurred to Jeremy that sneaking up on someone at a crime scene wasn't the brightest thing to do.

"Hello?" he called out.

"Yeah?" the man replied. The voice sounded cautious but not threatening. Jeremy heard footfalls heading his way. The same guy Jeremy had watched entering the museum waddled out to the entrance hall. He wore jeans with sandals and a gaudy yellow aloha shirt that couldn't contain his wiry black chest hair. He was bald except for two tufts of black hair on either side.

"Is the museum open?" Jeremy asked. Playing dumb. Buy some time, try to get whatever information he could. He was a dry, cracked sponge that would soak up the tiniest amount of water.

The big man frowned. "Naw, buddy. Place just got robbed. I'm a claims adjuster for the insurance company. My bad, I should have locked the door after I came in."

Jeremy peered in at the main exhibit hall, at the shattered display cases that once housed the list of items he'd read in the police report, the numbered tags delineating the crime scene, and at the lack of items the museum now had to display. The place had really been gutted, he realized.

"Sorry, pal, but you gotta go," the claims adjuster said. "Nothing much worth seeing here anymore, anyways."

"I can see that," Jeremy said, turning and walking back toward the entrance. "Sorry to bother you," he said, pulling open the front door and stepping back outside.

He heard the lock *snick* closed behind him.

Jeremy didn't know what he'd expected to find in there, but the portly claims adjuster certainly wasn't it. He thought there would still be some police work going on. *Must have been pretty straightforward. Doubt they found much,* he thought, crossing back over the bridge to the Fresh Catch parking lot.

And he did learn one thing. Jeremy reached his Bronco and glanced back at the museum before climbing in.

The Sandy Cove Maritime Museum was insured. Perhaps that was where the reward money was coming from? Jeremy wasn't sure, but he took out a notepad he kept stashed in the glove box and wrote a reminder to see if the source of the reward was publicly available. Was it all coming from the city or was some of it coming from Dallas Draper himself?

-34-

REVERSE LOOKUP

"Zero results found for your query."

Matt Knox grimaced at the message box the database presented. There was no match for a boat named *Davy Jones' Locker*. So what did the key's inscription refer to? Matt didn't know, but he was tired of thinking about it for now so he opened his desk drawer and dropped the key inside, onto a tray of rubber bands and paper clips.

Deciding he should hide it better, lest John Samson get a little snoopy, or even the cleaning service people–was he growing more paranoid?–Matt lifted the removable supplies tray out of the drawer and dropped the key into the space beneath it. His breath caught as he saw the object in there. A cell-phone.

Sal's.

He stared at the object in fascination. He'd completely forgotten about it. He flashed on himself back in Sal's apartment. It was as if he were an actor starring in a movie, doing the deed, as he now thought of it, then swiping both his phone and Sal's—at least he assumed it to be Sal's—from Sal's kitchen counter before leaving. He'd been relieved and annoyed at the same time to get his phone back, since he'd reported his lost handset to the service provider (told Summer he'd dropped it overboard from their Whaler on the way to work) to have it cancelled. He'd already ordered a replacement which was on the way via next day FedEx. Amazing how addicted modern society has become to their little gadgets, Matt thought, plucking Sal's device from the desk. Everybody from power sales reps to pot-smoking gang leaders just had to have one. Outside his office he heard John's desk phone ring one-and-a-half times before he picked it up.

Matt wondered if the battery in the phone still carried any charge. He flipped the phone open and watched as it lit up. Message notification icons told him Sal had waiting texts and voicemails. Matt looked at the latest texts. One thread from someone named Pablo. Matt's mind played a moving picture of a skinny Hispanic man jumping aboard the Chris Craft...saying "Hey, man," to Sal...dropping museum items into a sack...

The last text from him read, "Stuff is at the drop."

Matt stopped breathing as he contemplated the meaning of the message. He scrolled back through the thread.

From Sal: U there?

From Pablo: Y

Sal: Which unit?

Pablo: Move&Store, #122B

Sal: Just needed the # No names

Pablo: Sorry

Matt snickered. These guys weren't the brightest bulbs on the tree. Then again, that just made it all the worse that they had gotten the better of him. It pissed him off. Even after killing Sal, he could still feel a seething anger—almost a hatred—broiling within him. It surprised him, and yet he welcomed it at the same time, like some unknown force he didn't fully understand but had been expecting for some time.

Matt was tempted to send Pablo a text message from the dead man. On my way... He'd love to scare the shit out of him. But he thought better of it. This phone was quite the treasure trove. Literally, by the looks of things. With Sal dead, their plans for the treasure had no doubt been seriously derailed. It might well still be wherever they stashed it. No need to tip his hand just yet. They wanted him to rob a museum, after all. To the thief went the spoils. Those stolen goods were his. He would take from those who would take from others, from those who would force others to do their unsavory bidding.

Matt perused Sal's phone some more, scrolling through text threads and even emails. Sal was a busy little beaver for a guy with no real job, Matt thought. Fairly enterprising, directing his loose cadre of thugs and semi-drifters with what looked to Matt like some sort of a shotgun approach (literally, in some cases, he had no doubt). He knew some of his little schemes wouldn't pan out, but it was a numbers game. As a salesman, Matt could relate to that.

At least a few of Sal's contacts appeared to be busy as well. Not all of them responded right away. Like this one guy, Matt thought, scrolling through a text…Josey…The name brought Matt back aboard the Chris Craft. Chunky Hispanic dude clamoring aboard, falling into the skinny one…*Pablo*…as he jumped over the rail. *"Yo watch it, Josey,"* Pablo had said. A casual flick of the wrist in return.

Matt's cerebral cinema came to an abrupt end there, probably because he'd began asking Sal what the hell was going on. *Fat-ass bastard, helping that pompous ass Sal to force a guy he didn't even know to rob a museum.* Why the hell shouldn't he make that motherfucker pay?

Scrolling through the phone's contacts, Matt wasn't surprised to see that there were no physical addresses entered for Sal's associates. Just phone numbers and in a few cases, e-mail addresses. *Fuck it,* Matt thought eyeing his appointment calendar on his PC. Slow work day. He looked up at a framed picture on his wall—"The worst day fishing is better than the best day working"—the kind of humor that tended to go over well with would-be yacht buyers. *Time to go fishing.*

He called up the text conversation from Sal to Josey, the last message being from Josey to Sal, reading Waitin on u. Must have to do with coordinating the transfer of the museum loot after the actual theft, Matt conjectured. He stroked the stubble on his chin (hadn't been shaving quite as regularly the last few days) before applying his thumbs to Sal's keypad.

Josey-it's me Sal. U there? Matt clicked Send and his desk phone rang, startling him momentarily, as though the text he'd sent from a dead man had summoned an immediate reply. But he recognized the number on the telephone's display as a regional business. He fielded the work call, an inquiry about renting a yacht for an executive team building workshop. Ten minutes later, Matt hung up and glanced back at Sal's phone.

WTF-who this?

The grin crossing Matt's face could only be described as devilish. He eagerly composed a reply, adopting Sal's texting style he'd seen from reading his other messages. *He's on the line–reel him in.*

Its Sal. I aint dead. Dont tell nobody. Got a crazy-azz plan for the museum shit, u in it.

He jumped in his chair as the tinny strains of some gangsta rap song blared from Sal's cell. The screen lit up with the incoming caller: Josey, a cartoon graphic of the business end of a double-barreled shotgun the icon chosen to represent him. Matt raised his eyebrows before hitting Ignore on the call and going back to the text.

Now what?

Cant' talk now. Where u at.

U ain't Sal. Fuckin cops.

Bet your life? Matt chuckled to himself.

Prove it.

Matt rubbed his temples while he thought on this. He was about to start typing when a knock came at his office door. John Samson's voice. Matt hid the phone from sight.

"Working on something, John." He could feel the beginnings of a workable response to Josey formulating in his brain—like the precursor chemicals of some primordial stew that would someday form life. But right now they were still indistinct, and Jon's knock had scattered them back into oblivion.

Samson opened the door and stuck his head through. "Heading out to the Grog N Grub—you want to go?"

Matt stood up and pounded a fist on his desk. "Damn it, John I said *I'm working on something!* Get out."

John started to close the door, his face twisting into a display of angry confusion. He halted just before the door closed, standing outside the office but talking through the still open door.

"I don't know what's gotten into you lately, Matt, but you've been a real dick." He slammed the door the rest of the way shut.

A few seconds later Matt heard the outer office door open and close. He pulled out Sal's phone again, Josey's last reply still the latest message. *Prove it.*

A surge of adrenaline shocked Matt into a ramrod straight position in his chair as inspiration struck him. His mind's eye took him back inside the museum during the robbery and he picked out the details. Details only someone who was there could know. His thumbs marauded over the miniature keys until he hit Send with a flourish:

Bobby held up the pearls, said he wanted to give his girl a pearl necklace. U said I already gave her 1 last week. He started to bitchslap u and I told u both STFU.

Ten seconds elapsed before the reply came.

Where u wanna meet?

-35-

RENDEZVOUS

Matt flipped the dealership's door sign to "Gone Fishing–Back at 1pm," and stepped outside to their dock. That dirtbag Josey was cleaning boat hulls over at an industrial section of the harbor. Told him to come on over. "Sal" said he'd be there in thirty.

A large Hatteras, a sailing sloop and the same old Chris Craft occupied their dock space. None of these would do, Matt thought, scanning the dock area for something else. He could drive home and use his Boston Whaler, but that probably wasn't the brightest idea. The dealership had a runabout as well, but with SANDY COVE YACHT BROKERS emblazoned on both sides. Pass.

Matt's eyes narrowed as his gaze alighted on a small inflatable workboat tucked between the sloop and the Hatteras. It was owned by an old salt they hired sometimes to do detail work on the yachts. Matt recalled the guy asking if he could leave it here for a couple of days until he came back with the parts he ordered to complete his job. It was weathered and battered, but functioning, like at least a hundred other dinghies around the harbor. No one would look twice at it. Matt approached it and checked for the registration stickers. One on each side, both up to date. Didn't need to get pulled over. *Perfect.*

Matt tossed his backpack into the dinghy and untied its lines. The outboard (an Evinrude, for Christ's sake, probably made four decades ago, Matt thought—it cracked him up how these old guys would rather die than use something not made in America) came to life on the fourth pull. Matt kicked the gas can, felt it slosh, and nosed out between the yachts into the channel.

He turned left at the main waterway, heading deeper into the harbor, away from the ocean. He cranked up the throttle a bit as he passed a NO WAKE sign, glancing at his watch. Gotta get there.

He passed a shipyard, cranes stretching into the sky and boats getting repairs done up on lifts. He continued east, toward the mountains that loomed in the distance. He slowed his dinghy as the passages became narrower in the harbor's upper reaches. Matt reached into his backpack, pulled out a baseball cap with a marlin on the bill and a pair of polarized, horse blinder sunglasses and put them both on. Josey would recognize him for sure. He relied on the element of surprise.

He would scope out the scene, Matt reasoned as he turned a corner into one of the most inland canals. If Josey was just sitting up on the dock on the lookout, this wasn't going to work and Matt would simply turn around before he got too close. He'd just have to play it by ear. Hopefully the loser would be doing what he said he was doing, though—cleaning boat hulls.

Cleaning Nauti Girl.

Matt recalled Josey's text and then pictured the boat. He was familiar with it—a Stingray cruiser that had been with the brokerage for a time a few years back. *Nauti Girl indeed, Matt thought, flashing on the owner's wife taking her top off at a cocktail party on board the boat Matt had been invited to after selling it to them.*

He spotted the boat now, several slips down. Paintjob was different but other than that it was easy to recognize. Same lines, same name. Real quiet back here in this part of the harbor, too. Houses on only one side, an open field on the other that supposedly they were going to build something on one day when they got done fighting over the zoning laws.

Matt dropped the motor down to idle and eased over to the opposite side of the canal from *Nauti Girl* as he approached. An old boat cleaning skiff was tied up alongside the cruiser, its deck space occupied by coiled hoses and an air compressor—Josey's hull cleaning rig.

No one on board.

Josey was down below, underwater. Matt cut his engine and let the momentum carry him to the slips on *Nauti Girl*'s side. The engine would be quite loud underwater, Matt knew, and if Josey saw him gliding up he might come up to investigate. Not that he would be expecting Sal to arrive by boat.

Matt docked the dinghy a half dozen slips away and got out onto the dock. He walked casually down to the *Nauti Girl* as if he belonged there, like he was invited or perhaps was working on her.

The boat was docked nose in. Matt was visible to the houses from the dock, but once on the boat's rear deck he'd be largely hidden from view, except from the water where traffic was light. Matt shouldered his backpack as he stepped aboard, the boat rocking gently with his weight. A seagull cawed in the distance.

He walked along *Nauti Girl*'s port rail and stepped out onto the aft deck. He liked what they'd done with the boat, adding the grill on the stern rail, and the custom seat cushions, Matt couldn't help but noticing. He'd have to find out who did that later.

Right now, what interested Matt was the skiff tied to *Nauti's* stern rail, and the rubber hose extending from it that dropped out of sight below, where Josey breathed from it through a SCUBA regulator.

-36-

ANCHORS AWEIGH

Matt watched Josey's bubbles percolate to the surface off the *Nauti Girl's* stern. The harbor water wasn't clear enough for Matt to be able to see him, but he could picture him well enough, wearing the standard boat cleaning gear: a black wetsuit with lead weight belt to keep him from floating up into the hull he was trying to clean, a diving mask, a SCUBA mouthpiece leading up to the air compressor on the skiff. A sponge or cleaning tool of some kind for wiping the inevitable layers of marine growth from the boat's hull.

Should have stuck to your boat cleaning job instead of robbing museums, you punk, Matt thought as he eyed the air compressor. Shutting it off would cease the flow of air to Josey. Only a few feet underwater, the diver would be in no real danger, but it would bring him right to the surface, where Matt wanted him. He hefted his backpack but set it down again without opening it. The old musket inside might not be so effective here. Josey's thick wetsuit and mask would effectively shield him from much of the musket's blast. Its report would also be quite loud in this quiet residential canal area.

Matt's gaze landed on the rusty anchor lying on a pile of rope in the skiff's bow. About a foot long, a classic small boat style anchor with a shank and four folding tines. Matt shuffled to it and picked it up, untangling it from its own anchor line. With the tines folded in, it was basically a straight length of metal pipe. Matt hefted its weight.

Substantial, yet still easy to swing. The yacht salesman glanced around the neighborhood as he tried a couple of practice swings.

Then he undid the metal catch holding the tines back and let them open, like the petals of a metal flower. Now he had something resembling a grappling hook, still tied to a line from the shank end.

While he considered his weapon of opportunity, Matt psyched himself up, thinking about his prey. *Fucked with the wrong guy this time, buddy.* Josey was a piece of shit who deserved to die cleaning someone else's toy.

Matt folded the tines back in. Extended, one of them could pierce Josey's mask faceplate or if Matt was lucky, his windpipe or even skull, but if it wasn't a perfect strike there was a decent chance the tine would glance off its target without doing any real damage. Matt wasn't looking for a fight. Would it be nice if Josey recognized him before he died? Oh yes. Definitely. But that was not the primary objective here.

One good blow to the head from the folded anchor ought to do it. Matt looked to the compressor. Just about time to shut it off. But first, let's see what soon-to-be-not-of-this-Earth Josey has got laying around. *Probably not much.* Matt found his sweatshirt draped over the steering console. He rifled through the pockets. No wallet. A loose ten dollar bill, which he left in place. He looked back into the recesses of the console beneath the steering wheel, where there was a small storage compartment. Matt snickered at a couple of joints back there, but he could find nothing interesting. On second thought, Matt grabbed the joints and tossed them on deck. *Maybe the cops will think it's drug related.*

Then he moved back to the air compressor. Located the switch to turn it off. He picked up the folded anchor in his right hand, making sure the rope tied to it wasn't tangled down around his feet. He located Josey by his bubble stream. Perfect. He was right off the Nauti's port stern—if forced to come up he'd be between the Nauti and the skiff. With a last look around at his immediate surroundings (no one in sight!), Matt flipped the air pump switch to OFF.

It spooked Matt a little how quiet it became without the din of the compressor. The only sound was the gentle lapping of water against the boat's hull. But there was no time to have second thoughts now. Josey's bubbles stopped their march to the surface. *And here he comes, ladies and gentlemen, right on cue.*

Matt could see Josey's dark, wetsuit clad form emerging from underneath the Nauti Girl's hull. *Damn.* He wasn't coming up as close to the skiff as Matt had hoped. He was much closer to the Nauti, gasping for breath as his head broke the surface.

Change of plans. He couldn't just stand here. A tarp lay in a crumpled heap in the center of the skiff, used to cover the equipment when not in use. Matt lay down and pulled the tarp over his body. He heard Josey mutter some epithet and start to swim toward the skiff, heavy splashing shattering the stillness.

Did he see me?

From beneath the tarp Matt could see the edge of the skiff in the foreground and the *Nauti*'s barbeque in the background. Couldn't see the water, it was too low. He knew the tarp would look weird to Josey if he thought about it, but hoped he'd be focusing on the compressor. He forced himself to wait.

Before long a dark, wet hand clamped onto the skiff's rail, inches from Matt's face. Matt saw the dive mask whiz past his limited field of vision as Josey tossed it into the boat. He heard Josey's exertions as the museum-robbing boat cleaner swung a leg up and began pulling himself into the floating work platform.

Matt sprung out from under the tarp. In seconds he was on two feet, looking down at Josey flopping into the boat, anchor raised above his head. Josey's eyes first narrowed in recognition and then widened in terror as Matt brought the anchor down on Josey's left temple.

There was a muted crack and then a stream of blood tracing its way down Josey's cheek.

"What the fuck?" Matt's victim sputtered, hands up to shield himself from further blows as he rolled over on his side. Matt raised the anchor again and felt the catch holding the tines together come undone, the metal flower blooming in his hand as he brought the anchor down once more. This time the anchor caught Josey in the back of the neck, one of the tines actually embedding itself there. The big man was instantly still. Matt stared into his lifeless eyes for a moment, finding it hard to believe that Josey was dead.

Then he shoved the big, weighted body overboard into the water, pulling the anchor with it, where it sank out of sight.

Matt calmly walked back across the *Nauti Girl* to the dock. Five minutes later he was motoring the dinghy down the harbor's main channel back toward Sandy Cove Yacht Brokers.

-37-

NOSE FOR NEWS

Cove 6 news reporter Carol Tepper munched on a Caesar salad inside the van while she argued with her cameraman, who was in fact a man, by the name of Sander Clothier. Recently assigned to work with Tepper, Clothier was still getting used to her. He thought of it as he getting used to her, and not they getting used to each other, because, as he'd come to notice the longer his tenure in the business wore on, the career drive of the reporters he filmed tended to exceed his own. He wasn't going to win an Emmy or a Pulitzer or whatever the hell awards they give to news teams these days. He was just doing a job, counting down the months until retirement.

"We have plenty of time to get to the dog show. Seriously, where's your sense of adventure, Sander?"

"It's in the bedroom, where it belongs. I prefer my work to be boring and secure."

Carol cracked a smile but said, "Shhhh," while she turned up the volume on the police scanner they sometimes used to sniff out breaking news. "This sounds good, listen," she said, before turning back to her lunch.

Sander occupied the driver's seat next to her. Carol's senior by a good thirty years, he'd worked with many on-camera personalities during the course of his career, and he recognized a real go-getter when he saw one. Still, getting them live on some sensational story at any expense wasn't in his job description. They got paid to cover specific stories handed down to them from on high, and while some—even many—of those stories might be banal or trivial or boring, however you wanted to put it, the fact remained that there was an audience for them the station's sponsors had identified, and so they had a job to do. Rarely was there nothing to report, even in the small town of Sandy Cove.

Furthermore, Sander thought, Carol had some talent. She was no Kronkite or Sawyer, but he'd seen her turn something as mundane as a local little league game into a galvanizing human interest piece. Unlike a lot of up-and-comers who wanted the glory before the work, she did do a good job with the assignments she was given, but she wanted more.

Bitch is hot, too, he acknowledged, casting a sidelong glance at her naturally blonde hair arranged in a tight bun with a pair of chopsticks sticking through it, beautiful blue eyes over a pert, upturned nose, and a slim figure decked out in some fancy designer shit. He was sure there was some percentage of viewers—and not all of them men, either—who'd watch her deliver a report about how fast the grass was growing in front of city hall.

Carol's drive, in addition to the looks, sort of put Sander on edge. Her job was secure as it was. The station would be happy to have her in her current capacity for as long as she kept showing up. But at the age of twenty-seven, he guessed she had at the very most two more years before some rich guy married her and she got out of the business. Maybe she sensed this herself and that's why she felt the urgency to tackle more important stories? There was no polite or politically correct way to express this to her, however, and so Sander, himself happily married for close to two decades to a woman his own age, obliged her chance-taking.

The dispatcher on the police band was instructing a field unit to one of the harbor's residential canals in that detached monotone police dispatchers had down to a tee. "...boat owner called in that the water in the slip next to his was red in color, that maybe it looked like blood. Caller was referred to Harbor Master to check for red tide reports, but a second caller phoned in twenty minutes later about a boat cleaner's skiff found unattended in the same slip."

The reply from the patrol unit was garbled and static-filled, but the dispatcher's response was clear as she recited an address and said, "10-4. Adam 17 please proceed to the scene."

Carol snapped shut her clear plastic salad to-go container and tossed it onto the dash as Sander put the van in gear.

"We'll check it out," he said.

"Thanks, Sander."

-38-

HER AGAIN

Jeremy Washington pulled his Bronco into the lot for Sandy Cove Hardware & Lumber. He had been heading home after his museum visit, but when he saw the hardware store he pulled in. He was pretty handy with tools, after all, and he needed a job. There weren't a lot of cars in the lot, Jeremy noticed as he made his way to the entrance. The building was small, not like one of the big box home improvement stores that could be found not too far outside of town. Jeremy had been here once or twice in the past, but it had been a while and he couldn't remember the last time.

He pushed open the double glass doors, setting off an electronic chime. A man of about fifty years of age with light brown hair and blue eyes leaned his head out from the counter, to the left of the front door from where Jeremy entered. The man smiled as Jeremy walked in. The two had seen each other around town, but didn't really know each other. Mild acquaintances at best, Jeremy thought, but hey, when you're looking for work any association helped. Jeremy knew him to be the manager of the store. He tried to think of his name as he walked up to the counter.

"Hi there," the manager greeted Jeremy. "Jeremy, right?"

"Morning, Paul," Jeremy said, nodding. Then he remembered a sort of mnemonic device that helped him to remember the guy's name. "Paul Wright, right?"

"The one and not the only. Been a while, Jeremy. You doing okay these days?"

He knows, Jeremy thought.

"Looking for anything I can help you with?"

"Actually, I'm looking for work. You guys need any help cutting lumber, or stocking, anything like that? I'm real handy. I'd take something part-time if that's all you need."

Paul frowned as he seemed to consider Jeremy in a new light— someone who sought money from him rather than a customer here to give him money. "No, sir, it's just me and one other guy these days. Don't need anyone else. I've been in one form of customer service or another my whole career, and let me tell you, times have not been good lately. As you can see, we're not exactly slammed around here." Paul waved an arm at his aisles.

Jeremy nodded as he looked back at the store, all of two customers visible, nitpicking through the wares on the shelves.

"Hard times on everyone right now," Paul continued. "You ever consider moving down to L.A.? Lot more jobs."

It was Jeremy's turn to frown. Relocating was not something he wanted to consider. Especially not to L.A. Almost his entire life had been spent in Sandy Cove. The thought of big city life didn't appeal to him in the slightest, and he knew Alisa felt the same way.

"Not really. Like to stay here," he said. He was starting to turn around to leave when the television mounted above the counter behind Paul caught his attention. The same blonde reporter who'd handled the museum robbery live coverage was now reporting from somewhere inside the harbor, a BREAKING NEWS banner marching across the bottom of the screen. Paul followed Jeremy's eyes to the screen, and they both lapsed into momentary silence while they watched the report.

A city ambulance was visible in the background while the camera focused on Carol standing at the water's edge of a boat slip, face composed in a dead-serious expression while she seemed to stare right through the camera at each and every viewer.

"A body was pulled about fifteen minutes ago from this very boat slip in a canal along Spinnaker Drive. Apparently the victim—an as yet unnamed adult Hispanic male approximately thirty years of age—suffered some kind of head trauma.

"In fact," Carol continued, while turning to peer into the harbor, "the water is still red here, ostensibly from the blood of the victim, whose name is not yet being released pending notification of family. We can confirm, however, that this is the boat cleaning skiff the deceased man was working from at the time of the incident. Police say it is possible that the man suffered propeller injuries from the large boat he was cleaning, this one here."

The camera followed Carol's pointing finger out to the *Nauti Girl*, with the skiff still tied to her stern rail, both floating on water that was indeed tinted a distinctive red. The camera zoomed on a thick smear of blood on the skiff's deck. Jeremy's pulse quickened. *That's Josey Jiminez's skiff!* Jeremy knew Josey was an on-again-off-again member of Sal's criminal enterprises. He didn't know for certain whether he was involved in the museum job, but what he did know was that two people were now dead in the wake of that job.

"You okay?" Paul asked. The news had just moved onto another story, but Jeremy had been staring at the TV, lost in his thoughts.

"Yeah, just surprised, that's all. Don't see a lot of bodies fished from our harbor."

"True. Wow, did you see that red water, though? That's a lot of blood. Reminded me of one of those Japanese dolphin slaughter videos. I guess the water way back there in those slips doesn't circulate much."

-39-

TOMMYKNOCKER

"Any luck today?"

Jeremy had been expecting the question from his wife, but it didn't make it any easier. Their daughter, Star, tugged at her mother's skirt in the kitchen while she prepared dinner.

"Nothing yet. Stopped in at the hardware store to see if maybe they could use somebody there, but it seems like that place is just barely hanging on as it is."

Alisa continued to pull cans down from the cupboard while saying, "That all?"

Jeremy flushed. "Checked the craigslist ads and the paper, too, nothing." He flashed on his time earlier at the Fresh Catch. "Maybe I could be a fisherman?"

She laughed. At least he got her to laugh. "A fisherman? What do you know about fishing?"

It didn't escape Jeremy that every time he ventured forth a possible occupation for himself, Alisa prefaced her reaction with "What do *you* know about xyz?" The implied answer, naturally, being nothing. Which, he had to admit, in this case at least, was quite true.

"It's unskilled labor. How hard can it be? I've seen those TV shows. Deadliest whatever. Snap hooks onto a line. Toss some fish into a hold. Swab the deck."

"Well if you think you can do it, go check it out. Like tomorrow."

Jeremy thought about that. Might be a good idea, give him more reason to hang around the harbor. "I'll do that. I know the owner at Fresh Catch, maybe I'll ask him what boats are hiring."

Alisa smiled, giving Star a piece of cucumber she was slicing. "Come up with some other leads, too. Just in case being a fisherman doesn't work out, okay?"

"Good idea." But Jeremy's mind was already back on the museum case, returned there instantly by mentioning the Catch.

"Actually that reminds me, I took down some notes on a few leads when I was out today. I'm going to get them out of the truck. Want to be ready for tomorrow."

Alisa looked up from the counter. "Wow, I'm impressed. Dinner's ready in ten."

Jeremy went out to the carport and climbed into his Bronco. He took the trac phone out of the glove box, which was the real reason for his visit here. He hadn't checked it all day. Didn't know what we was expecting, but he should at least check. The red LED on the phone was blinking. Since no one but Tommy had the number, it must be him. Probably telling me about Josey Jiminez' skiff and the body in the harbor, Jeremy thought, clutching the phone to his hear. *Would like to hear more about that.*

Jeremy dialed into the voice mail. Yep, message from Tommy left a couple of hours ago. "Yo, got some 411," Tommy led off, not using Jeremy's name. "Lotta shit going on." *Great, Jeremy thought.*

"First, the stiff they pulled from the harbor this afternoon—you probably saw it on the news—that's Josey Jiminez, man, and check this. Dude was fucked *up* with a huge fuckin' hole in the base of his skull. We're talking instant death with a lot of applied force. Somebody was highly pissed off at this guy. He's one of Sal's goons."

Jeremy nodded with the phone to his ear, looking out on his complex's driveway from his Bronco as he listened to the one-way conversation. A dog barked somewhere nearby as the recording played out.

"Speaking of fuckin' Sal, he's dead too, man—before Josey, even. You must've seen that on the news by now. His little crime ring must have bit off more than they can chew this time around. Crazy shit, the way he went out, and this is why I'm calling you, man. Crime scene guys had a helluva time figuring out what happened to him, because his face was all fucked up, not quite as bad as if it was from a shotgun, meaning it was still there, but all hamburgered up from some kind of firearm they couldn't place at first."

Jeremy involuntarily shivered as he pictured Sal's dead face. Tommy's matter-of-fact account rolled on.

"Anyway, turns out there was some black powder residue left behind that they ID'd as coming from a modern supplier of gunpowder used in replica muskets, like old timey revolvers and shit like that, you hear me? And they say the thing was loaded with crushed fuckin' glass and carpet nails–because they recovered those all over Sal's place and from his face–and that Sal was blasted at close range with some kind of old musket type weapon spraying that shit out."

Jeremy could hear Tommy exhaling. "Man, I wasn't there personally, but I saw one of the crime scene pictures of Sal, and it ain't pretty what this thing did to him. I never seen *nothin'* like it, and you know I've seen guys shot up pretty bad."

"Anyway, thought you should know. Don't take a genius to connect a thug like Sal to a local robbery, and then one of the stolen things was a musket, and Sal was killed by one, right? We need to find that stolen loot, man. That's the thing that's gonna get you—get us–the reward. Another thing. Sal had nothing of value in his apartment. Just a little weed, a regular handgun, normal shit. I'll see if I can put some pressure on Sal's guys. Talk later."

The message ended and Jeremy put the trac phone back in the glove box, slowly, moving like a sloth as his mind kicked into overdrive with this new information.

-40-

THE LONE GUNMAN THEORY

The next morning found Jeremy pulling into Pablo's auto shop. Tommy was onto the fact that getting one of Sal's gang to tell them what they had done with the loot was key, and Pablo seemed the most likely candidate. Jeremy didn't know the other guys associated with Sal nearly as well. With Josey dead, Pablo would hopefully be more talkative.

The Bronco's dash clock blinked off at 10:07 as Jeremy killed the engine and stepped out into the parking lot in front of the garage. He hadn't come in as early as he might have. Wanted to give Pablo a chance to get a little work done, maybe be ready for a little break, Jeremy thought, walking across the parking lot. He could see a couple of customers inside the glassed-in office cube, but the work garage didn't look busy.

It had also given him the chance to scour the web classifieds for more jobs, but a no-experience-required security guard position at the harbor was all he could find. The hardware store guy's suggestion haunted him as he stepped over a yellow plastic chain separating the work area from the parking lot.

Why dontcha move to L.A.?

Jeremy spotted Pablo at the far end of the garage, now working under the hood of a yellow Ferrari. The work stall adjacent to his was empty.

"Almost done with my ride?"

Pablo lifted his head from the engine. When he saw it was Jeremy his eyes narrowed from behind his clear safety goggles.

"Well, if it isn't the snitch. Need more information to help you get that reward, eh?"

Jeremy wasn't pleased that his agenda was so out in the open, but it was the truth, and there was nothing he could do about it. He stepped up to the sports car, ogling its lines for a few seconds while Pablo wiped his hands on a grease rag. "I'm trying to help you, Pablo. But you have to help me."

"How are you gonna do that?" Pablo asked, throwing his rag to the concrete floor.

"You heard what happened to Josey?"

Pablo's look softened. "I did, man–*shit.*"

Jeremy pressed on. "Was Josey in on the job with you?"

"That's none of your business." Pablo scuffed his feet on the garage floor.

"I know he was in with you guys in general. Now he's dead along with Sal. You think that's a coincidence, Pablo? What the hell is going on? You guys fighting over how to divvy up the loot?"

Pablo rubbed his palms together and looked around the garage. Satisfied they had ample privacy, he turned his attention back to Jeremy, lowering his voice. "I don't know what the fuck is going on, man. Who's doing this. The loot is still secure, man. All there, I checked it *this morning*. None of the guys would do this fucked up shit."

All of a sudden Pablo looked extremely distraught, like he might even start to cry, Jeremy thought. It wasn't some kind of an act. His disbelief was as genuine as could be. And something else registered in Jeremy's brain. The loot. *If he checked on it this morning, then it must be somewhere nearby. It hasn't been sold yet, or at least not delivered to their black market buyers.*

Jeremy mustered up the most sincere look he could. "Pablo, I'm worried about you, man. Two guys on that job are dead. You say you still have the loot. What is it?"

Pablo exhaled deeply, looking up at Jeremy then back to the floor.

"Okay, here. How about this," Jeremy said, producing a folded piece of paper from his pocket—the museum job stolen inventory list he'd gotten from Tommy. He handed it to Pablo, whose eyes scanned it with recognition.

"Is this the stuff you stole? Look at it carefully."

Pablo looked up from the paper, transferring his gaze to Jeremy himself, looking his body up and down. "You're not wearing a wire, are you?"

"No. Everything you say is just between you and me."

"Lift up your shirt real quick."

Jeremy did so.

"Turn around." Again, Jeremy did as he was asked. Satisfied, Pablo turned his attention back to list.

He traced a finger down the printout, eyes occasionally darting to the side as his brain searched his memory before continuing down the list. After almost two minutes, Pablo said, "Yeah, this is it, except..." His pointer finger meandered up the paper. "The muskets," he said with finality, jabbing the paper on that line item. "We don't have any muskets and I don't remember anybody taking those."

"They were taken. Two of them. The case they were in was unlocked but not smashed."

Pablo shrugged, puzzling over the information presented to him. "We covered most of the main area but I don't think we got every single thing. I swear, I don't remember seeing any guns in there, except Sal's .38 that he brought in with him. I don't remember seeing any old revolvers or whatever."

Jeremy shivered. This was what scared him most of all. He gently pulled the paper from Pablo's hands. He wanted his full attention. "Pablo, do you know how Sal was killed?"

"I saw that picture you showed me, but no, what did that to him?"

"Crime scene guys say it was some kind of projectile spray weapon. A weapon that would be commensurate with—that means could have caused—Sal's injuries. An old musket, like the two that were taken from the museum the day you robbed it."

Pablo could not hide his look of surprise. "Sal was killed by a musket–for sure?

"Yes. Ballistics turned up black gunpowder residue in Sal's apartment that is only used in these kinds of weapons. Firearms database searches have turned up nothing, no lead shot ammo buys, but weapons this old don't have to be registered, and they can shoot almost anything. Sal was treated to a nice cocktail of ground up glass, rat poison and carpet nails blasted with gunpowder out of a packed muzzle."

"Damn. That's old school."

"Yeah, like seventeen-ninety fucking five. But modern day terrorists pack the same kind of shit into their homemade bombs. But you're not here for a history lesson. Point is, your buddy Sal got schooled just like that at point blank range to the face. Here's a little reminder of what this old-ass weapon did." Jeremy pulled his camera from his pocket and called up the image of Sal's musket-blasted face.

Pablo pushed away Jeremy's arm that held the camera. "Yo, man, why you playin' me like that?"

"Because you're next, Pablo!" Jeremy poked Pablo's chest with each of his next three words. "You. Are. Next. Unless you can help me nail whatever sick bastard is doing this."

Pablo gave Jeremy a half-smile. "How do you know the two deaths are related? Because with Josey, it wasn't a musket. They said on the news he was clubbed with something and found dead in the water, maybe drowned."

"Normally the different methods of killing might suggest a different perp, but come on, Pablo, when two guys who committed the same crime are both killed a few days later..." he let the sentence hang and noted that this time Pablo did not deny that Josey had been in the museum that day. But he did say, "What if it is different perps, but they're working for the same guy or organization or whatever? Like each guy kills a different way, according to his specialty."

Jeremy shot him a doubting look. "This isn't a kung-fu movie, Pablo. Do you really think there's a group of killers prowling around Sandy Cove, each killing someone by a different specialty? Really?"

Pablo shrugged sheepishly. Jeremy went on.

"It's not impossible, okay, but it could definitely be one guy. If I were a crime boss, I'd send one guy at first to see if he could handle it. The more guys you send the riskier it is, right? Bigger footprint, more chances one of them will get caught."

"Makes sense," Pablo conceded.

"But there's something else that so far makes me think it's one guy."

"What's that?" Pablo said, now starting to wipe down the Ferrari with a cloth.

"Both murders were very close quarters kills, with even more force than needed to make the kill."

"So?"

"So it's like this guy—if it is one guy, which is my theory—hated Sal and Josey. Think about it. A professional hitter doesn't usually get that close. Inside Sal's apartment. On Josey's little workboat. It's like this guy *wanted* to get close."

"With a club or an old musket you have to get that close."

Jeremy nodded. "The weapon choice would dictate that, but they are kind of weird choices, especially the musket. They can't be all that reliable."

"Weird shit, man," Pablo agreed.

"Pablo. Take me to the loot."

Pablo shook his head as he pulled a cart with engine diagnostics equipment over to the Italian sports car. "No can do, Mr. Private Detective, or whatever it is you call yourself now that you're not a cop. I tell you where the stuff is and it's like we went through it all for nothing. You just want the reward, and I understand that, but I can't feel sorry for you because I asked you if you wanted in and you declined. So I've told you some things to help you catch whoever's doing these murders, 'cuz that's fucked up shit, man, but I ain't telling you about where the loot is, no way, no how. Forget about it."

Jeremy gave Pablo a hard stare, but said nothing. He was right. If he knew where the stolen goods where, what then? Use the information to collect the reward, which means the loot would be taken from

Pablo and company. Funny how with Sal out of the picture that Pablo was the new number one man in the crime ring, Jeremy thought. Even if his people were dying around him.

"Be careful, Pablo," Jeremy said before walking away.

-41-

TWO BUCK CHUCK

"Gavin, Caitlin, we're leaving. Remember, no TV or video games until you have your homework done. I'll be checking when we get back. Thanks again for babysitting, Amy."

"No problem, Mr. and Mrs. Knox," the local teenager said. Have fun at the party." Summer blew a kiss at her children before she and Matt walked out the front door.

"So whose party is this one, again?" asked Summer, taking Matt's hand as they began walking down the sidewalk.

"The Eks. Saw Mattias out on the water earlier this week when I took the boat to work, he told me about it."

"They have a lot of parties, don't they?"

"Yeah, well they rent, here from Sweden only for one year to do a job, so why not, right?"

"Right, well, we didn't have anything great, but I brought a bottle of two buck Chuck from Trader Joe's, and a French loaf."

"That'll be fine. Mattias is usually pretty buzzed at these things, I doubt he'll notice or even care."

"Should be fun. I'm ready for some wine."

"I could use a glass or three myself."

Summer laughed as they strolled through the neighborhood. Sunset wasn't far off, and they passed the usual compliment of dog walkers and children playing. Ahead of them they could see another couple also headed to the party, evidenced by the picnic basket they carried, bottle of wine protruding from one end.

They arrived at an L-shaped, two-story waterfront house situated on a corner. A walkway led to the open front door, guests streaming in and visible milling about in the entrance hall. Matt and Summer filed into the house, exchanging pleasantries with the other party-goers, generally an older crowd, most of whom they either knew from the neighborhood or had seen before at similar social gatherings.

Reggae music wafted through the house at low volume. Several guests flitted about a table laid out with cheese and crackers and an assortment of wines. Mattias Ek, dressed for his role of party host in black jeans and a flannel shirt, spotted the Knoxes and stepped over. "Well if it isn't the lovely Knoxes! One of you is lovely, anyway," he added, raising his eyebrows at Summer while jabbing Matt softly with an elbow. "Welcome to paradise."

Someone else at the table added, "Don't mind the bodies," to a couple of laughs.

"Two deaths in a week is a lot for our little harbor town," Mattias concurred.

"Three bodies, if you count our dog." Cathy Sullivan, who had been reaching over the food table, now retreated from the small crowd there in order to glare at Matt. "There's the animal killer!" she said in a loud voice, pointing a dip-slathered celery stick at him that dripped onto the floor as if to add another dimension to her accusation. "You murdered our Alex!"

Mattias found Jim Sullivan in conversation with another man and pulled him aside. Matt saw Mattias point at Cathy, and Jim went to her, grabbed her by the hand and pulled her deeper into the house, both Sullivans giving Matt hateful looks as they went.

Mattias refilled his wine glass while he gave Matt a concerned stare. "What's that all about?" He still smiled but it was now infected with a certain uneasiness, no longer one hundred percent carefree. Matt took the bottle from Summer and found a wine opener on the table while he answered.

"They blame me for what happened to their dog, when it was the dog who came after my family. It was acting crazy, maybe it had rabies, I don't know, but I left before it ended up in the water. I understand they must be going through a grieving process."

"I think they're batshit crazy!" Summer said. "Matt saved us from their out of control beast that they let *run around loose!*" She finished her sentence by cupping her hand to her mouth and turning in the direction of the departing Sullivans.

Matt presented Summer with a glass of their wine. "It's okay, babe. Let them deal with their loss."

Summer smiled at her husband. "You know, I really think that dog ate the Johnsons' cat. Literally. You remember how it went missing? Hey, I love this song!" she said, grabbing Matt by the hand. "Let's dance!"

She pulled Matt out to the living room floor, where one couple gyrated awkwardly. When the song ended they refilled their wine glasses and then mingled with the flow of guests out to the backyard, where a fire burned in a large clay urn, casting its glow on the water in the canal below. Matt recognized Mattias' boat in a slip in front of the house.

A barbeque was set up in a corner of the yard, the smell of cooking meat permeating the atmosphere. Matt and Summer chatted briefly with a few guests. Matt was about to get some food from the grill when he spotted Dallas Draper, engaged in close conversation with a beautiful but older woman. Matt saw him shake his head. They spoke in hushed tones. Then the woman put a hand on Dallas' shoulder and squeezed. As he turned and walked away from her, Matt could see a tear on Dallas' cheek reflected in the firelight.

Matt couldn't remember when the last time he'd seen an adult man cry, certainly he'd never seen Dallas cry, he thought. And then he was surprised when Dallas saw him staring at him and came over to him and Summer. "Hi Matt, Summer," he said, wiping his cheek. "Sorry, I'm not very composed right now," he said.

"What's the matter, honey?" Summer asked in her semi-flirtatious way. She put a hand on his shoulder and Dallas slid out from under it when he saw Matt's eyes follow the gesture.

Dallas shook his head. "It's okay. I'm fine really, it's just the museum. You heard about the robbery?"

Summer said yes, while Matt nodded silently. Was Dallas playing with him? If so, he couldn't detect any sign of it. His distress appeared genuine.

"They took *everything*," Dallas said, choking back a little sob. "All that stuff I collected for decades, in all my travels. I'll never be able to replace it."

"Don't worry, Dallas, they'll catch those scumbags," Summer declared.

"Police make any progress on the case yet?" Matt asked. "Last I heard, on the news, they didn't know much, or at least they said they didn't."

"No, they really don't," Dallas said. "They lifted a fingerprint in there that they say is probably from one of the looters, but they ran it and it doesn't come up in the system."

"That's unusual, isn't it?" Summer asked.

"Yes. They said it looked like a professional job, and professional thieves usually have some kind of record, even if it's something minor."

"Couldn't it be one of the museum visitors, or one of your employees?" Matt said.

Dallas paused to smile and wave at a couple walking by. "They're actually testing all the employees, just in case, not that it's any of them. I know none of them would do something like that. But they don't have many leads so they're doing everything they can think of."

Summer reached out again and put a hand on Dallas' arm. "I hope you get your things back. We really enjoyed taking the kids there—just last summer, right, Matt? Matt?"

Matt was lost in thought, staring at Dallas. "Sorry! Yeah, I was just thinking how interesting everything there was. I'm real sorry, Dallas. Hopefully that reward will help people to come forward."

"Yeah, it's going up, too. Doubling to fifty grand. I'm still putting up the same twenty-five, but now the city stepped up and they're matching me. Mayor tells me it should be on tomorrow's news. This kind of thing makes the whole town look bad, you know, a major waterfront landmark all of a sudden gutted..." He paused to take a deep breath. "I'm sorry, you two, I know you came here to have a good time. Don't let my pity party interfere."

"Not at all, Dallas," Summer said.

A drunk guy in a T-shirt emblazoned with Gamefish of California came up to the three of them. He was rumored to have retired early due to some kind of Internet 2.0 stock options, but whenever there was a party that he wasn't at, talk quickly turned to speculating on the true source of his apparent wealth and whether he had taken out a second mortgage on his home, whether he ever did any kind of work at all. Typical talk for the cove.

"You guys going to the fireworks show tomorrow?" he said without preamble.

"I can't believe the Fourth crept up on us so quickly this year," Summer said. Seems like the pirate party was just last month.

"Yarrrrhg, that would be a limey year ago, lassey," the fish guy slurred. The annual fireworks display on Sandy Cove Beach was a veritable institution for the town. Another woman leaned in as she was passing by the group.

"Glad we won't have to wait long for another party!"

The woman's boyfriend–rumored to be staying in her house when she was away–a big no-no for the neighborhood association–caught up with her, encircling his arms around her waist briefly before waving at Matt, Summer and Dallas. "That's why we live here, right? This is the life."

"Cheers to that," Matt said, raising his glass of two buck Chuck.

-42-
INDEPENDENCE DAY

Matt sat at his desk behind the closed door of his home office. Sal's phone was open in front of him while he scrolled through its contents. He was getting nervous about using it—about even having it around—since he knew the GPS feature could potentially be used to locate it, and with Sal murdered, an investigation was to be expected. He would get rid of the phone today.

A soft double-tap came at his door. Matt slid the phone off the desktop onto his lap as the door opened and Summer came in, dressed in form fitting white shorts and a red halter top, crowned with a black pirate hat and an eye patch.

"Pirate party! You're going to dress the part, right?"

"You bet," Matt said, patting a wide belt with twin revolver holsters on his desk. "The rest of my outfit's upstairs, I'll go throw it on in a minute."

"Okay, we're ready to leave in about fifteen," she said. "I have everything packed—picnic basket, blanket, jackets for tonight."

"Great, I'll be right out, just wrapping up a referral."

"Okay, don't be too long or there won't be any parking left and we'll have to walk a long ways."

Summer closed the door and left. Matt picked up Sal's cell again. Yes, definitely time to ditch it, he thought, scrolling through a few screens he'd seen before while he thought back to the day of the robbery. *There were four of them, including Sal. Sal's out of the picture, and*

*Josey. That leaves...*Matt racked his brain, willing it to replay scenes from that fateful day. He could hear his kids squealing upstairs while they chased each other around, their footsteps thumping on his ceiling. In his mind's eye he saw Sal addressing the skinny one, *Pablo.*

Pablo's number was in the phone's incoming list. But Matt didn't think a direct call with the ploy that he was Sal and still alive, come meet me in secret, would still work. Too much time had gone by, and with Josey dead, too, it was too questionable. But he knew where he worked, because of a text that said he'd be at the auto shop, and Sal had replied, U still at Pep Boys?

No, cove collision repair.

That message was only two weeks old, so there was a decent chance he was still there, unless he made enough from his share of the museum loot that he decided to quit his job, Matt thought. Which would be stupid, so soon after the robbery, but these guys weren't going to be the sharpest knives in the drawer now, were they? But it was a lead.

As for the other gang member, Matt could picture him—a thirty-something Hispanic, squat, looked like he lifted weights, tattoos, shaved head. But for the life of him he couldn't recall his name, and he couldn't deduce it from the content of Sal's phone. Matt pulled the battery from the phone, flipped the device open and ripped it in half. He put the pieces in three separate bags and put one in the waste basket underneath his desk while pocketing the other two. He would dispose of each piece in a different location.

Out in the house he could hear the trammel of footsteps down on the first floor now. *Almost time.* He unlocked his bottom desk drawer and drew out the two muskets. With Sal he had only used one of them, since he was then unfamiliar with the weapon and wanted to focus on making sure that he could effectively handle one. Today his costume called for two, however, and so two he would use.

He pulled out the black gunpowder container, a coffee can filled with crushed glass, and a spray can of rat poison. Checking first to make sure the curtains were closed over his window, Matt proceeded to carefully load and prepare his weapons. When he was finished, he put the ammunition supplies back in the drawer and locked it.

Then he stood up, put on his belt holster, and inserted the two muskets into the holsters. Pleased with the fit, he added a cheap plastic sword and scabbard toy decoration to his outfit so that it would be that much more likely anyone casually noticing the muskets would consider them fake by association. He'd been to the Cove Fourth of July beach day many times, and he was confident this ensemble would pass muster as one of the many pirate costumes that would be on the beach.

Ten minutes later, Matt was behind the wheel of his SUV on the way to the festivities, wife and kids talking about how nice the weather was, and did you bring enough sunscreen...Matt filtered most of it out. He would have went for Pablo today were it not the 4th. It troubled Matt that he still seethed over being made to rob the museum, but it was like he had to make Pablo pay, even if he knew it was wrong. He tried to reason with himself: *what was the big deal? They made you do it, not like you had a choice. But afterwards, those decisions are yours and yours alone. You could have stopped after killing Sal, but you didn't...*

"Honey? You passed the turn."

Matt snapped out of it and looked at the road. He'd gone straight through an intersection instead of making a right. A turn that came on a drive he'd done hundreds of times.

"You thinking about something?"

"Just how much fun we're going to have!" he said.

The "Yeahs!" from the backseat confirmed that his enthusiasm had been infectious, and by the time he'd corralled the SUV onto the correct road, the family was discussing on which part of the beach they should stake their claim in order to best view the fireworks that evening.

-43-

HAPPY 4TH

By the time the mayor of Sandy Cove walked onto the small stage that had been erected on the grassy picnic area next to town's only beach (the rest of the Cove's waterfront consisting of either harbor or rocky shoreline), there was hardly a patch of sand visible between all the blankets and towels. The smell of sunscreen and barbecue wafted through the air. The grassy park area next to the beach was also filled to capacity, all of its grills having been in non-stop operation all day. The playful shouts of children at play—throwing footballs and Frisbees if they could find enough room, splashing through the water, body-boarding and skimboarding—mingled with hundreds of relaxed conversations playing out across the packed beach.

The Knox family had arrived early enough to secure a relatively large patch of sand. As was customary, many beach goers had dug sizable pits to more clearly stake out a claim to their sandy piece of real estate, pockmarking the entire beach with recreational foxholes. Matt had dug one for his family using a collapsible camping shovel, almost an hour's effort resulting in a roughly oval depression about fifteen feet long by eight feet wide, and three deep. His kids had helped him to shore up the walls by packing the sand in tight. They made a slide entrance leading into their architectural creation, which Caitlin had decorated with little crenulated sandcastle turrets around the perimeter, molded from buckets of wet sand imported from water's edge.

The crowning touch was a skull and crossbones flag on a pole, protruding from the top of a sandy mound shaped for that very purpose. Then they'd lined the pit with their blankets and towels, arranged their cooler, mini-grill, beach chairs and umbrella, and ground was broken at Castle Knox with a champagne toast for Matt and Summer, sparkling cider for the kids.

Around them, people dressed as pirates walked from pit to pit, stopping to chat when they found someone they knew, or thought they knew, or wanted to know, as the case may be. Some of the pirate costumes were rather elaborate, making their owners difficult to recognize, not to mention the fact that as the day wore on more and more beverages were consumed. Radios blared from a few pits, especially those occupied by the college kids home for the summer, and some even featured live music in the form of acoustic guitars, harmonicas and bongo drums. Completing this festive environment was a barge anchored about half a mile off the beach, to be used as a floating pyrotechnics platform from which to launch the evening's fireworks display.

The tap-tap-tap of a hand on a live microphone got the attention of the beach throngs. A man looking out of place in a suit cleared his throat. "Good afternoon, ladies and gentlemen, everyone, your attention please! I present to you the mayor of Sandy Cove, Ms. Gina Adams."

The mayor thanked the man for the introduction and stepped up to the podium. Although her exact age was a topic of speculation around town, Gina was in the neighborhood of sixty and was enjoying her fourth consecutive two-year term as mayor, after a long run on the city council before that. A two-time divorcee, Mayor Adams had overseen expansion of the town's harbor, in spite of the protests from both environmentalists opposed to wetland destruction and those who simply wanted their small town to remain small. Even the 7th annual Fourth of July Sandy Cove Beach Fireworks Display and Pirate Party had been her gift to the town, although those who had lived here long enough knew that the tradition had started out informally long before it swelled with taxpayer dollars.

"I just got back from vacation and was a little worried at first that our town had been overrun by pirates, but then I remembered what day it was. Happy Fourth of July, Sandy Cove, glad you could make it!" Gina led off with an exaggerated wave. She wore a simple blue dress with matching sun hat and oversized sunglasses.

Cries of "Hi Gina!" and "You go girl!" died down as the mayor looked out across her beach. She smiled at a young man who had been tossing a football.

"We turned the good weather on just for you! Let me tell you, I just got back from Costa Rica, where I went snorkeling, and sure it's nice down there, but they ain't got nothing over Sandy Cove!" The beach erupted in cheers. "I think we've got the best beach in world, right here in our own beautiful backyard!

"Let me tell you what else we've got."

"Beer!" a joker called out from one of the sand pits.

Gina raised an eyebrow and pointed his way without commenting.

"The best damn fireworks show in California!" More cheers. Behind Gina on the grass a small platoon of city police officers kept a close eye on the mayor. Sandy Cove wasn't known for having more than its fair share of nutjobs, and small town mayor wasn't the kind of high profile post that brought the would-be assassins out of their rotten woodwork, but it was a show of force for the city, a chance to remind the taxpayers of where their money went–to protect the mayor so that she could throw them a big party now and then.

Mayor Adams continued. "As the sun sets and we get our pyrotechnics show underway, take a moment to remind yourselves of our great nation, founded on great principles and strong community, and how we, as residents of Sandy Cove, have adopted those values and made them our own cherished way of life.

"Fifteen minutes until the fireworks start—enjoy the show!" Gina stepped away from the podium to hearty applause.

In the Knox pit, Matt was having a swordfight with his kids while Summer talked to one of her tennis club friends about how inadequate the night lights were on the new court. After a couple of minutes the friend asked Summer if it would be okay if she stayed in their pit to watch the fireworks show. "I come bearing gifts," she said, hoisting a bottle of white wine from her oversized handbag.

"Oooooh, great idea," Summer said, followed by, "Darn, I left a bag of stuff in the car and it has the wine opener in it. Hold on..."

"Matt?"

Matt was pushing his squealing kids into a corner at the point of his sword. "Arrrrgh, ye walk the plank, then, ye will!"

"Matthew!" Summer called, louder.

Matt turned around, holding his hands up as if to say, *what?*

"I left the wine opener in the car. Do we have another one down here?" Matt's wife asked.

He shook his head. "Got a beer opener."

Summer held up the bottle. "That won't do. Can you be a dear, please and go to the car and get it? There's just enough time if you go right now before the fireworks start." She shook the bottle in her hand. "Pretty please? You want to get me drunk don't you?"

Summer's friend laughed. "Nice costume, Matt," she said.

"Enough, you two. I know when I'm being buttered up. I'll go. But in return I'll be sharing a glass with you."

"Deal," Summer said. "Hurry! Like ten minutes."

Matt climbed out of the pit and walked past Summer toward the end of the beach where their car was parked. "For you dear, any-thing," he said, before breaking into a trot down the beach, threading his way between sand pits.

"You're the best!" he heard Summer call out behind him. He slowed his pace to what could barely be called a jog as he encountered numerous people and obstacles such as coolers and beach chairs in his way. Around him, the sounds of small fireworks set off by those in the crowd who couldn't wait for the professional show began to pop and whistle.

As he neared the far end of the beach the crowd thinned somewhat and became a bit rowdier. Matt smelled marijuana wafting out of one pit, the dark figures within obscured by shadows. Hard rock music emanated from another sandpit, and Matt saw some men passing a bottle back and forth singing *Yo ho ho and a bottle of rum...*

A stand of eucalyptus trees marked the edge of the road and Matt left the beach. Under the tree cover it became dark enough that he had to stop for a moment to let his eyes adjust. Then he walked up the slight grade until he found the family vehicle on the left side of the road, wedged between two other cars so tightly it'd have to be airlifted out, Matt thought bitterly. Hopefully at least one of the drivers who'd boxed him in would leave before they did.

Matt opened the hatchback of his SUV and found a white plastic store bag inside. He grabbed it and checked its contents: a wine opener, a cutting board and a cheese slicer. Just as he pushed the hatch closed he heard the *ka-boom* of the first fireworks detonating. He turned around and looked over toward the beach in time to see a scarlet flower bloom in the night sky.

Damn. Matt took off at a leisurely run, not unlike when he'd jogged through his neighborhood after killing the dog (*getting into shape lately, maybe I should make it a regular thing*), and passed back through the stand of trees onto the beach.

The tang of fireworks assaulted his nose while a pall of dark smoke cut visibility to a few yards. There were fewer pits dug here compared to the central section of beach the Knox's had staked out, but despite the open spaces, a hectic medley of amateur pyrotechnics infused the beach with a dangerous energy. Matt dodged a minefield of sparklers, ladyfingers, bottle rockets, M80s, roman candles, spinners and smokers. If he'd been walking slow it would have been easier, but he continued to run, wanting to get back to his pit while the main display was still on.

A professional explosion lit up the ocean off to Matt's left, casting a purplish glow over Sandy Cove. He looked over at it, momentarily taken by its beauty–the contrast of the brilliant radiance against a black sky, the intricate patterns–and then he registered a flash of harsh, white light to his right and felt himself knock into a warm body.

He turned and saw that he'd run into a man who'd been kneeling to set up a bottle rocket. He'd just lit the fuse a second before Matt plowed into him and the guy stumbled to get up in the sand, reaching out for the fallen rocket in order to right it.

He was too late, though, and the mini-explosive detonated just before his hand reached it.

"Oh, *shit*!" The man let loose a string of curses as he clutched one hand in the other, staggering to his feet and hopping about. Matt was surprised to see that he wasn't some teenager but a middle aged man like himself, perhaps a street person, he couldn't be sure in the low light.

"Sorry, you okay there?" Matt said.

The man stopped jumping around and looked at Matt. His eyes narrowed, causing the reflection of a scarlet firework from the barge Matt saw there to shrink with his closing lids.

"Dumb asshole! Watch where the fuck you're going!"

Matt reflexively shrunk back from the hostility. "Hey, take it easy. It was an accident. I apologize. You need any help with that hand?"

Matt glanced down the beach, looking for his family pit, but he was still far away. Around them, no one seemed to have noticed their collision. Apparently either this guy was alone or else had wandered off from one of the pits on his own to light his fireworks.

The would-be pyrotechnical wizard looked down at his hand, still wrapped in his good one, and then back up at Matt.

"Yeah, give me some money. I'm gonna have medical expenses."

Matt held his hands up in a gesture of helplessness, the store bag swinging from his wrist.

"Sorry, buddy, I can't do that. I can call an ambulance for you, though, do you want me to do that?" He started to pull his cellular from his pants pocket.

"No. Gimme that bag, then."

Matt glanced down at the bag containing the wine opener.

"I can't do that. I need it."

"You gotta give me something. This is your fault." He shook his damaged hand in Matt's general direction.

Matt sighed as more fireworks boomed out over the water. He needed to get back to his pit before he missed the entire fireworks show, which would piss Summer off.

"Fine," he said, slipping the bag from his wrist. He took the things out of it and put them in his pockets and then held out the empty bag, a facetious offering that fluttered in the sea breeze.

"What the fuck is that!"

"You said you wanted the bag."

Matt could smell the guy's breath now. Alcohol.

"Gimme the stuff that was in it."

"No way. Look pal, you've had a lot to drink. Who are you here with? I'll take you back over there, make sure you get some help if you need it."

"Here by myself. Now gimme the stuff you clumsy oaf."

Matt's next thoughts rode along with the low whistle that represented a new firework rising from the barge as it shot into the night sky, propelling itself higher. As the whistle increased in pitch and intensity, Matt's thoughts did the same, until, when the incendiary device detonated, Matt's neurons had delivered to him a full-blown idea.

And not a good one.

-44-

LIFE'S A BEACH AND THEN YOU DIE

Matt swiveled his head around, scoping out the sand in their immediate vicinity. Small groups of teens and various ne'er-do-wells were still preoccupied with setting off their cheap Mexican explosives or drinking heavily and watching the city pyrotechnics. The odors of cordite and marijuana mingled into a single, distinctive scent, at once offensive and intoxicating.

The yacht salesman drew his twin blunderbusses, aiming them in the belligerent guy's direction.

"I don't think so. Nobody's taking my stuff."

The guy looked at Matt's guns and appeared as though he was trying to contain himself, before bursting into guffaws of laughter.

"That's so funny, man!" he said, wiping a tear from his eye with the back of his blasted hand. Then he grew serious, face taking on a scowl. "You can keep your costume. Gimme the other stuff."

"These are real."

"Yeah, and my name is fuckin' Blackbeard," The guy started but said nothing further after he took a closer look at the pistols, their antique engraved metal gleaming dully in the colorful ambient light.

Matt saw him lean in a little closer, a stupid expression on his stupid face as his stupid brain tried to process what he was looking at. Matt started to squeeze the triggers.

He aimed the blunderbuss in his right hand at the guy's idiotic face, and the one in his left at the dirty wife beater T-shirt covering the bloated belly. While he took aim, Matt timed the firework intervals from the barge. They were nearing the end of a big sequence now, and a series of rapid rocket releases were producing a predicable rhythm of booming blasts.

He applied pressure on both triggers, waiting...waiting for the next percussive blast...

The concentration on Matt's face must have scared the guy because he started to back away at the last second, but he was too late.

The gun in Matt's right hand triggered first, ripping off the guy's face, followed one second later by its twin, which sprayed its deadly cocktail of carpet nails, glass and rat poison at the guy's belly, where it tore though into his gut.

Matt's victim flopped wordlessly onto the sand.

Matt quickly holstered his weapons and looked around. A huge volley of rockets was going off now and he'd hoped that his reports had blended in. No one seemed to be looking his way.

In the strange kind of high-functioning daze in which he'd found himself lately, Matt Knox picked his way slowly and carefully back to his central beach pit, where he could see Summer, her friend and the kids seated in beach chairs, chatting happily and watching the show.

He entered the pit and Summer rose to greet him.

"Matt! That took forever, I was starting to worry. Did you get the wine opener?" Her gaze accused his empty hands. He pulled it out of his pocket and handed it to her along with the cheese grater and small cutting board that he'd tucked into his waistband.

"Thanks, honey! What happened to the bag I had the stuff in?"

"I used it to clean up some trash on the beach."

-45-

TIME'S UP

"You've got to get that security guard job today! We can't wait any longer."

Jeremy Washington looked at his wife across their kitchen table but said nothing. He had been watching the small TV on the kitchen counter where Carol Tepper stood on Sandy Cove Beach, amidst the aftermath of the previous day's celebration. The sound was muted on the television but Jeremy could see the garbage-strewn beach, littered with cans, plastic bags and firework debris. City workers were visible in the background picking trash and driving a sand grader.

For the first time in the last five years, the Washingtons had stayed home from the 4th of July celebration. The last thing Jeremy wanted to do was be out around the whole town right now, recently fired and out of work. Skipping the tradition had put a damper on Alisa's mood, though, and being at home all day gave her plenty of time to needle Jeremy about his job situation. He'd had time to try, nothing was working, they needed money yesterday, there must be something else he could do....

And of course it was all true.

The past week hadn't gotten him any closer to the museum reward money, either. He'd been in touch with Tommy, but the Sandy Cove PD was equally stalled and dealing with two murders—Sal and his boat-cleaning gang member—that had also produced no leads. His only real remaining connection to the case was Pablo...

"Jeremy? Jeremy!"

Alisa's voice brought him back.

"Yeah."

"You can always keep looking for something better. Just get a security guard job. Something. Anything."

"Okay. Alright, I'll do it. I'll go down to the mall today."

Alisa stood up and grabbed her purse. "Good. Full day today for me. Claire told me I might be able to pick up her hours besides mine, because she's going out later to celebrate her husband's promotion."

"Good for him." He was staring at the TV again, where Carol was pointing and motioning her hand toward a patch of sand.

"Hey, if I can pick up a few extra hours because of it, that's a good thing, Jeremy. Don't be jealous. You'll get your groove back, baby, I know you will. I've got to go."

She gave him a peck on the cheek and breezed out the door. Jeremy got up and turned the volume up on the TV, where the camera now focused on a human form lying in the sand, blocked off by yellow police tape. A red banner crawled across the bottom of the screen: ...BODY FOUND ON SANDY COVE BEACH IN WAKE OF 4th of JULY CELEBRATION...

Carol Tepper continued her reporting from off-camera.

"Police have not yet positively identified the body of a deceased adult Caucasian male found here in the sand early this morning." The camera zoomed in on the human figure sprawled on the beach. The body was clothed, feet unshod and caked with black grime. The frame deliberately cut off the head while the reporter spoke.

"I've been talking with police here on the scene for the better part of the last hour, and I can say that at this point the cause of this man's demise is a matter of conjecture, although several unsubstantiated theories have been unofficially put forth. One early one was that the man had fallen asleep or passed out on the beach last night and failed to wake up this morning before a sand raking machine ran him over, as happened to a tourist last month in Los Angeles. Another possibility is that the victim was injured by amateur fireworks. Hold on, Sander."

The camera's field of view shifted toward the corpse's head. Jeremy leaned in closer to the TV and turned up the volume even more to better hear a muffled vocal exchange. It sounded to him like Carol was having an argument with her cameraman. Whatever it was it was brief, and the camera steadied while Carol's voice came through again.

"I warn you that if you're squeamish you should look away." Off camera a male voice was heard shouting "No, no! Get that thing out of here!"

"Hurry up, Sander," Carol was heard saying.

Jeremy's little TV screen filled with the image of the dead man's face. It seemed to him that news shows grew more graphic with each passing year, but in this case he was thankful for the detail. He didn't recognize the face, but that would have been difficult with the degree of damage.

As the camera steadied on the still visage, Jeremy recoiled– not in horror at the severity of the wounds, although they were bad—but in seeing how similar the type of injury was to what had happened to Sal. The shredded flesh—extensive but not as forceful as a shotgun from close range—the strange wound pattern. He'd been a cop for ten years and had never seen an injury like Sal's.

Now he'd seen two in as many weeks.

Jeremy flipped off the TV, where the blonde was remarking how this was the third death in Sandy Cove in recent weeks. He grabbed his keys, stepped outside, and got into his Bronco.

He paused with the keys in the ignition, not yet turned, debating with himself whether he should stake out Pablo today—he knew where the goods were, he *was* the answer–but then decided he had to get that security guard job. Once he had some money coming in, any money, he'd have more slack to work on the museum case.

Ex-cop Jeremy Washington put his old Bronco in gear, flipped on his police scanner, taking comfort in the familiar voices, and drove toward the Sandy Cove Mall.

DON'T COUNT YOUR CHICKENS

The room in the behind-the-scenes section of the mall was a lousy little affair, fluorescent tube lights casting their flickering glare on a no-nonsense metal desk behind which sat the Chief of Mall Security, according to the placard on his desk. His considerable bulk overflowed the simple metal folding chair that he dominated. A corkboard festooned with photocopied schedules and occupational safety forms graced an otherwise sterile wall of painted cinderblocks.

In front of the desk on a plastic folding chair sat Jeremy Washington, a raft of partially completed paperwork spread out on the edge of the desk before him. He had completed the first page and was hard at work on the rest of it when the Chief (Jeremy doubted he would ever be able to call this buffoon Chief, so firmly did he associate the term with the police force), rapped his knuckles on the desk next to Jeremy's paperwork.

"Hold up there, Mr. Washington."

Jeremy stopped writing and looked up from his form.

"I'm looking at what you've got so far. Says here under Reason for Leaving Your Last Job that you were terminated."

Jeremy nodded.

"Can you elaborate on that for me?"

Jeremy stared at the man, flustered. He hadn't expected to be quizzed in any real detail; it was a mall security guard job for crying out loud. He'd thought they'd take any warm body and that the hiring process would be a mere formality.

"After working nearly ten years on the force, I was let go due to..." He paused while wondering what the most suitable euphemism for "taking bribes from a gang" would be. Mall Chief tented his beefy hands, seeming to study Jeremy's face as if he could read something into his expressions like some kind of amateur psychologist. He raised his eyebrows in a silent prompt.

"...for...procedural violations."

Mall Chief narrowed his eyes and set his hands down. Then his countenance seemed to brighten. "Wait a minute! I know you!"

Jeremy shrank back a little in his chair. These days, that kind of recognition was rarely desirable.

"Pardon me?"

"I saw your picture on TV not too long ago. Ex-cop. You were fired for accepting protection money or something like that."

"It wasn't *protection* money, whatever that is."

"What was it, then?"

Jeremy felt that this question was crossing too far into his personal business and normally he'd decline to answer, but he needed this job, so he went with it.

"It was just money, to...*expedite* certain activities."

Mall Chief leaned back perilously in his chair, the discount metal protesting under his shifting weight. "Activities, yes, that's right. I remember now. Bribes. You were fired for taking bribes while on duty, is that correct?"

Jeremy looked at the man in his eyes.

"Don't lie about it, it'll just come out in the background report. Save us both the time."

"That's correct."

At length, Mall Chief plucked from Jeremy's hand the pen he had been using to fill out the forms.

"I'm sorry, Mr. Washington, but I can't hire you. I don't even want to waste your time by having you complete the application." Jeremy looked down at his incomplete forms in shock.

"It's not like I was trying to hide it. Where it asks, Have you ever been charged with a crime, I put Yes. It even says..." He snatched the paper from the desk, reading the fine print: "Past convictions do not necessarily preclude you from consideration." He looked up at Mall Chief, who now frowned in Jeremy's direction.

"In many cases that's true, if the crime has nothing to do with the job here. If you were busted for smoking weed ten years ago, I'm not gonna hold it against you. But taking bribes, recently..."

Jeremy brightened. "Actually, that's exactly the type of crime it was. I wasn't even convicted of any crime for the bribes, I was just let go. Administrative action only, not legal. You can look that up with the courts."

He slowly shook his head and waved a hand, as if shooing away the can of worms Jeremy's background represented. "I just can't do it."

"Why not? I'd make a great security guard."

The interviewer took a deep breath and shifted in his chair. He was losing patience.

"Because if you resorted to taking bribes when you were a cop—a job that paid probably three or four times what I can pay you—then what's to stop you from taking bribes here? I gotta worry that you'll copy a store key for somebody to make a few extra bucks? It would be *my* ass if anything ever happened. It's not like there's a shortage of people who can do this job. Sorry, but I just I can't do it."

-47-

CONFESSIONAL

Jeremy Washington entered his apartment and slammed the door shut. He crossed the worn carpet over to the couch and kicked the coffee table leg, hard, knocking over a couple of glasses that had been sitting on it. He sat on the couch with his head in his hands.

What had he been thinking? No one in their right mind would be able to give him a security guard job now, even if they wanted to. Professionally, he was dead to Sandy Cove now. The hardware store guy was right: maybe he would have to move to L.A so he could lie on an application and not mention he'd been fired. Not that a security guard job was the ticket to his dreams, anyhow. And L.A. wasn't cheap. Even if he did get that kind of a job down there, it wouldn't go very far.

So what the hell was he going to do?

He was still pondering this when he heard rap music coming from the driveway. It grew louder still until it died suddenly along with a car engine. The sound of a car door, then footsteps approaching his doorstep.

"Yo Jeremy, man, you here?"

Pablo.

Jeremy lifted his head. What could he want? Was he alone? For a fleeting moment a dark thought crossed his mind, one of fear. What if whoever had been behind the Sandy Cove killings had come for *him*—perhaps alerted by Pablo to his intentions of earning the reward?

And then an even more uncomfortable thought: what if Pablo *was* the killer?

It was possible, wasn't it? Pablo did stand to gain. With Sal out of the picture, he had advanced up the ranks of the gang. His share of the loot—from the museum job and whatever other enterprises they had going—had increased. He used to be a nice guy, Jeremy knew from their high school days ("daze" he and Pablo used to joke) and deep down he probably still was, but once you're a cop you know how human nature operates. When times got tough, the tough did what they had to, justified what they had to. Had Pablo changed that much over the years?

Jeremy stood and walked to the front door. He put his eye to the peephole and jumped when he saw an eye looking back at him.

"Jeremy you paranoid freak, it's me, Pablo, open up." Pablo pulled back from the peephole and Jeremy saw through the fisheye view that he was alone. Taking a deep breath to steady his nerves, he pulled open the door.

"What's up, Pablo?"

"Need to talk to you. Can I come in?"

Jeremy glanced at Pablo up and down—he could detect no hidden bulge of a weapon under his baggy clothing—and he seemed more or less relaxed. More so than him, even. He swung the door open the rest of the way and stepped aside, sweeping an arm into his apartment.

"Thanks." Pablo entered the apartment and looked around.

"She's at work," Jeremy said, knowing that Pablo was wondering if they were alone. His initial uneasiness had peaked. Pablo was just Pablo—the same guy he'd known all these years, the guy who used to be big into graffiti tagging. He even had some artistic talent at it, drawing those colorful, interlocking, bubbly letters that for a while made him some extra money on the fringe art scene. The guy he used to go surfing with in high school before class, back when they both still surfed.

"What you smiling about? You find a job or something?"

Jeremy wiped the grin from his face. "No. Just got turned down for one, in fact. I was just remembering that time when you painted that cool graffiti mural inside the hall in Sandy Cove High. How you told me to be sure and be early to school that day so that I'd see it before they painted over it."

Pablo's own features lit up in a grin. "That was so cool! Still have the pictures I took. And they did paint over it, shit was gone by second period. But everybody saw it, man, they all liked it. Damn," he finished, reveling in the memory for a second, before taking a seat on Jeremy's couch and turning serious. Those days were gone forever for both of them. Life was much more serious now—vastly more serious.

"Look, man, reason I'm here is cuz I'm worried. Real concerned. About this latest job," he finished, glancing around as if not sure he could trust the environment, as if not using the word "museum" would protect him if there did happen to be someone listening.

Jeremy remained standing across the coffee table from where Pablo sat. "What about it?"

Pablo's eyes were downcast as he spoke. "You know they upped the reward on the loot to fifty grand."

Jeremy nodded. "Lotta money."

Pablo fidgeted on the couch. "Jeremy, man..." he started, but then trailed off."

"What is it? Go ahead."

"I'm not sure what the fuck's going on, man."

Jeremy remained silent, but held eye contact with him, to let him know he had his undivided attention. Pablo continued.

"I think maybe..." Again his words fizzled out.

"Come on, Pablo. You think maybe what?"

"I think maybe that I should tell you where the loot is."

-48-

DOUBLE DEALING

Jeremy could hear their cheap wall clock ticking from the kitchen in the stunned silence that followed Pablo's statement. Too many questions were swirling through Jeremy's head—why come forward now? Was Pablo trying to trick him somehow? What was his motivation? He said nothing, apparently looking suitably astonished, because Pablo broke the silence first.

"I've been thinking about what you said, in the shop."

"Yeah? And?"

"I *am* worried that whoever killed Sal and Josie is coming after me. I've been seeing some strange cats following me, like in my car around town and shit."

"Like who?"

"I dunno. Weird rides, always on my ass. And the plan for the loot..."

Jeremy took the few steps over to the couch and sat down next to Pablo.

"Tell me about that, Pablo."

"I'm just going to give it to you straight."

"Shoot."

"With Sal gone, and Josey too, there's been a lot of arguing with the rest of us about what to do with the loot."

"Like when to start selling it or who to sell it to or what?"

"Both, yeah."

"Who all is in on this besides you now that Sal and Josey are out?" *Out for good*, he thought but did not say.

Pablo led off by shrugging as if to indicate that the answer was predictable. "Bobby—he was actually in there with us—and then the rest of the crew running support. Eduardo who drove the getaway van, some other dudes you don't know who are supposed to be arranging buyers, transport, that kinda shit."

"So there were only four of you who actually broke in and took all the stuff?" Jeremy pictured the dimly lit interior of the museum as he'd visited it with the claims adjuster–the extensive damage, the thoroughness with which the place had been gutted. He would have guessed a higher number, at least five, maybe six thieves.

"Yeah, there were only four of us. Well, five if you count The Saint."

Jeremy was in the act of pulling a stale saltine from the open pack on the coffee table, but abandoned that pursuit to focus on Pablo. "Count who?"

Pablo took a deep breath.

"There was another guy with us, not one of us—not in the gang, or any gang, but a local guy who lives in the harbor. I forget his real name, but Sal kinda knew him, called him the Saint because he has a squeaky clean record. It was Sal's idea to use him to get the keys to the place. He said he'd be above suspicion. He works in the yacht store and knew the owner of the museum cuz he sold him his yacht a while back. That's as much as Sal told me. So anyway–"

"Whoa. Back up the truck, brother. You're telling me Matt the Saint Knox, who manages the yacht dealership—you're telling me that he was *in* the museum with you while you robbed it?"

Jeremy was starting to wonder if Pablo was on drugs—imagining things, strange vehicles chasing him, people who weren't there...

"Matt Knox—yeah, that's his name. Shit yeah, man. I couldn't believe it, either, when Sal said he was gonna make him go in there with us. Cuz we were going to go through with it either way. But he did it. Went over to test drive a boat and then forced the guy to go with us. At gunpoint, man. Sal's fuckin' crazy. Was crazy," he added with a downcast expression.

"Whoa, whoa, hold on a minute…" Jeremy waved a hand through the air. "Take me through this. Matt the Saint Knox—I just had a job interview with him, by the way, didn't work out—but so he was walking around in the museum with you guys? What was he doing in there?"

"Yeah, Sal figured he'd get right back to work and no one would suspect a thing. So what he did was, he had the keys to the cases the stuff was in. For the ones that couldn't be smashed easily cuz they were some kinda hard plastic instead of glass, Sal had the Saint guy try all the keys until one of 'em fit."

"At gunpoint?"

"Yeah."

"And what was he doing when he wasn't unlocking cases? How did he act–was he telling you guys to stop or what? Did he try to escape?"

"Naw, he was pretty quiet. Looked pretty out of it, but I was busy, you know, I wasn't really keeping an eye on him. That was Sal's job. Me, Josey and Bobby had our hands full smashing and grabbing. The saint guy was just sort of there, like a ghost or something."

"A ghost…" Jeremy trailed off in thought.

"Yeah, like Casper the friendly fucking ghost, man, right there with the keys to lend a helping hand when you need it, and then when you're done he's just…gone!"

Jeremy did not share in Pablo's laughter. "And when you guys left, did you take the Sai—did you take Knox with you?"

Pablo shook his head. "Left him inside the museum. We got picked up out back. He didn't come back out before the van left, anyway. He was supposed to walk out through the front door and make a show of locking it from the outside in case anyone was watching, so they'd think he was doing something for the owner."

Jeremy was lost in thought. "What's weird is that he never reported anything to the police. Not even an anonymous call to report strange activity, nothing."

Pablo perked up. "How do you know? You ain't on the force no more."

That got Jeremy's attention. He'd let his guard down a little. *Slipped up. He doesn't know about Tommy and doesn't need to. Top of your game, come on.*

"I still have my police radio. I still have friends in low places. Trust me, he never said anything about it to authorities. Must have kept pretty tight-lipped about it with his family and friends, too, because there's no way something like that would stay a secret in this town."

"Doesn't surprise me. Sal said he threatened him if he did—we know where you live, that kinda shit."

Jeremy nodded slowly. "Yeah, yeah, but..."

"But what?"

"But Sal's *dead*. He's been dead for a week and Knox still hasn't come forward?"

Pablo appeared to mull this over. "Maybe he doesn't know he's dead?"

"It was all over the news."

"Maybe he's afraid someone else in the gang would get him. Which they might," he added. *A veiled warning?*

"Could be." Jeremy decided that while the Knox information was provocative, he had to get back on track to the loot quickly, before Pablo changed his mind. "So Pablo, you said when you came in that you were ready to tell me where the loot is?"

"Right. I don't like the way it's going, and with Sal gone, I dunno, man. Somebody's killing people...I'm thinking I want to get out of the gang. Too old for this shit."

"Good man, Pablo. You're doing the right thing. So where's the stuff?"

"Hold on. Not so easy. If I take you to it, you can take the credit for finding it, but I get half of the reward money."

Jeremy mentally divided fifty by three. About $17,000 each for him, Pablo and Tommy. At this rate, pretty soon he'd be sharing the reward with the whole damn town. Still, it was more than what he was going to get when it was only him and Tommy for $25,000. Seventeen thousand bucks or anywhere near it would make him—and Alisa—mighty happy right about now.

But the amount wasn't the problem. The problem was that he didn't want Pablo to know about Tommy's involvement. He didn't know why, exactly. He just didn't want all of his cards on the table yet. Call it a cop's (or ex-cop's) sixth sense. If Pablo led him to the loot and he successfully claimed the reward, he'd have to break it to him at that point that there's a third cohort, that his share was seventeen and not twenty-five. He'd explain that he couldn't have done it without his ex-partner's help, and Pablo would understand.

"I guess you're not okay with that."

Jeremy blinked his eyes a couple of times, snapping out of it.

"No, I'm sorry, Pablo, just spacing out. I am okay with it. You take me to the loot, I turn the stuff in, and we split the reward." *Split it three ways.* "Deal?"

Pablo extended his skinny, tattooed arm and pumped Jeremy's hand. Then he got up from the couch and said, "C'mon, let's go get that loot."

-49-

BACK TO WORK

Matt Knox breezed into the yacht brokerage. A lot of people took the day after the fourth off, but it was a good day for boat buying. In fact, John Samson was already here, dealing with a trio of potential customers. Matt gave them a pleasant wave but continued into his office without interrupting and shut the door.

If things with the customers developed past the looky-loo stage, John would come to his office. Sometimes the clients demanded to see Matt out of a desire to deal directly with the more senior person, but it was discouraged since most leads didn't pan out no matter how they were handled.

They'd worked out a system where if John knocked two times it meant, *not serious buyers don't waste your time*, and Matt would call out that he was on the line, be out in a bit. Three knocks indicated that they had somebody in the store who meant business, and that Matt should personally handle it.

Matt left his window blinds closed and sat behind his desk. He woke up his computer and used it to check the local news site, where a piece ran about the dead body found on the beach. A thin smile formed on his lips as he read the account. He flashed on the dim night, the black smoke from fireworks, the sharp odor, bright flashes, the drunken bum who'd challenged him...

The openness of it was the thrill. Killing homeless people for sport wasn't much of a contest. He wished he could identify the other members of Sal's gang. They should all pay for this, for making him break the law, for transforming him in this way.

What clues did he have that could lead to them?

He'd ditched Sal's phone for fear of being tracked, but he'd already gone through the useful numbers and written them down. There was the storage address where they were going to bring the stolen stuff, even what looked like a couple of codes—entrance gate, combination lock? But no doubt that was long empty. He leaned his elbow on the desk and scratched his temple. *Right? Surely they would have moved it all by now. Unless...unless they wanted to let some time pass before trying to sell the stuff.*

But what else do I have?

Then he remembered: the skeleton key.

Matt slid open his desk drawer and removed the top tray. He plucked the odd key from the space beneath. He held it up to the ceiling lights and turned it over in his hands. There was the inscription, the one Sal had seemed surprised by: *Davey Jones Locker.*

What could that mean? He tried to think about it from Dallas Draper's frame of reference. *Dallas has this strange skeleton key...What would he use it for? Something else in the museum they had overlooked? Was it just a semivaluable curio in and of itself? An antique? Davey Jones' Locker...*

He thought about who Dallas knew, pictured the houses and boats lining the canal adjacent to his home, getting farther and farther away until he couldn't be sure what they looked like...

There...wait a minute, back up...

Fifth house to the left when facing Dallas'. White house, small grass yard, boat slip out back but with no boat. What was that guy's name...he *doesn't like boats*...saw him at that party a couple years ago, he got some laughs after being asked why he doesn't want a boat even though he has a slip. He said, *I think it's my name...Dave Jones—bad luck, you know? Don't want to end up in my own locker.*

Matt dropped the key onto his desk in surprise.

I'll be goddamned!

He read the inscription on the key again: *Davey Jones' Locker.* And that's when three knocks came at his door. Matt dropped the key back into the drawer and got up.

50

WHAT WOULD YOU DO WITH ALL THAT MONEY?

Jeremy Washington instinctively clicked his seatbelt into place as Pablo drove them toward the *Move & Store*. Jeremy didn't like riding in Pablo's tricked out Nissan with the little fuzzy doll dangling from the rear fender, the ultra-dark tinted windows and aftermarket racing gear he'd added giving the vehicle a decidedly gangster flair, but they couldn't afford to have his Bronco recognized. As it was he wore an Oakland Raiders cap pulled down tight over a pair of cheap sunglasses. Just another gangsta. *Fine line between cop and criminal,* Jeremy warned himself.

"I really appreciate you doing this, Pablo. So glad you're doing the right thing."

Pablo looked over at his passenger. "No worries. I'm getting out of the game, man. This is the first step." He took a right onto a side street, then asked, "How long do you think it'll take us to get the reward money?"

Jeremy shrugged. "I don't know, a few weeks probably, as soon as they verify everything, but I wouldn't worry about it. It's Dallas Draper and the City, half each. They'll pay."

Pablo nodded as he gunned the accelerator to make it through a yellow light. "What are you going to do with your share?"

"Get my shit together, what else? I got no job, remember?"

"Sorry, right. If you find something before then, you might have extra cash, though. Like me, I'm gonna get a new ride. Trick that thing out!"

Jeremy smiled and shook his head. "I'm happy if I can keep food on the table for my family. That's all I want."

"Yeah, I ain't got that to worry about. Okay, bro, here it is up here on the left. Need you to duck while we turn in. Just in case somebody's there."

Jeremy unfastened his seatbelt and slid lower in the seat.

"You expecting anyone?"

"Nope. Just in case."

He slowed the car and made a left across a lightly trafficked lane to a gated parking lot. Several security cameras pointed at this entrance. Pablo reached out the window and punched a key code into the security apparatus.

A metal gate on rollers slid left. As soon as the car could fit, Pablo crossed into the parking lot. There were only a couple of vehicles in the lot, and those were parked directly in front of the office. He passed a long row of corrugated metal rollup doors set into a two-story building and turned the car into a space at the far end of the lot.

"That's the one there," Pablo said, pointing to one of the identical looking rollup doors. The number 166 was stenciled over the door.

"Who's name is the unit in?" Jeremy asked.

Pablo killed the engine. "I'm not even sure, man. Possibly Sal's or something he set up. We've been using this same unit for years now. I know the combination to the lock by heart."

He pulled his keys from the ignition. Both men exited the car and walked across the lot to UNIT 166.

A stout combination padlock—clearly impervious to bolt cutters and pry bars–stood guard through the door's hasp.

Jeremy was silent, looking around them while Pablo dialed the lock's combination. It opened with a *click* and Jeremy turned back around while Pablo heaved open the rollup.

"It's really not that much stuff," he said over the rumble of sliding metal. "With two of us we won't even need a dolly for it."

"I should say not," Jeremy said, gazing into the now open storage unit.

The small room with a concrete floor was eight by ten feet, and it was empty.

51

HALF OF ZERO IS...

Pablo's mind was so engaged with taking in the sight before him that his brain stopped sending signals to his fingers and his keys dropped to the ground.

"Pablo, if this is some kind of joke, it's not funny," Jeremy said. "What's going on?" But Jeremy had eyed his reaction carefully, and his cop's instinct told him that the emotional display was genuine.

Pablo remained silent, unmoving, just standing there at the entrance to the empty storage unit in frozen disbelief.

"Pablo! What's up?" Jeremy walked into the unit and turned around to look at him.

When he spoke it was in a low voice barely above a whisper. "The stuff...Everything's gone!" He looked like he was about to cry.

"Take it easy. Let's back up. Are you *sure* that this is the same unit the stuff was in? This isn't some other unit from a long time ago? Sal or his partners don't rent multiple units from this same facility?"

Pablo shook his head slowly. "No, man. I've been here a shitload of times. Look: on that inside wall right there, there should be a little graffiti piece I did that says SURF with a little cartoon guy peeking over the top of the letters."

Jeremy walked over to the wall Pablo indicated. Sure enough, a simple drawing that looked like it was done with a Sharpie graced the plasterboard wall.

Jeremy turned around to look at Pablo. "Okay, you've been here, but are you *positive* that you couldn't have been inside a different unit when you loaded in the stuff?" As a cop, Jeremy couldn't even count the times he'd seen witnesses to something swear up and down that they were remembering it correctly, only to sheepishly admit later when confronted with undeniable evidence that, oops sorry, I guess I was wrong.

"No, I saw my drawing then, too. This is definitely the right unit, Jeremy. Bastards took the loot!"

"What bastards?"

"Eduardo and them, I guess. The guys who drove the van, transported the stuff around. When Sal's murder hit the TV, they must've got spooked and bugged out with the stuff."

"Let's cover some more bases real quick. Has the bill been paid on this place? Is it possible that it was late and so the management here would have confiscated the stuff—locked it up in a different unit until the past due fees were paid up?"

"No, man. It's always been paid for years. It's on some kind of automatic bill pay that Sal set up. He was pretty good with accounts and transferring funds back and forth where they needed to go."

Jeremy nodded. "He must be. He passed the credit check at the yacht place in order to get that test drive."

"Yeah. Plus I've seen it before in this place when units don't get paid—they don't move the stuff out, they just put a big-ass lock on it until you pay, and if enough time goes by—like six months or something, then it gets auctioned off. No way that happened here."

Jeremy nodded. "What about just making a call to your people and asking them what's up with it?"

"I can't do that! What was I was doing here! We didn't have a meet-up scheduled. We were supposed to lay low for a month—let the stuff chill here while things cool down. But they haven't been cooling down—Sal and Josey are dead."

"Couldn't you say that you decided to do a security check? Just passing by, thought you would check in on it?"

"And all the stuff happens to be gone? They'd think I did something with it! C'mon, man!"

"But if you don't say anything about it all the way until the next meet-up, won't they think you did something with it anyway?"

Pablo rubbed his eyebrows in disturbed concentration. "I don't know, man. I don't know!"

"Relax. Who else has the combination to the lock besides you?"

"Sal had it. Whoever else he gave it to, I guess, but he was pretty tight on security. No one else I know of. I've always been the guy who opened it whenever I've been here, and if I was a couple minutes late the guys would be standing around waiting for me." Pablo lowered his voice and stepped closer to Jeremy.

"We've never had stuff worth as much as the museum loot before, all at one time, but it's not worth *that* much, you know? On TV they said a hundred grand, but that's a bullshit insurance price. I saw the stuff. Real street value's probably only half that, or a little less. We were used to having more than that per month, but coming in a little at time, three grand here in cash, five grand here in chop shop parts, maybe a couple grand worth of weed, that kind of thing, but moving pretty fast in and out."

"So you think having stuff worth this much all at once caused someone in the gang to go for it on their own? Take it and bail out?"

"That, combined with the weird stuff that's been going on, yeah. I don't think..." he trailed off in thought.

"Don't think what?"

"I don't see how even those guys would kill anybody over this loot though. Like I said, it wasn't worth all *that* much. To any one of us, yeah, it's a lot of money, but for our gang it wasn't a way high amount. It was more like a nice bonus compared to what we typically raked in, you know? Nothing any of us needed to kill over, man. I just don't get it."

Suddenly they heard the gate at the lot entrance start to rumble open. The two men looked at one another.

"Someone's coming," Jeremy said, stating the obvious.

"Shit!" Pablo started for the parking lot, then turned and darted back in. "What should we do, man? If it's Eduardo and them I can't be seen in this empty fuckin' place! They'll fuck me up bad. That was our agreement. Nobody comes alone without telling the others."

"Take it easy, Pablo. There's security cameras here."

"Fuck that, man. Nobody looks at that shit. They might not even be real."

They heard the squeal of tires and an engine accelerating.

"Only you have the combination, right?"

"Far as I know," Pablo's eyes were wide, the skin around them taught, his fists balled up.

"Quick, let's close it," Jeremy suggested.

"Lock won't be on!"

"Just hook it through the outside. From a distance it'll look locked."

Pablo's answer was to reach up and yank the door down by its rope handle. He snaked an arm out and slid the lock through the hasp, locking it, then pulled his hand back in, hoping it hadn't been seen, and shoved the door the rest of the way down to the concrete. He prayed that although the lock didn't actually stick through the metal loop on the door frame, that this fact wouldn't be obvious from a casual distance. The sudden darkness was not pitch black, but it was too dark really see anything. A sliver of light eked its way in around the door frame.

Then they heard the car engine grow louder until it was parked directly outside the unit, not five feet away by the sound of its idle.

"Oh shit, man," Pablo whispered. "This is fucked up. This is so fucked up."

A thought so uncomfortable as to be revolting welled up inside Jeremy's brain. Here he was, alone with Pablo inside a storage unit, hardly anyone around, and a vehicle all of a sudden drives up to them. Coincidence? Or Pablo setting him up to get worked over by his goons as a warning to lay off the snooping around? Or even worse. People had been dying lately, after all. Suddenly he was furious for having allowed himself to be put into such a vulnerable position. Was he already losing the situational awareness he had developed over his decade as a cop? Was that a use-it-or-lose-it kind of ability?

This possibility only added anger to his confusion. Jeremy whirled and grabbed Pablo with both hands by his hoodie sweatshirt and slammed him against the wall.

"Are you setting me up, Pablo? You think I'm stupid? Lure me out here and have your guys do a number on me? Think you can play me like that!" He moved his hands to Pablo's neck and began to squeeze.

"Noooo," Pablo managed to rasp out of his compressed throat. His eyes pleaded with Jeremy through the near darkness. The ex-cop braced himself for a knee to come up at him—he'd been in this kind of confrontation plenty of times—but instead Pablo only looked at him and then past him to the door, reminding him of the imminent threat just outside.

Jeremy relaxed his grip just a bit. He didn't want to hurt Pablo.

"Not a setup," Pablo breathed.

The engine shut off. They heard the car door open, heard it shut, and then heard shoes falling across the pavement coming toward unit 166.

MIGHT AS WELL CHECK

Matt Knox stepped out of his SUV into the Move & Store lot. The client John had ushered in to see him had indeed turned out to be a promising lead (although Matt had to admit that the thrill of closing a substantial deal—something that used to excite him—seemed to hold less luster for him now), but one for which not much could be done today. He'd given Matt his criteria for a boat and Matt let him know they didn't have anything worth seeing at the moment, but that he'd locate a few options and get back to him.

This left him with a spot of free time, and after further pondering he'd decided that it was worth it see what was going on at Sal's storage unit. The skeleton key's purpose eluded him for the time being, but checking out the storage was a simple enough thing to do. He reached behind his back to feel the butt of the blunderbuss he'd brought along, reading the numbers above the unit doors.

164...165...166!

He fished a scrap of paper from his pocket as he approached the unit's door. *Combination lock?* He squinted as he focused on the lock.

There it was! He'd gotten through the gate, there was a storage unit with the number 166, guarded with a combination lock; the information gleaned from Sal's phone looked like it was accurate.

Could the stuff from the museum still be in there?

It occurred to him that he could be on camera right now–that he probably already was when he drove in, his vehicle license plate possibly recorded. But he knew that those videos were usually only retained for a couple of days or so. If nothing was reported within that time, it would be overwritten. And even if Sal's partners in crime did notice right away that their unit had been broken into, they couldn't very well report it to the cops, now could they?

But that was all theoretical. The truth was that he really didn't give a shit. He was going to look inside this unit. After that, he didn't know. One thing at time. He told himself not to worry about anything anymore. Just wasn't worth it. A reggae song he'd last heard at the wine party went through his head on his way up to the door.

Don't worry, about a thing...

His conscious tried to tell him that this was ridiculous. He was breaking the law the minute he'd used the ill-gotten gate code. Only a few short weeks ago he'd never even have considered such an act. Now the simple trespassing barely even registered for him. Like it was his right to be here or something. Opening the unit—that would give him a rush, but just being in the parking lot—nothing. *Guess my tolerance for this stuff is rising.*

He could always say he was checking on a unit for a friend but he forgot what unit number they gave him.

...Cuz every little thing, gonna be alright...

Matt shone a mental light on the shadow of his conscience and put his hand on the lock. He was about to try the combination he'd written down when he realized that the shackle had swung loose and was not actually locked.

An oversight? They forgot to lock it, or maybe they thought it was locked but it popped out later? Seemed odd for a group of professional thieves. Had it been picked or tampered with?

Matt slid the lock from the door as he mulled it over. The lock was in one piece with no obvious damage to it. No one had tried to pry it or shoot it or smash it off. Which meant...

Could they be in there now? Matt leaned his ear closer to the door. He listened for a full minute but heard nothing.

He clicked the shackle into the lock and turned the combination wheel. Locked. Then he tried the combination he'd written down from Sal's phone. Three sets of double-digit numbers...

Click!

This was the lock. He opened it and put it back on the door, unlocked, the way he'd found it. He took a quick look around and saw no one. Stooping to grab the handle at the bottom of the door, Matt the saint Knox opened someone else's storage unit.

He gazed inside, not wanting to step into the space before his eyes had fully adjusted. But he could see right away that an adjustment period wouldn't be necessary.

The unit was bare. He felt a twinge of disappointment.

Everything's already been moved. No wonder they didn't bother to lock it.

-53-

HIDE AND SEEK

Jeremy Washington gripped Pablo's bicep, a signal to remain quiet. They'd just heard the metal door roll up. From their place of concealment in the crawl space above the unit's drop ceiling tiles (Pablo had boosted Jeremy up onto some metal water pipes that ran above the tiling, and then he had leaned back out to haul in his accomplice who hastily replaced the tiles after him), they could hear but not see into the unit below. Sitting on the pipes like high-rise construction workers, their feet dangling to just over the ceiling tiles, the two men steadied one another for balance in the near darkness.

Even in the dim light Jeremy could tell that Pablo's eyes were wide with fear. He was concerned that he would just start screaming or trying to crawl away or something. He whispered to him, "Probably just a security guard." *A job I'm not even qualified for myself.* Not to mention, Jeremy thought but did not say, if it was security and they were just stopping by to see if they needed any help (they were the only customers in the place by the look of the parking lot, after all), then what would they do when they saw there was no one in the unit even though they probably saw them walk into it on the closed circuit cameras?

Jeremy looked around the cramped space. There was nowhere to really go from here; they had to keep their heads low or else bump into the fiberglass insulation that marked the beginning of the floor above. The pipes that supported them disappeared through solid walls to either side.

Footsteps echoed in the unit below. Jeremy stopped breathing.

The shrill jangle of a mobile phone shattered the quiet.

Pablo involuntarily jumped at the sonic intrusion and then Jeremy heard the sound of skin sliding over metal and reached out and grabbed Pablo, whose hand had slipped on the pipe.

The magnitude of the adrenaline jolt to Jeremy's system was almost incapacitating. It was his phone that was ringing! Not his cellular, which he had powered down before stepping into Pablo's car. Out of habit he silenced his phone whenever on any kind of stakeout or sensitive operation. But he'd forgotten about the trac phone. The only person who had the number was Tommy, and although he wasn't scheduled to call, he hadn't heard from him in a while.

You idiot! How could you forget that!

Jeremy scrambled to reach the cargo pocket the phone was in without wobbling off of his precarious perch. He could hear Pablo hissing at him but he relegated that to the back of his consciousness while his fingers felt the smooth plastic and hit a button—*any damn button, just make it stop!*—silencing the trac phone.

They heard footsteps in the unit below. Tentative—a couple in one direction, then a couple more in another...

And then the rollup door clattered as it was pulled shut. Whoever had come in was now leaving, probably assuming the phone came from someone on the second floor. Jeremy and Pablo waited a few seconds to make certain the intruder had truly left the space. When it was clear that he had, Jeremy said, "I need to see who that was."

"Gotta be Eduardo."

They heard the car engine start up again outside.

"What's he drive?"

"When he's not driving the van? El Camino.

"The car outside didn't really sound like an El Camino to me."

They heard the car shift and begin to drive.

Jeremy began to slither off of the pipe.

"What are you doing?"

"Getting down. Want to see who that was."

"Careful what you wish for. They might want to see you, too."

Jeremy hung from the pipe until he could kick out one of the ceiling tiles. He dangled from the pipe with his feet sticking through the open tile space into the airspace of the storage room below. Let himself drop.

"Okay?" Pablo called down.

"Yes, come on down."

Jeremy reached out to pull the door open. For a second he had a sobering thought: what if whoever just left had locked the padlock in place? But he was relieved to feel and hear the door slide up on its rollers. Then another sobering possibility: what if there were two people in the car and one of them had stayed behind for some reason? He'd be walking out right into them.

He poked his head out the doorway and looked right toward the entrance. No cars. Looked around the parking lot. No people.

He'd missed the visitor.

-54-

REAP WHAT YOU SOW

Matt Knox made the drive back to the yacht dealership without incident and eased his SUV into a parking space. His little sortie had been for nothing, but that wasn't unexpected. Just a little drive, no big deal. He wondered what had become of the loot, though. Had it been sold already? Was some lady in Beverly Hills walking down Rodeo Drive right now wearing a sea otter shawl? Who would have bought all those pieces of scrimshaw, and the old brass compasses and ships' bells? Seemed odd they could move that kind of inventory so quickly. Or maybe they just transported it to another location out of caution—didn't want to leave the stuff in one place for too long?

Matt reflected on what the public knew of the case. Not much, he decided, walking across the parking lot back into work. The museum had been robbed, the stuff was still missing, no named suspects yet. Loose talk around town sort of suspected Sal's gang, but no one actually knew for sure. There was too much crime in the general area for Sal & Company to be responsible for all of it.

Inside the brokerage John was still dealing with a customer who'd been in earlier. Good sign, Matt though, as he ensconced himself in his office again. *Take care of business, John. I've got to figure something out here...*

Matt eased into his chair behind his desk and opened a drawer. He pulled the blunderbuss he'd taken with him (*why did you bring that with you, Matthew? Were you going to hurt someone with it again, if there had been people in the unit—Sal's people? You would have blasted them, wouldn't you?)* out from under his shirt and stashed it in the bottom drawer underneath a stack of old issues of *Yachter's World.*

He closed that drawer and opened the top one, lifting the tray of supplies to reveal the space beneath. From it he removed the skeleton key.

Back to this. He bounced the key in his hand, appreciating the weight. He marveled at its inscription once more.

Davey Jones Locker.

He replayed the same mental tour he'd taken earlier, the one that led to Dallas' neighbor's house. It was just too coincidental, wasn't it? His name was Dave Jones, and the key was to Davey Jones' Locker? As far as Matt was aware Dallas Draper and Dave Jones didn't have any business enterprises together. They didn't even hang out together, even though they were neighbors living a few houses apart and about the same age.

And even if it was Dave's, what the hell would it open? The man didn't own a boat, not that it looked like a boat key. His house? Weird key for a house. Something in the museum? In Dallas' boat? Matt sure as heck wasn't going back to either of those places. Dallas' house?

Matt shook his head as the questions multiplied like bacteria on a sugar-laced Petri dish. The puzzle eluded him for now. He put the key back into the drawer.

Maybe it was nothing. Sal had gotten a pretty good look at the monkey's fist, after all, and he hadn't shown any interest in it when Matt first gave him the keys. And in his apartment, just before...

My first kill! That's what it was. My first. You always remember your first.

Just before that, Sal had pretty much scoffed at the key, right up until he read the inscription.

I'll be goddamned.

Maybe Sal knew Dallas' neighbor? Matt didn't think so, but then again, there sure was a lot that he hadn't known about Sal Jonason, wasn't there?

He pulled the key out of the drawer again.

With the treasure already moved out of the initial holding place Sal's gang had for it, Matt wasn't sure why the key even mattered anymore. Everything of value associated with the heist seems to have already been processed. And yet he felt incomplete. He *hated* that at least two of the people who had forced him to rob the museum were still out there, going about their lives in whatever state of affairs passed as business as usual for them, while he was left to come to terms with this altered mental state, changed in such unexpected ways by his forced cooperation.

The fact that he was starting to enjoy his new mindset mattered little. They hadn't known nor cared whether he would grow into this new lifestyle, much like a person who spits out an orange seed into the dirt is not thinking about whether it will one day grow into a tree. And certainly not whether the fruit of that tree will turn out to be poisonous.

Follow the treasure and I'll find them. Most pirates sought a map to a treasure. For Matt, the treasure *was* the map—to the pirates, his victims. That was the real mother lode.

The skeleton key might or might not lead to the cache, but he had one simple possibility to follow up on. He pocketed the key and opened the drawer with the blunderbuss.

Time to go for a little boat ride. He could wait until tomorrow and take his Whaler, but Summer would think it odd that he wanted to take the boat to work now that both cars were in perfect working order. Better to take the old workboat again. He stood there a moment, wondering if he should tell John he'd be out again for a little while. He shoved that thought aside as he stuck the barrel of the blunderbuss into his waistband and under his shirt. *Who gives a fuck.*

Matt Knox walked out of his office onto the main retail floor, where John Samson was talking on the phone with a client. Out of the corner of his eye he could see him gesticulating silently, like he wanted him to come over and see something on the computer while he talked. Matt gave him a casual *see ya later* wave on the way out the door.

-55-

MATCHMAKER

Jeremy let the headrest of Pablo's bucket seat support his neck while they drove away from the Move & Store. They'd left without encountering anyone at all but Pablo still maintained a white-knuckle death grip on the wheel, furtively glancing at his rear view mirror.

"Relax, Pablo, nobody saw us."

"Somebody was *in* there while your phone went off! What the fuck is wrong with you, anyway? You crazy or something?"

"I'm sorry. My mistake."

"Whoever that was must have heard it. It was loud as shit, man!"

"They probably assumed it was someone on the second floor."

Pablo shook his head in silence as he coasted through a yellow light. At length he said, "So who was it, anyway?"

"Who was what?"

"Who called you back there? I just want to know what was so important that almost got me killed."

Jeremy knew why Pablo was upset. With the cache of stolen goods gone, he now had no hope of the reward that he was going to use to set him on the path to straight and narrow.

Did he still need him, though?

After all, if Pablo didn't know where the loot was, he was of no help in collecting the reward for its safe return. Yet he had meant well. He had told him things he wouldn't have otherwise known, like the storage location. He was still Jeremy's main connection to any flow of information from the gang.

"It's another one of my contacts helping me to find the stolen loot, Pablo. That's all I'm gonna say. I haven't heard from them in a while, they finally decide to call me, of course at the worst possible time. But they didn't know that."

Pablo took a left off the main drag onto the side street that led to his place. "Fair enough. I know I'm not the only guy in the world who might be able to get you that reward." Jeremy nodded his appreciation for Pablo's understanding.

"So what'd he say? Or she?"

"They didn't leave a message," Jeremy said, keeping with the deliberately vague pronoun. He pulled the trac phone from a pocket and turned it on. "I need to return that call."

"Does this contact of yours know everything—like that we just went to the storage place?"

"No, not that much. Mostly been helping with basic casework like alerts if the stolen items show up in certain places, getting me police reports, that kind of thing."

"I'm guessing it's one of your ex-cop buddies."

"I can neither confirm nor deny that," Jeremy said, holding the trac up to his right ear, the one farthest away from Pablo.

Tommy's voice came on the line after the second ring.

"About time you fuckin' called. Finally got some good info. We got a break," Tommy said. Jeremy was grateful that his ex-partner's voice wasn't booming loud. He wouldn't have to worry about Pablo hearing anything out of the speaker.

"What have you got?"

"Lab results came back on some prints. Got a match! Scary shit, though. You with me?"

"Go on."

"Lab turned out a positive match between the only print lifted from the museum, and—get this—a print lifted from Josey Jiminez's work boat. Not the print of Josey himself. Remember this was the guy who turned the harbor red with his blood from a massive trauma wound while diving to clean a boat, the poor sonofabitch. He was known to associate with Sal's gang but he wasn't one of the worst ones. No prior felonies, at least."

"Hold up. You said 'the only print lifted from the museum,' but what about all the museum staff—they get checked out yet?"

"Right, they were all interviewed, prints checked, and none of them come up as the slightest bit suspicious. The print we got was from the main exhibit area targeted by the thieves, and it was fresher than the employee prints that cover everything from routine use."

"Okay, so that print was a match for another print found on Josey's work boat?"

"Correct. Which means that whoever killed Josey Jiminez was also in on the museum theft. That elevates this whole thing, man. We're not talking simple burglary anymore, this is murder."

Jeremy wrestled with telling Tommy that Pablo didn't know where the loot was any more, about the Move & Store trip. To do so would be to bring Pablo into their inner circle. He wasn't sure if he was ready to do that yet. He could wait until later...

He was still wrestling with this when Tommy said, "Hey listen, I'm getting a call. Gotta split, but that's what I had for you. Get back to me with what's up on your end, okay? Later." Tommy clicked off and Jeremy set the trac phone down in his lap.

The same guy who killed Josey Martinez was also in on the museum theft.

"What's up, everything okay?" Pablo asked.

Jeremy watched a row of palm trees pass by outside in a blur. If the print that linked to no criminal record belonged to whoever had murdered Josey, then that person couldn't possibly be Pablo Martinez. He looked over at his old friend driving. One of the perks of being a cop was that it was possible to look up your friends and neighbors, just for the heck of it were you so inclined, and he knew for a fact that Pablo had a record. Nothing to brag about, by gangster standards, but there was no possible way he would come up clean as a whistle like this print did. And if Pablo himself didn't represent the danger (he now felt bad for ever thinking that), then he must be *in* danger.

"Not really. Pablo, I've got some bad news."

"I thought I already got my share of that today, but lay it on me."

The storage episode would corroborate the 'in danger' theory, Jeremy thought. "You know that print I told you about that they lifted from the museum?"

"Yeah, it was the only one."

"Right. A print found on Josey's boat cleaning skiff matches the one taken from the museum."

Pablo unconsciously pressed his foot down harder on the pedal, as if the increasing speed fueled the processing power of his brain. He said nothing, though, only drove.

"Somebody inside the museum with you was also on Josey's work boat, which means almost for sure that he's Josey's killer. Slow down."

The Nissan's speed decreased. "It wasn't me. Let's get that out of the way."

"You don't have to worry about that. I know your prints wouldn't come out clean."

"But none of our prints would come out that fucking clean, man. Unless Sal figured out how to do some kind of identity switch or he burned his fingertips off or some crazy shit."

"No, this is a perfect print. I've seen prints left by people who tried to burn or mutilate them—they don't even really have fingerprints anymore, it's just scar tissue. I guess it's possible Sal could have done something to manipulate his record, but I know from experience, Pablo, that the correct explanation is usually the simplest. Sal didn't burn off his fingertips or figure out how to hack the FBI databases."

Pablo turned off onto his street, slowing to an appropriate speed for the residential lane.

"So what's the simplest explanation?"

Jeremy took a deep breath and looked at his friend. "The simplest explanation here, Pablo, is that the print belongs to the one guy who was there that we know doesn't have a record."

"But we all have records." Pablo turned into his driveway and stopped the car right there at the end.

"You're not seeing the forest for the trees. You told me before that someone else was in there with you."

"Well, yeah, there was The Saint, but he's not in the gang."

The Nissan's engine made clicking sounds as it cooled.

Jeremy forced himself to remain calm, to summon his patience. He flashed on their early school days, how Pablo almost had to be held back in the ninth grade because he just wasn't comprehending basic things. But he had a feeling that his life now depended on understanding what was going on.

"Pablo, why do you call him The Saint?"

The gang member answered without hesitation. "Because he's a model fucking citizen, man, squeaky clean, he—"

Jeremy watched with satisfaction as Pablo cut himself off in mid sentence. He finished with one word that said it all.

"Shit."

-56-

DAVEY JONES' LOCKER

Matt Knox boated up to the slip fronting Dave Jones' house, ripples from his forward progress spreading out across the still water. No one was visible in any of the waterfront houses, including Dallas Draper's, three down to Matt's right as he faced them. He looked across to the other side of the canal, where all was quiet except for an elderly gentleman spray washing a forty-foot pontoon boat. He was six houses down toward the end of the canal where it ended in a 'T', with the crossbar representing two dead-end passages lined with close packed residences. The only way back to the main harbor thoroughfare was to retrace the way he'd come, which Matt was thankful for since it meant traffic here was low and he'd see any vessels that approached from the main channel.

The yacht dealer cut the outboard on the borrowed work dinghy and let the boat glide up to the end cap of Mr. Jones' dock. He looped a line over a cleat to secure the boat. Grinning at the sight of a grimy ball cap with a sportfishing logo crushed beneath a five gallon bucket, he swiped it from the deck and put it on. A pair of salt encrusted work gloves lay not far from where the hat had been and he donned those as well. Just doin' some work, nothing to see here.

Speaking of, he thought while he scanned Dave's house more carefully, what exactly was he doing now? He fingered the skeleton key in the pocket of his Levi's. Taking in the view of Dave's immaculate looking house–damn near a mansion, Matt thought (the Joneses were keeping up just fine)–he held out little hope that he would find a lock that fit this key anywhere on it. Posted signs with a security company moniker were spiked into the lawn at either end of the yard, boldly proclaiming *Protected Property*. Matt snickered at the sign's image of a fierce dog in a menacing perma-growl. He enjoyed a mental image of a bloody skateboard for a split second before forcing it aside in order to focus on the task at hand. He looked around, taking in more details. The front door was a rock-solid oak affair with a peephole. On the second floor a wraparound balcony featured closed (and no doubt locked) French doors with drawn curtains.

Perhaps the key opened something that was inside the house, say a jewelry box? A chill coursed through him–not a particularly unpleasant sensation, either–as he imagined himself finding a way into the Jones' house. He tried to picture the rest of the family: wife, he forgot her name but she was nothing special to look at, two grown daughters, off doing their own things somewhere. That was all he knew about the Joneses.

He averted his gaze from the house where his mind, almost unconsciously, had begun calculating various methods of entry. He looked at the empty dock. How ridiculous to have a waterfront house with dockage and not have a boat, Matt thought, eyes tracing the empty expanse of floating platform along its U-shaped design. Not even a kayak sitting up on the dock.

To each his own, I guess, Matt thought. And then he saw the dock box. It was a white fiberglass locker—about three feet high and maybe four wide with a hinged lid. Every dock had one, so the fact that there was one here was certainly not unusual. What surprised Matt, though, was that Dave's was locked. They were used to store boat related equipment that didn't make sense to carry back and forth or leave on the boat—hoses, boat covers, cleaning supplies and life jackets, little used fishing gear, that sort of thing. Almost all of them were locked, too, so Dave's wasn't unique in that regard either, although for a guy with no boat it did make one wonder what he was keeping in there.

What really caught Matt's attention, though, was the lock itself: an odd shaped black metal contraption. The Saint took a few steps closer to the dock box, squinting as his eyes soaked up the details: dimpled casing spotted with rust, a U-shaped shaft that was on the thin side.

Why would a person with no boat want to lock his dock box?

And then his focused stare reached the lock's keyhole. A large opening matched the shape of the skeleton key held in his hand. Not very secure. No doubt it could be opened with other implements besides its intended key. But then again, it wouldn't necessarily need to be that secure, Matt thought, taking the remaining steps over to the dockbox. No boat usually meant no stuff in the dockbox. The old lock was probably just a token attempt to keep space-hungry watersports enthusiasts from appropriating his storage box.

But did his key fit it?

Glancing around the area, Matt saw no one except for the power wash guy, who was now on the opposite side of his boat, hidden from view, blasting away. Matt knelt in front of the dock box and held the lock in his left hand. He tugged on it to check that it was actually locked (that Master lock in the storage place had looked like it was locked, too, but wasn't), but it held firm. He started to remove the bulky work gloves, then halted. *Probably shouldn't leave any more fingerprints lying around.*

Fumbling with the skeleton key between the fingers of his right glove, he managed to mate it with the lock. He could see now that the metal of the two pieces—lock and key—shared the same texture and appearance. For them not to be a pair would be quite a coincidence indeed.

He turned the key.

When it clicked open he jumped a little. He didn't know what he was expecting, but the key was a perfect fit. He pulled the lock open and slid it from the dockbox, setting it down on the dock. Matt stood and dusted off his knees, then pocketed the key.

He glanced about once more. Nothing had changed around him. He lifted the container's lid and propped it all the way open on its hinges.

Removing his sunglasses, Matt Knox peered into Dave Jone's locker.

-57-

SCARE TACTICS

Jeremy Washington was glad to get back into his own car again. Pablo had dropped him back at his place before heading to his mechanic job, and now, as he eased his Bronco out onto the road, Jeremy's mind turned back to the case.

Matt the Saint Knox.

Inside the museum during the theft. Prints found on Josey Jiminez' floating murder scene.

The stolen loot gone, at least according to Pablo. Jeremy tried hard but couldn't think of a reason not to believe him. And if he accepted that, he had to accept that someone had come looking for the stuff this morning and had come way too close for comfort to finding them inside the unit where the loot was supposedly stashed. He could have been killed, right then and there.

He thought of Alisa and the kids going on without him. *Was this worth it?* Risking his life–and for what–the *possibility* of a reward? He knew how these kinds of public offerings sometimes turned out–even when helpful information was received, the reward may not be disbursed because there was other information from different sources that also helped lead to the recovery or conviction. And the city of Sandy Cove already had a bone to pick with him, he thought, reaching into his center divider console for the trac phone–*the Tommyphone*, as he'd taken to calling it.

But the city's reaction to his misdeed in that case was out of his control and so, as he had taught himself in the years in and years out on a job where he was confronted with uncertainty on a daily basis, he willed his mind to corral all the little things he could control, to herd them into a cohesive unit of determination and resolve until he had a stampede that could at least face, if not trample the unknown.

Jeremy pulled the Bronco into the parking lot of a nearly empty strip mall. He didn't need anything here, but he had to concentrate on the call he was about to make and didn't want to add distracted driving to his repertoire of misdoings. He dialed the only number saved into the trac.

While the phone rang, he noticed a Help Wanted sign in one of the store windows. A donut shop. The cop cliché had some truth to it. *Great. I can serve donuts to the guys I used to work with.* Then he noticed that the place wasn't even open yet, and upon closer inspection still, that it likely wasn't even open at all anymore. The owners had just up and left, Help Wanted but never found. So even that humiliation wasn't an option.

Tommy picked up after six rings. "Yo, Jeremy, what's up?"

"Need a favor. Got a minute?"

"What do you need? Stayin' outta trouble?"

"Barely. Listen to this." He filled him in on Pablo's disclosure that Matt Knox had been with them in the museum and that he had said he was going to take him to the stolen goods but when they arrived it was missing. He didn't want to be completely alone with this information at this point. He needed to tell someone.

"Wow! You got lucky, Jeremy. You need to take it easy. But you're way closer to it than the official line over here so far. Like we thought, Flannery's just going through the motions."

"Fuckin' A Flannery."

"The one and only. He issued all the usual bulletins, you know the drill, but they haven't been really pulling out all the stops, I guess because nobody's gonna get their panties in a wad to get back a bunch of insured knick-knacks for a rich guy like Dallas Draper.

"But they would over murder."

"That's what they're focusing on, yeah, but until now nobody was thinking the murders and the museum theft were connected. Sal's gang is kind of always a possible suspect for any crime, but usually they knock over gas stations, not pull museum heists like a Tom fuckin' Cruise movie, so they weren't connecting them. And they *damn* sure don't know shit about the Saint. No way I can bring that up to 'em either, without some kind of evidence that would have led me to it outside of our little secret partnership, know what I'm saying?"

"I've got an idea."

"Uh-oh."

"Hear me out."

"I've got to get back on my beat, but tell me quick."

Jeremy relayed how he had interviewed with Knox for a job at the dealership.

"Sounds like a real prick. How's that going for you, anyway–you find some work yet?"

"Still trying. But listen, here's what I think would be good. You go down to the yacht place on lunch or break, just go in there on personal time–but in uniform–and say you're thinking about buying a boat, and say you want to talk to Mr. Knox about it. Use his name, even if he's there himself."

A beat of silence passed while Tommy digested this. Jeremy continued. "*If* he actually did anything wrong, that would scare the shit out of him, right?"

"And if he didn't, he'd probably just think I was sending a message, *you're a jerk for kicking our boy when he's down.* I like it. Put some pressure on him. Guys slip up when they're under pressure."

"Let's hope he does."

-58-

WHAT DO WE HAVE HERE?

Matt Knox blinked a couple of times to make sure he wasn't seeing things that weren't there. The dockbox was full to the brim. It nearly overflowed with...he leaned over to get a better look...with things...nautical things. Pearls! Scrimshaw. Glass fishing floats encased in rope nets. Sheathed cutlasses. And there were several closed cardboard boxes.

I'll be goddamned.

He lifted his head out of the box to have a look around. Coast was clear. He turned back to the items. Matt reached a hand into the storage locker and reached down into it, probing to see how densely packed it was. He felt something exquisitely soft and scrunched his fingers around it. He moved a few other things out of the way with his other hand and saw that it was an animal fur.

He tried to reconcile this chaotic pile of stuff with the museum layout he'd seen. Could all of the stolen items fit right here in this box? He recalled the duffel bags and supposed that, unorganized as it was, that it probably could. It was amazing, he thought, noting in the far recesses of his mind that the spray washing across the way had stopped, how little space the things actually occupied when they were all crammed together like this.

He closed the lid so as not to attract so much attention to himself while he evaluated this new development. The treasure was right here?! *Why here?* Didn't matter. This was it, what else could it be? He recognized most of the stuff. What was in those boxes, though?

He scanned the area for signs of anyone observing him. Finding none, he propped open the lid of the locker again. He darted an arm inside and shuffled some of the items around until he was able to extract one of the cardboard boxes, selected because it was the first one he came across that he could easily grab and remove from the locker.

He pried it from the sea of items inside, set it on the edge of the locker and pulled apart the flaps. Inside, two revolvers—blunder-busses exactly like the ones he had–rested on a contoured velvet tray. The sight of the weapons started Matt's heart racing. Did he have his revolvers? Did he actually know where they were or was it possible that somehow they'd been stolen back from him?

He took a deep breath and forced himself to calm, calm, calm down. When was the last time he saw them? Fourth of July. *(The bum!)* Conscious of the fact that he was standing out in the open on someone else's property holding a case of guns, Matt moved to re-box them, but at the last second (*do it do it do it*)he removed one of the pistols and tucked it in his waistband, as he had grown accustomed to doing lately. Then he let the little box, now relieved of half its contents, fall back into the riotous jumble of stolen keepsakes.

This new blunderbuss felt heavier to him, but he attributed that to the variation that must have been present in the manufacturing processes of the period. But he had seen the gun exhibit and there were only two blunderbusses. He was positive of that. And if there were only two, where did these two come from? *Maybe Sal or one of them found some more in another case that I didn't see.*

Matt brought the lid down to rest on top of the box. A little warning bell rang in his head: *Been here too long now, time to move along.* He looked at the work boat, still bobbing in place, tied to the dock, then back to the dock box. It occurred to Matt that there were a lot of valuable things in the box. *Should I take some with me, at least something easy to carry and conceal—the pearls, maybe?*

But he couldn't muster the enthusiasm. He just didn't care about the stuff. He only wanted who it would lead to. The other gang members. He had no idea how it ended up in Dave Jones' dock box—he didn't see any association with Mr. Jones and Sal's gang—but someone had put it here and so someone would be coming back for it at some point.

He went over to the box and put the old black lock back on it while he thought it through. How would he know when someone returned for the loot? He wasn't some technical guru who could snap up a wireless camera surveillance system that would beam images to a secure website. He couldn't stand around here all day. There was really only so much he could do. He'd just have to get a little lucky.

He turned the skeleton key clockwise in the lock, clicking it into place. He'd have to start taking his boat to work every day, that's all. That way he could swing by once in the morning on the way in, then again at lunch—possibly even more if little job related errands best accomplished by water came up—and finally on the way back home. He'd have to think of a way to explain his sudden desire to take the boat to work every day to Summer, but he'd come up with something.

He pocketed the skeleton key and took a look at the nondescript locker. Amazing that all this stuff that everyone is looking for is right here, pretty much smack dab in the middle of Sandy Cove right in plain sight.

...everyone is looking for...

He stood ramrod straight as the idea came to him. There was a reward out for this stuff. Fifty grand altogether. He didn't want the stuff, but who in their right mind wouldn't want fifty grand? If he went to the police and said, I know where the stolen museum goods are, then surely they would listen. He was Matt the motherfucking Saint! Beyond reproach. Of course he'd have to figure out how he came to know where it was without tipping his forced (and then not so forced) involvement, which wouldn't be easy, but he had fifty thousand reasons to figure it out.

Something else to work on back at the office, he thought, starting to turn around for the work boat. But he froze in place when he heard the voice somewhere behind him.

"Hey there!"

-59-

DON'T I KNOW YOU FROM SOMEWHERE?

"I said hey there! Excuse me?"

Matt Knox had heard the voice behind him the first time. He was stunned that he had been snuck up on. Had he been so lost in concentration staring into the dockbox that he had been oblivious to the sound of approaching footsteps or perhaps a boat? He hoped his shirt was covering the old revolver tucked against the small of his back. *Who is it?* His right hand started to wander toward his lower back. Just in case.

He turned around to face whoever confronted him, steeling his nerves.

Matt stared at the gentleman from across the way who'd been power-washing his yacht. Definitely not as bad as it could be, but still not good. Now he had a neighbor who could place him at the dockbox. Was he about to accuse him of something?

"Sorry to interrupt, but I saw your boat and that you're doing some work over here and thought I would ask if you're available for a temporary job today? Been working on my boat..." He turned a little to point it out..."and I need somebody who can siphon out some old fuel from the tank and dispose of it for me. Could you do that?"

Matt sized the guy up. About sixty, pretty decent shape for his age, bald head gleaming in the sun with smears of sunscreen still visible, dressed in a yacht club polo tucked into a pair of khaki shorts with a canvas belt and matching topsider deck shoes.

Cell-phone in a leather sheath clipped to his belt on one side, some kind of multi-tool on the other. Matt had done business with literally hundreds of guys just like this.

"Hi there. Sorry, but I'm not set up for that right now. Just came by to do a quick repair to the dock. Got to get going, in fact..." He made a show of glancing at his watch, which was a little too nice looking for something the workboat guy would be wearing; titanium mariner's chronometer instead of maybe a plastic band digital, if he wore a watch at all. Should have taken it off. *Next time.*

"Sure, I understand. Just thought I would try since you were a stone's throw away. Do you happen to know someone who could—say, you look familiar."

Matt cocked his head to the side, awaiting the man's realization while hoping it wouldn't come. He didn't recognize him, he was reasonably sure of that.

"Pardon?"

"You're from the yacht dealership, right?"

Matt's stomach churned.

"I've seen your commercials on TV. Good stuff!"

He felt his intestines join in on the action. The local TV spots were something he'd rather forget. A couple of years ago the owners had wanted to try something new, marketing-wise, and they thought Matt had a gregarious enough personality to pull off a thirty-second promo. It had come out okay, some silly humor involving a guy in a rowboat getting dwarfed by a forty-foot Bayliner, but in the end it left him feeling a little like a used car salesman, and thankfully they decided not to renew the spots.

But even worse than that was the fact that he was wearing what he had thought of as a partial disguise, the workman's gloves, hat, shades, boat. So much for that.

"I didn't realize you got out of the office. Haven't seen you on repair jobs before."

This just gets better and better.

"Yeah, well I don't usually, but sometimes you gotta do what you gotta do, right? Tell you what: I've got the number of a guy who's licensed to do fuel disposal. You got a card or something—an email? I'll have him get in touch with you."

The man reached into one of his cargo pockets. "Yeah, sure, that'd be great." He extended an arm with a business card pinched between two fingers. "Appreciate it, thanks."

Matt pocketed the card without looking at it. "You have a good day, now."

The boater said thanks again and stepped into his little raft, powered by a small electric trolling motor. He glided silently back across the channel. *No wonder I didn't hear him coming.*

Matt stared at the back of his shiny head as he returned to his yacht. He reached back and petted the outline of the blunderbuss for a second or two.

In his mind...

Matt aimed his old revolver at the back of that shiny dome and pulled the trigger. The old man slumped at the back of his dinghy, his arm pulling the tiller of the trolling motor as he fell to the deck, his now pilotless craft continuing on in a tight circle, around, around, around, while blood congealed in the sun.

Matt took himself out of the fantasy and hopped into the workboat, untying its lines. Time to get back to the shop.

The mind crimes just weren't cutting it anymore.

-60-
CALLING CARD

Matt Knox tied the workboat to the dock in front of the yacht dealership. He jumped out onto the dock and strode to the door of his place of work. Inside, John Samson was on the phone, eying Matt closely while his boss ignored him and walked to his office.

Matt shut his door, closed the curtains and sat behind his desk. The message light was dark on his phone. *Good.* He removed his new blunderbuss from his pants and examined it under an architectural drafting light that he used to show boat plans to clients. Funny, it *looked* the same as the other two, but somehow it seemed a little different. He'd have to compare it side by side against the other two once he got home. Fire it, too. He put the blunderbuss in his bottom desk drawer.

No sooner had he closed it than three knocks beat against his door. *John's got a hot prospect.* He told him to come in. The door swung open and Samson entered the room, a small piece of paper in one hand. He headed straight to Matt's desk.

"Got some good news, Matt. Guy came by a few minutes ago—you just missed him—said he was real interested in buying a sailboat, wanted to see you about it."

Matt yawned. The adventure of locating the museum treasure had given him a big rush, and now that it was over he felt like he needed a strong cup of coffee.

"Thanks John. Leave me his card, I'll get right on it." Matt opened his cell and checked the messages while John placed the business card on Matt's desk.

John turned and strode for the door. Usually he would chat Matt up about pretty much anything—the girl he liked at the Grog N Grub, the weather, the beach bonfire party he'd went to over the weekend...but lately it hadn't been worth the effort. He had just reached the door when Matt happened to glance over at the card on his desk.

It featured the Sandy Cove PD badge logo, green and brown motif. Matt felt a rush of adrenaline, the hairs on his arms standing up. He held up a hand as he swiped up the card.

"Hold up—John?"

Samson stepped back inside.

"Who's this from—police came by?"

"Yeah, a cop—name's on the card—came by on his lunch break, he said, to buy a sailboat."

Matt read the name on the card—half hoping it was that disgruntled ex-cop he'd done that lame job interview with—what was his name? *Jeremy something...* He could deal with that loser.

But the name on the card was not Jeremy.

"That's what he said—he wanted to buy a boat?"

John looked at him like he was trying to fit a square peg into a round hole. "Uh, yeah Matt, he wanted to buy a boat, or at least think about it. That's why people come in here, remember?"

"Well I'm glad that's what he wanted. Thought you might be in trouble or something!" He gave his employee a big grin.

Glad to see Matt assuming a sliver of his jovial side which he hadn't seen much of lately, John smiled and stepped back into the office. "Only if being the best damned boat salesman this side of the Mississippi is a crime. Seriously though, I can't take any credit for this one, if it pans out. He asked specifically for you."

Matt's thought processes seemed to freeze, as if the blood coursing through his brain had suddenly thickened and slowed.

"You mean he walked in here and said he wanted to buy a boat, lemme talk to the manager?"

"Not exactly. He did say he wanted to buy a boat, but he asked to speak with you by name. He was in uniform but said he was on his lunch break. I told him you were out for lunch, and he asked when you'd be back and I told him..."

Asked when I'd be back!

"...couple hours or so. Where were you, anyway? I saw the work-boat was gone. You went to check out the destroyer, didn't you? I hear that thing's pretty sick!"

Currently a naval vessel was anchored just offshore of the harbor and they permitted the general public to tour the ship.

"Yeah, I had to check that out!"

"Cool, shoulda told me, I woulda went with you. How was it?"

"It was sick! Those guys can handle anything. Great to see where our tax dollars go. Anyway, John—thanks for letting me know about this. I should give this guy a call back right now."

He held up the card and John backed out of the room, giving him the thumbs up. "Set that hook, buddy!"

Alone again in his office, Matt stared at the cop's card. *Holy fuck. Whatthefuckisthis?* He fought back sensations of panic and helpless-ness. Buy a boat? Seriously? He reviewed what John had told him. *In uniform...asked for me by name...left a card, asked when I'd be back.* He glanced down at the drawer he'd just dropped his new gun into, saw that it was open a hair, and kicked it flush.

If they knew something they'd just arrest him, wouldn't they? Why wait? *Stop over-thinking everything. Fuck this. Remember who you are.* Matt the fucking saint Knox doesn't need to run away from jack shit. He stared at the card, turning it over in his fingers. Nothing written on the back. He thought back to shooting the bum, shooting Sal, crushing that loser's skull in on the boat. It made him feel better. Gave him courage.

You wanna keep doing that kind of stuff you're going to have to learn to deal with cops. This fucking pig wants a boat, give him a goddamn boat and send him on his way. It would be weird not to call him back.

He picked up his desk phone and dialed the number on the card.

-61-

FAMILY PHONE PLAN

The Tommyphone rang for the second time that day. A surprise to Jeremy, since Tommy rarely called, and a surprise to Alisa as well. She stared in puzzlement at her husband's unlit cellular on the countertop, then followed the sound of the generic ringer to Jeremy himself, who froze in the middle of the living room on his way to the couch.

"What is that?" she asked him.

Jeremy hadn't yet told his wife about the trac phone, about his quest for the reward, his quasi-partnership with Tommy—none of it. As far as she knew he was looking for a job every waking minute.

"It's a phone." The ringing continued. He knew he'd have some explaining to do to Alisa, but right now his curiosity over what Tommy had to say overrode that. He pulled the trac from his jeans pocket.

"You have a second phone?" Alisa's voice went in one ear while Tommy's now came through another.

He held up a finger to his wife. "Excuse me, baby. I gotta take this."

Into the phone, he said "Jeremy here."

Alisa smiled and mouthed the word, *Job?* and although he knew it would make things more difficult for him later on, he nodded. Tommy already had his full attention. Besides, it was a job of sorts, wasn't it?

"Yeah, so guess who just called me at the station?" Tommy didn't wait for an answer. "I went down to the yacht place today, and the Saint wasn't there but I left a card with your old high school chum. What's his name?"

"Samson."

"Yeah, John Samson. He seems like a nice guy. Anyway, the Saint just called me back."

"And?" Jeremy drifted deeper into the living room, feeling Alisa's eyes on his back as he went.

"I have to say, man, dude seems on the up and up. Just like a salesman, a little pushy, super gung-ho attitude, but there was nothing I could tell just by talking to him on the phone that made him seem shady."

"Well thanks for going down there. You never know, he could be rattled but be good at hiding it."

"That's why I thought I'd pursue this to its obvious conclusion." Tommy stopped short as if to invite Jeremy to guess the implication, but with Alisa tracking into the living room after him, blatantly eavesdropping, he wasn't in the mood to play games.

"And that is?"

"He invited me to come have a look at some boats. I'm going down there for a test drive tomorrow."

Jeremy stopped his pacing.

"A test drive?"

"Yeah, well it would seem pretty strange if I went in there and said I wanted a boat and then didn't come back to see 'em, right? And who knows, maybe I'll even find a deal on that yacht I've been wanting!"

"Good luck on that. Plus it gives you an excuse to shadow him some more."

"Right. I'll ring you tomorrow after the appointment."

"Be careful," he added, but Tommy had already dropped off the call.

Wow, Knox actually set an appointment with him. Guess he's not too scared. Then again, if he was guilty, then what else could he do but to play along? If he flat out refused to acknowledge the visit…

Jeremy's wife broke into his thoughts. "Who is that and what do they have to be careful about?"

He turned around to face her. "And what are you doing with that phone?" she added before he could respond to her first two questions.

-62-

ANOTHER DAY AT THE OFFICE

Matt Knox stood at the helm of his little Whaler, easily passing a boat cleaner on his way to work in his barge. The barge guy gave him a puzzled stare as he watched him pass. Matt used to keep pace with the slow moving work boat. He no longer even consulted his GPS to see if he was within the NO WAKE harbor speed limits. He doubted he was and didn't much care. There were more exciting things to worry about now.

Such as who was it that stashed the museum goods in Davey Jones' Locker? Matt cut back on the throttle a bit as he made the turn into the canal where Dallas and Dave lived. No traffic at all in here. He reminded himself of a circling shark as he passed by Dallas' fancy wooden boat, then the Jones' dockbox (still locked, nothing looked any different), into one of the dead end canals where he made a U-turn and passed by the Jones' again and back out into the main channel.

On Patrol. He'd do the circuit again at lunch and yet again on the way home. If someone noticed him, so what? He probably sold them their boat. Matt the Saint Knox owned these waters. But for now it was time to get to the dealership.

He cranked up the throttle and threw a big wake the rest of the way over to the yacht brokerage. The boats berthed in their slips there were still bobbing up and down after being displaced by his entrance as he made his way inside. He mentally reviewed what he knew of his work day while he walked into his office. *Call that one guy back about the Hatteras...tell John to stop creating a new file every week for the summaries, just edit the same one...oh shit!-later this morning that cop's coming by for a test drive...or is it more than that?*

"Hey Matt! Boatin' to work, huh? That's the way!" John Samson greeted him.

Matt paused in the doorway to his office, one hand on the handle, ready to pull it closed. "Yeah. Decided it's time to get out there more, you know, really get hands on with the boat buying community."

John gave him a thumbs up sign and turned back to his workstation on the main floor. Matt shut the door to his office and retreated to his desk. He worked without distraction for a couple of hours until his desk phone lit up with a call from John. He picked up.

"That cop's here to see you, walking in right now."

"Great. Go ahead and prequalify him with a credit check now, would you?"

"You bet. Should I send him your way while he waits for the result?"

"You can send him in as soon as he fills out the forms, but if he doesn't pass the check, let me know right away. You remember the radio code for that, right?"

They'd worked out coded language to let each other know if a potential buyer failed to pass a credit check in case they were already out on a test drive because they'd been expected to pass or if the results were late coming back. It happened; they ended up using that code about three or four times per year.

"Roadrunner to Coyote, call ACME."

-63-

A PICTURE IS WORTH A THOUSAND WORDS

Matt sat at his desk across from Tommy. Damn cop. Was this guy onto him? Did he know he was in the museum? Did he suspect that he'd killed Sal, or Josey, or even that stupid bum? The cop glanced at his watch and muted his annoying, squawky radio.

"Didn't know I'd have to fill out a bunch of forms just to look at some boats," he began with a frown.

Matt flashed him his one-point-three million dollar luxury yacht smile. "I do apologize, Tommy, but it clears the waters, shall we say, for smooth sailing later on. Now we can focus on finding the perfect craft for you without the distraction of hoops yet to jump through."

"Yeah I get it, now that I have more time invested I'm that much more likely to not want it to go to waste, meaning I feel that much more compelled to buy, is that the idea?"

Matt appraised him critically for a few seconds while maintaining his amiable visage. If this guy was acting, he was damned good at it. If he wasn't, he was...deliberately trying to piss him off, testing his temper?

"Well now, nothing gets past you, does it, Tommy?"

The cop shifted in his seat. "I've seen it all. So's my buddy Jeremy, by the way—he's the guy you turned down for a job not too long ago."

Wow. Try as he might, Matt could not contain his surprise at that one. This guy pulled no punches. The cop spoke again before Matt could muster a reply, controlling the conversation.

"So about a sailboat. I was looking at the ones parked out back here," he said, glancing over Matt's head toward the slips fronting the brokerage, "and they all look really high end. I just want–"

Matt waved him down, glad to be back on familiar territory. "I get it, I get it. You just want something affordable that will be right for you and your family. Married man, I presume? I see you wear a ring."

Tommy nodded. "Fifteen years."

"Kids?"

He nodded. "Two. One just started high school, one in junior high."

Matt paused for just a second, processing this information continuing.

"Okay, so we're talking family outings, right? Something with enough space for the four of you and maybe a couple of good friends, but without breaking the bank."

"That sounds about right."

Fucking pig with his gun on his belt, a baton and all that other aggressive shit. In his mind...

Matt forced himself not to start a mind crime. He no longer needed those. But what if this pig was recording this with one of those voice-activated mini-jobs—maybe even sending it live back to the precinct! *Fuck.* He never should have agreed to let a cop in here.

He had to force himself not to look down at the drawer where his new blunderbuss resided, to check if it was closed. He knew it was, but he felt like one of those people he'd seen TV shows about who have some kind of obsessive compulsive disorder where they can't leave the house without checking a dozen times that they'd locked the door or turned all the lights off.

You should check the drawer, check the drawer. What if he comes behind the desk to look out the window at the boats.

"Let's talk boats."

Checkitcheckitcheckit.

"Great, so I think what might be right for you is a twenty-six foot Catalina that we should have in few days. It's not one of the ones out there right now but I can show you a picture of one just like it."

Matt reached across his desk to grasp one of the framed photos that adorned its edges. This one depicted a sailboat with a smiling couple aboard. The picture was signed in a flowery script: "Ahoy Matt—thanks so much for finding us the perfect boat! Cheryl & Tom."

Matt handed the frame to Tommy. "That's a twenty-six foot Catalina there. Have a look." He glanced down while Tommy took the photo.

Drawer's closed.

Tommy inspected the photograph while Matt looked on.

Open the drawer, whip out the pirate pistol and fuckin' blast this shithead. He tried to shake off the sentiment by concentrating on Tommy's words.

"Looks about right. I'd have to learn how to sail, but...be here in a few days, you said?" He looked up from the picture to address Matt, who'd been staring at him intently. The salesman snapped out of it and stood up rapidly.

"I think I've got a brochure on one from the company. This one'll be used, not new, of course, and maybe a different model year, but it has all the same specs."

"Yeah, I'd like to take a look at that," Tommy said.

Matt went to an old file cabinet against the wall. His back was turned to Tommy while he rummaged through the drawers, murmuring something about John's organizational skills while he looked for the literature.

Tommy glanced over at Matt and back at the picture of the couple, eyeing its glass frame. The cop's hand sliced out to the framed picture and reeled it back to his body in total silence. He dropped it into the pocket of his windbreaker with the merest whisper of nylon.

"Aha!" Matt exclaimed.

Tommy sat up straight in his seat.

"Here it is!" Matt added, extracting a glossy folder from the cabinet. Tommy relaxed a bit while Matt walked back to his desk and took his seat again. Matt slid the folder to him across the desk, where it landed not far from where the picture had been.

"Why don't you take this and I'll give you a call as soon as the boat's in so you can come in for a guided tour and a test drive. Sound good?" Matt flashed that smile again.

Tommy stood also. "Sounds good," he said, reaching across the desk to pump Matt's hand. "Sounds real good."

-64-

WHAT IS IT WITH PEOPLE THESE DAYS?

John Samson knocked on Matt's door as he pushed it open. Matt looked up from the computer where he'd been locating a Catalina 26. Cop or not, the guy had seemed serious about buying a boat.

"Came by for the play by play," Samson said, taking the same seat Tommy had just vacated. "He seemed pretty happy on the way out. How'd it go? Anything you need me to follow up on?"

"Actually, yeah, there is." Matt swung his computer monitor around so that John could see it.

"I told him I'd bring in a Catalina twenty-six footer for him to take a test trip on with his family, decide if it's right for him. I found one for sale by owner right now in Morro Bay. I'm going to call him today, and if he takes my offer, I'll need you to go over there and tow it back here."

John nodded.

Matt squinted at his monitor. "Says family circumstances force sale, so I should be able to score a deal."

"Work it. Been a little while since we sold a Cat 26, hasn't it?"

Matt shrugged. "Yeah, you know, they're on the low end of what we do, but the idea is in a few years they come back for an upgrade. But I did sell one last summer to the—"Matt's finger froze in mid-point along with his words in mid-sentence as he looked across the desk, right at the edge in front of where John sat.

"Something wrong?"

"Oh, just looking for that picture the MacAllisters gave me of them in their Catalina. I handed it to the cop to look at for reference." He looked around the desk, expecting to find it slightly out of place. John's gaze followed his own around the desk. "Maybe it fell off. You see it on the floor over by you?"

John looked down around his feet. Shook his head.

Matt stood up and walked over to the side of the desk and checked there. He circled the entire desk, and then when he'd gotten back to his chair he got down on his hands and knees and looked beneath the desk.

"What the *fuck*!" he said, loudly, as he stood back up. John jumped just a little in his chair, so unexpected was the outburst. "Take it easy! It'll turn up."

"Well it goddamn better turn the fuck up! You don't have it, do you?"

Samson looked at him for a moment before responding, as if backing away from an animal that only moments before had seemed approachable but had suddenly turned unpredictable.

"No, I don't have it, why would I have it? Never mind. Matt, you look a little pale, are you feeling alright? Low blood sugar maybe, something? You want a Snickers bar?" John started to reach into one of his pockets.

Matt yelled at him, "No, I don't want your fucking Snickers bar! I want to know what the goddamn hell happened to that picture! It was right here!" He pointed dramatically at the edge of the desk, to a blank spot between a snapshot of an elderly couple on the fly bridge of a large motor yacht to the right and some kind of children's day camp racing little sunfish sailboats in the harbor on the left.

John took a deep breath. "Maybe Tommy took it?"

Matt stared at his employee. "Why would he do that?" *To get my fingerprints!* "Who just takes something off of someone's desk without asking permission? What the hell is wrong with people these days?"

John waited to see that Matt was done posing rhetorical questions before asking, "You said you showed it to him while he was in here as an example?"

"I did," Matt said in a lower voice. He settled back into his seat.

John nodded enthusiastically, eager to placate his boss. "So he probably took it home with him to show his wife. He'll bring it back."

"Well he better fucking bring it back," Matt said, mostly under his breath.

John gave him a hard stare and then stood. "I'll go work on buying that boat." He turned around when he reached the door and pulled his pockets inside out. "Notice I'm not taking any of your pictures with me."

Matt glared at him until he left.

-65-

PICTURE PERFECT

Jeremy scooped up the Tommyphone, glad that Alisa was now at work. It had been a long hard morning convincing her that perhaps-just perhaps—his ex-partner might be able to help him get back on the force. A long shot he told her, but worth the price of a disposable phone.

Tommy talked to him rapid fire while he felt his blood race.

"You did *what?*"

"I got him to hand me a picture, and later, after he put his thumb right on the glass, I dropped it into my jacket pocket."

Jeremy released a sigh of disbelief at the treasure trove of potential evidence Tommy had scored for them. "That's ballsy, man! Nice move. But we can't use it as official evidence, right?"

"Nah, you know the deal on that. Illegally obtained. I don't want Fuckin' A Flannery to even know about it, but I got someone in the prints lab who owes me a favor, if you get my drift."

"So you'll have them run the prints for you and tell you the results without them being listed as part of the official casework."

"Yeah. But then we'll know, bro, we'll *know*."

Jeremy paused. Up to now, he'd felt like he'd done the brunt of the real work in this partnership, but this was a huge break, one that had come with some risk to Tommy.

"What if he noticed the picture is gone from his desk after you left?"

Jeremy heard the sound of police sirens in the background from Tommy's end.

"I doubt he will. His whole desk was cluttered with pictures of boats, but I suppose if he does call me out on it, I'll just say I really wanted to be able to show it to my wife to get her excited about buying the boat, because I couldn't remember what kind it was, wouldn't know what to look up, some horseshit like that."

"Well, that makes—wait a minute, what's that? You're going back there again? What for?"

"To take a look at this boat. Follow through with the charade, right? Plus the kids will have a fun time out on the water for a day. What's to lose?"

-66-

BUYER BEWARE

The Office. Not the most original name for a boat, Matt Knox thought as he watched John Samson maneuver the Catalina 26 alongside the brokerage dock. It had been an uneventful last couple of days and he was glad John had been able to score the sailboat and get it down here so soon. Matt pointed to a section of dock further away from the storefront.

"Bring her over there. It's not the best looking boat. Let's keep the prime dock space clear for something prettier."

Samson shrugged. "Nothing coming in today that I'm aware of, but suit yourself."

"You think it needs much prep work to get it ready to show today?"

"No, she's in good shape for what she is. Pretty turnkey, just like the guy said." Samson engaged the trolling motor to finagle the craft into a finger dock on the perimeter of their little section of marina. After a minute he had tied the boat up and walked over to Matt, who walked with him back into the dealership.

"Good work, John. Client's coming over later today. I'll take it from here."

"Sounds good. I'm headed over to the Grog N Grub for lunch later, you game?"

"Thanks, but I need to do a little paperwork on some other leads. This old Catalina's not gonna do that much for our bottom line."

"Push those superyachts!" John headed over to his desk on the main floor while Matt retreated to his office.

At lunchtime, after checking to see that John had left, he went outside to *The Office* and stepped aboard. About fifteen minutes later he was back at his desk.

A couple of hours after that his desk phone rang and John told him that Tommy was here to see the boat.

Matt emerged from his office and walked out to the main floor and there was Tommy, wife and two kids (a boy and a girl) in tow.

"Brought the whole clan, I see!" Matt greeted them.

"Yeah well, like I said, this would be a family investment, so I want the whole family to see it before we make a decision."

"Can we take the boat out?" The boy asked, jumping up and down.

Tommy looked at Matt.

"You bet!" Matt said. "Let's go have a look!" He led the family outside to the docks and walked with them out to the sailboat, where the wife chuckled as expected over the name, and Matt suffered through the obligatory "So when I say I'm at the office..." jokes.

Matt glanced at his watch. "Listen," he began, "I have a couple of things to attend to back at the office—my other office, that is!—but I'll come back in a few minutes after you've had some time to get acquainted. Go ahead aboard and have a good look around—feel free to check it out thoroughly—you can touch anything, turn anything on, whatever." He looked at Tommy's wife. "There's a galley—that's kitchen in boat speak—with a full service stove—feel free to turn it on, try it out, cook something on it if you want. Whatever. Make yourselves at home."

And with that the policeman and his family boarded *The Office* while Matt walked back to the dealership.

-67-

WHERE THERE'S SMOKE

John Samson stood in the doorway to Matt Knox's office eating a submarine sandwich. Matt asked him, "I thought you went to the Grog N Grub for lunch? Isn't that a Cali Tom's hoagie?" He frowned while John answered between bites that spilled lettuce onto the floor.

"No...just between you and me...food sucks there. I ate a crappy little frozen cheeseburger and drank a couple of lukewarm draft beers just so I could sit at the bar and have an excuse to talk to Sandi...but afterwards I stopped at Tom's to pick up some real food."

"Man, you've been working on that piece for I don't know—"

They heard a dull *thud* from somewhere outside. "You hear that?" Matt asked.

"Yeah." John stepped into Matt's office and they both looked out the window. A column of dark smoke rose from the far side of the dock.

"Fire over there!" Matt said.

"Let's check it out," John said, already out the door, leaving his unfinished hoagie on Matt's desk.

"Probably a truck backfiring on the bridge," Matt conjectured as the two of them stepped out the back entrance onto the dock area.

John immediately broke into a run. *"The Office!"*

Matt followed the smoke plume down to its source—the Catalina 26 and a thick fire raging inside its cabin. He took his cellular out as he ran behind John toward the blaze. "Fire! Fire!" he shouted as he ran.

He dialed 911 and held the phone to his ear as they sprinted over the uneven wooden surface.

John stood there helpless for a second, not believing what he was looking at. The entire boat was engulfed in a thick orange fireball laced with black tendrils. He ran to a fire extinguisher on a piling and smashed the glass with his elbow. It felt like a squirt gun as he emptied its contents onto the flaming boat.

"Fire on the way?" he screamed at Matt, who was now yelling into his phone: "Boat fire, boat fire! Sandy Cove Yachts. Possibly people on board! Hurry, please!" He dropped his phone and ran to the edge of the pier in front of The Office, where the heat was almost unbearable.

John depleted the extinguisher and let it drop to the pier as he looked on helplessly, eyes tearing. "You see anyone? You see anybody?" he screamed, starting to walk further down the pier alongside the yacht, hoping to see human forms in the water or climbing up onto the dock.

Because the only way one could have survived the conflagration inside that fiberglass tube was if they weren't still in it.

"Jesus, Matt—*do* something!" He turned to his boss, who was hailing a passing boater, asking him for his fire extinguisher.

John turned back to the sailboat, which now canted to one side, a trail of debris—paper plates, Little Debbie snack cakes still wrapped in plastic, a magazine—floating away from the wreckage. People had begun to gather on the balcony of a restaurant overlooking the waterfront—pointing, shouting, making phone calls, a few of them running down the stairs toward the spectacle.

"Here comes the fireboat!" someone shouted from a second crowd that had begun to gather on the pier a little ways down from Matt and John, at a safer distance from the inferno.

Matt dove into the water fully clothed, shoes and all, submerging for a few seconds before surfacing into a crawl stroke toward the flaming boat.

"You see anybody? See anybody!" he called out periodically as he swam around the boat perhaps a few feet closer than what would be considered a safe distance.

And then the harbor fire team arrived and began firehosing the stricken craft while a small raft deployed, one of the men hauling Matt up into it.

When the flames had been doused, the entire craft lay submerged just below the waterline, only the mast protruding at a low angle, extending over the dock as if in a final attempt to remain above the surface.

-68-

SAFETY FIRST

Fifteen minutes later the Harbor Fire crew had *The Office* up on the dock by crane, flames doused, still smoldering, water streaming from the fractured hull. A fireman stepped from the cabin and vomited on what was left of the boat's rear deck.

Matt and John were close enough to hear some of his emotional reply to his colleagues. "...know how many...body parts...*bad*." Police arrived on scene and a couple of them boarded the charred boat alongside two more fire specialists.

A firefighter who'd been talking to the one who had just came out of the cabin went over to Matt and John.

"You with the yacht dealer?"

Matt nodded. "I'm the sales manager, Matt Knox, and this my employee, John Samson."

The fireman nodded grimly. "Do you know how many people were aboard?"

"F—" Matt started but then choked off into a quiet sob. "Four!" he said when he recovered.

The firefighter looked at John for confirmation. Samson looked him in the eye and nodded agreement.

"Was it one of your boats?"

A Sandy Cove PD officer walked up to them, notebook out, pen in hand.

Matt nodded. "Just bought the title to it today—John here brought it down from Morro Bay this morning and gave it a sea trial. Was working fine, right, John?"

"Yes. No issues at all. I don't see how the little three gallon gas can it had for the outboard motor could have done this. There's no big diesel tank or anything like you'd find on a powerboat. It's a small sailboat. What the hell happened?"

They heard a yell from the boat and looked over to see a firefighter holding up a metal fragment with an assured air suggesting it meant something to him.

"Propane tank." One of the firemen talking to Matt and John gave them a knowing glance.

"Pro-" Matt cut himself off as if lost in thought, then looked to John.

"I don't see how," John said, looking confused. "The first thing I did before I left Morro was to open the cabin hatch and doors, open the bilge, air everything out. I sell boats for a living. Been doing it for close to three years. That's basic safety stuff."

Propane tanks for cooking were known to be a common cause of boat explosions. If a leak developed anywhere in the system, the gas was heavier than air and would sink to the lowest part of the vessel. Any spark or flame, even static electricity, could then touch it off.

Matt looked down at his feet, then back up to the cops and firemen. "Look, John, I know I was pushing you to get that boat down here ASAP so we could make that sale today. Is it possible you forgot to ventilate it? When people are considering a purchase, you know how they turn everything on, try it out. If they turned on the stove..."

John appeared to mouth the word, *What?!* in disbelief, without vocalizing anything.

Matt continued, the officials looking on earnestly now, a couple of them scribbling rapid notes. "I mean, you said yourself you had a few beers at lunch..."

John's face turned crimson. "Are you...are you trying to blame this on *me*?"

Matt looked at the officials and shrugged. "Hey, I'm just—" He turned back to John in time to see his right fist connect with his left eye, a solid blow that knocked him off balance. But one of the fire-fighters steadied him and the cops easily pulled the two men apart.

"Easy, easy. Hold up. Nobody's accusing anybody of anything," one of the policemen said. "We're just trying to figure out what happened. We've got four people dead here. We'll get to the bottom of this. Just calm down."

John glared at Matt like an injured wild animal. "I don't know what's wrong with you, Matt. But you're fucked up. You're so fucked up! You need to see a shrink or something."

One of the cops eyed the other and nodded, pulling something from a pocket. "You mind blowing into this, Mr. Samson? Breathalyzer."

John's eyes widened. "I already told you I had a couple of drinks, but it was after I brought the boat down."

"But maybe you would have remembered to ventilate it if you hadn't gotten drunk at lunch," Matt said, his voice calm.

The cop standing between them stood ready to keep them apart. The crowd of onlookers had grown. A television news crew could be seen trotting down the dock ramp.

"That's ridiculous!"

"How about you, Mr. Knox," one of the other cops said. "Take a breathalyzer? Help us clear this up?"

Matt stared at the device in the cop's hand. He appeared surprised at first but a smile formed slowly on his lips. "Why, certainly."

The cop brought the machine to his mouth and he exhaled. After a few seconds the cop addressed his gathered colleagues.

"Negative."

"Mr. Samson?" A new breathalyzer was offered to John.

"Forget it. I'm not saying anything else. Get me a lawyer."

-69-

BAD NEWS

Jeremy buttered another piece of toast and made a show of scanning the job ads in that morning's Cove Gazette, but his mind was elsewhere. He knew Tommy was down at the yacht place today, but that was only follow-up work compared to that print he lifted. He wondered if Knox had confronted him about the missing photograph.

But it was difficult to concentrate with Alisa standing next to him, saying, "What about that one?" every few minutes as she jabbed her fingernail into the fine print of the classifieds.

He had to give her credit, though. After she found him on the trac phone working with Tommy she had been more understanding than he would have guessed. *The whole town would love to catch whoever robbed the museum, myself included*, she'd said. *And the reward would be the best thing ever.*

True, he'd left out all mention of the storage encounter with Pablo or anything that would highlight potential danger, but still. Then she'd given him a serious look. *Just promise me one thing, Jeremy Washington. Look me in the eye.* He'd met her gaze. *Don't do anything stupid. Please. We can't afford it.*

And really that had had more impact than anything else she could have said—any lecture on how he should be looking for work or not associating at all with an organization that cast him out. She was basically *trusting* him to do the right thing for their family.

And was he?

"...Jeremy! Take a look at this." He snapped out of it as Alisa spun their little kitchen TV around on its lazy Susan so that he was looking at...*an action movie?* Smoke in the sky, fire trucks, cops walking around, talking to people...Why does she want him to watch TV? And then he saw the news logo blink on, the blonde reporter from the local news station appearing on camera.

"I don't mean look at *her*, either," Alisa kidded.

Jeremy snatched up the remote and turned up the volume. "I only care about what she's *saying*, dear!"

On screen, Carol Tepper was pointing dramatically into the water, her blond bangs fluttering around her face in the breeze.

"...explosion of some kind at this dock right here, just behind the Sandy Cove Yacht dealership." Then she turned, the camera following her gaze to show the charred hull of *The Office* dangling from the crane that had extracted it from the harbor.

"A dismal day for Sandy Cove as we learn that a local family of four has perished in an explosion and resulting fire aboard this sailboat, a twenty-six foot Catalina named *The Office*."

Jeremy leaned closer to the television at the mention of the type of boat it was. *Catalina sailboat...why did that sound familiar?*

"Fire officials say an onboard propane system appears to be the cause of the blast."

Carol cupped her hand over her mouth and spoke to someone just off camera. "Can we? Okay."

"That's terrible," Alisa said. "Seems like a lot of bad things have been happening at the harbor lately, doesn't it?"

Jeremy was about to respond but Carol's next delivery stunned him into silence.

"I've received word that next of kin have been notified—in this case the victims' grandparents, and so we are cleared by authorities to release the name of the victims." Carol looked down briefly at an index card in her hand before continuing. "I'm told that Sandy Cove police officer Tommy Dione and his wife and two children have perished in the boat blaze that happened here only about an hour ago."

Alisa shrieked at the mention of Jeremy's partner's name. "Oh my God," she said softly, clutching his arm. The two families had been friends for years, with countless barbeques, play dates and beach days behind them. That all four of them could now be gone was unthinkable. Yet, as Carol Tepper forged onward on camera, now approaching the throng of onlookers on the pier, it was clear that it had happened. She thrust her microphone under the chin of a sunburned man of about fifty, wife of a similar age by his side. He wagged his floppy hat clad head back and forth several times before speaking.

"Surreal. We were up there at the oyster bar—What the Shuck—" Carol's cameraman followed his point to pan in on the establishment, where a crowd of people still leaned over the balcony, watching the scene unfold on the dock. "—when we heard this *boom!"*

"It was so loud," the witness' wife chimed in. He nodded.

"At first we thought it was one of those festive cannons going off, like the kind some of the yachts have that look like old pirate cannons, but a second later everyone was pointing out over the water so I turned around in time to see the top of the cabin blow off and a fireball—I mean literally a huge ball of fire, not just a little tongue of flame like when someone puts too much lighter fluid on a barbeque— shooting straight up."

"My next thought was they were shooting a Hollywood movie," the wife added, Carol quickly placing the microphone near her.

The on-scene interviews continued, but Jeremy phased out the TV and leaned on his wife for support, overcome with nausea. Tommy! He never should have let him go back to the yacht place. *Accident? Yeah right!*

He had to do something. What were the chances that Matt Knox had nothing to do with this?

Tommy stole that picture!

The frame was already at the lab for fingerprinting. He didn't know how he'd get the results, though, without Tommy. But he needed to find a way.

"You were just talking to him yesterday! And the *kids*!" Alisa said, tears flowing.

"He told me he was going down to the yacht place again. He..." Jeremy hesitated. Tommy was *dead*.

"He what?" Alisa gripped his arm.

"He went there before, and he stole a picture off Matt Knox's desk."

Alisa bit her lower lip like she did when she was confused. "Why would he do that? And why was he even there—he buying a boat?"

"We suspected Matt Knox is somehow involved with the museum robbery, and so Tommy went in pretending to be interested in buying a boat."

"Wait a minute. Matt Knox? The guy from the yacht place who had those ads on TV? He donates to that children's charity every year? Don't they call him Matt 'the saint' Knox?"

"That's the one."

"You think *he* helped to rob the museum?" She looked back at the TV, which now showed a parking lot full of ambulances, fire trucks and police cars.

"All I know for sure is that there's fingerprint evidence from someone with no criminal record whatsoever found both inside the museum and..." Jeremy realized too late that he'd just run right to the edge of You're Giving Her Way Too Much Information and launched himself off.

"And where else?"

"On the boat of one of Sal's gang members who also helped to rob the museum."

She paused to process this while an appropriately grim faced Carol Tepper said, "Back to you in the studio."

"So why'd he take the photo—what was it of?"

"It was just a picture of the same kind of boat he pretended he was interested in buying. But it was framed and he knew Matt's prints would be on the glass, so he took it. It's possible that Matt noticed it was gone afterward."

Jeremy braced himself for the onslaught of his wife's are-you-trying-to-get-yourself-killed tirade, but instead she shook her head and let go of his arm.

"I don't know, Jer. Matt the Saint? Really? That's your big suspect?"

Jeremy looked at her, expecting some kind of follow-up, but there was none. "Well, yeah, you heard about the prints, right. And now this," he pointed at the TV, where they had moved on to the weather.

"What does the Department think?"

The Department. In other words, the *real* cops. "Tommy s—" He choked up a little at the mention of his dead ex-partner's name, but struggled on. "Tommy said Fuckin' A Flannery wasn't taking the robbery very seriously, didn't think a bunch of insured nautical curios were too important, until people started dying, that is—first Sal, then Josey."

"So they don't think it's the Saint."

"I don't think so, no. But I don't think they've done much in the way of genuine investigating, either."

She frowned and shoved a pile of envelopes toward him on the counter. "I'm going to go lay down, honey, maybe call Linda. This is terrible news. Here's the mail."

Jeremy dragged the pile of letters listlessly toward him. *She doesn't think it's Knox.* As he sorted through the mail—more bills he couldn't pay, some junk loan offers, a letter from Alisa's mother (maybe she sent money)... he worried that no one else would either. Especially now with Tommy dead, he had no one helping him on the inside. He had sorted the mail into two piles—toss and keep, when he saw that one piece remained.

Manila 5x7 envelope, post office stamp dated yesterday. He scanned the return address and saw, *Forensic Laboratories, L.L.C.*

Goosebumps raised along his limbs. This was one of the independent crime labs the department contracted with. He flipped the envelope over, as if examining a strange artifact. *Tommy had the lab send the fingerprint test results to me?* Jeremy looked around, as if his wife might still be standing over his shoulder waiting to see what was in the envelope. He was alone, could hear the fan running that she turned on when sleeping for the white noise.

Picking up the envelope carefully, almost as if made of glass, he examined the seal. The metal clasp had been fortified with scotch tape. Jeremy reached into a drawer and pulled out a small paring knife.

He sliced open the envelope and removed its contents.

-70-

FROM BEYOND

It would be a long time before an ex-cop like Jeremy Washington didn't recognize instantly a forensic lab results card when he saw one. This one focused on fingerprints, he saw right away when he slid the card from the envelope.

Tommy's chickenscratch handwriting filled one page. He'd read enough of Tommy's reports over the years to know beyond a sliver of doubt that he had written this. And that also told him he'd went to some trouble to make sure he got this. He'd gone to the lab, called in some favor he was owed by having the results sent to Jeremy, with a personal note dropped into the envelope. The lab could get in trouble for that, no doubt. Tommy was going out on a limb for him yet again. He was really starting to put some energy into solving the museum case and earning that reward, Jeremy thought. Maybe he wanted to earn that reward money and use it to actually buy a boat? Overcome with grief, he dropped his head into his hands.

At length he picked up the note and began to read:

Wanted you to get these in case I couldn't meet up next few days-FnA Flannery's got me on some out of the way beat—I think he knows I've been snooping around a bit on the museum case—he doesn't know about you, though. Plus I got the yacht store visits to take care of. So here you go. I haven't seen the results yet—I'm dropping this note off as I leave my contact your address– didn't want to have it sent to 2 different places—just tell me what the results are. Comparator is museum print. Submitted is the print lifted from Knox's pic. Is this our guy? Talk soon—T

Talk soon...nope, try talk never. Never again. He slammed his fist on the counter, causing a few loose coins to jangle as they wobbled briefly before settling once again.

That bastard, Knox. You better hope it's not you, motherfucker.

He picked up the card that displayed the results of the fingerprint analysis:

ARTICLE A: comparator print set
ARTICLE B: submitted print set
RESULTS: MATCH/NO MATCH / PARTIAL MATCH

Jeremy sucked his breath in sharply. The word MATCH was circled. The prints from Matt Knox's own photograph frame match the unknown set found in the museum, which in turn match those found on Josey's workboat.

It seems Matt the Saint Knox isn't so holy after all, Jeremy thought.

Thank you, Tommy. Thank God you had these sent to me.

Jeremy had what he needed. Proof that Knox was not at all what he seemed. As to why an upstanding citizen would stray this far off the straight and narrow, Jeremy had no idea. But he didn't need an idea. Didn't care. As a cop he'd seen all kinds of people in various shades of weak moments. They almost always had an excuse. It was the rare person facing charges who simply owned up to what he or she did. And he sure as hell didn't expect that to happen with Knox now. This guy was dangerous, on a binge of killing. And now with Tommy gone, it was Jeremy and Jeremy alone who had the responsibility to bring this predator to justice.

He swiped the lab results card from the counter and headed out the door for his Bronco. It was time to pay a visit to the Sandy Cove PD.

Jeremy thanked the receptionist and made his way through the all too familiar cubical labyrinth, dispensing curt hello's, quick nods, and a general no-time-to-chat-now aura as he passed among his surprised former coworkers until he reached a row of private offices in the back. He got some grim satisfaction on watching a couple of the guys' eyes quickly cast glances to his hands, is if he might be some disgruntled monster who came to slay his former co-workers.

Jeremy quickly moved past the door he knew belonged to the Chief of Police and stepped up to another with a nameplate reading Detective Joseph A. Flannery. He took a quick look behind him to see if anyone was coming to escort him off the premises (not yet) and then banged on Fuckin' A Flannery's door.

-71-

A DAY LATE AND $50,000 SHORT

Jeremy heard a phone slam back into its cradle and then a higher register voice said, "Get your ass in here."

He opened the door and walked in, shutting the door behind him without taking his eyes off of Flannery. The detective was shaking his head and muttering to himself while jotting something on a piece of paper. He dropped his pen.

"Can you believe those fuckin' guys over at Central, they—" Flannery froze mid-sentence when he looked up to see Jeremy standing there. He rose quickly.

"Jeremy, what—" Flannery looked him up and down carefully, as if probing for the outline of a weapon hidden under his clothing. Not seeing one, he looked Jeremy in the eyes, squinting as if trying to see into something bright.

"Relax, Joe. I've got something that'll help you out. Got five?"

The detective loosened his posture but remained standing. Jeremy held out the lab card with the fingerprint results. "Take a look at this, will you?" He frisbeed it onto Flannery's desk.

"What the fuck is it? I'm busier than a set of jumper cables at a Mexican wedding." His eyes bored into Jeremy's, looking for a twinkle that would suggest his humor had registered. He didn't see one, so he changed the subject. "You find a new job yet? That's not what you're here about, is it? 'Cause I can't help you."

"That's not why I'm here."

"Then what is it? I'm sorry about Tommy—I guess you heard?" He picked up the card, staring at it while peering over the edge at Jeremy.

"Me too. I have new information about the maritime museum robbery, information that links an individual from the robbery to the murders of Josey Jiminez and Sal Jonason."

Flannery remained standing. His expression changed to one of pity.

"Washington, listen to me. You're not a cop anymore. I know it's a tough thing, but you've got to move on. Other guys have done it, guys on the force even longer than you. You can do it. Got no choice. Forget about casework. Get some work, period."

"Let me assure you that I have no illusions about being a cop. I'm just after the reward money—fifty grand. I've got proof of who's behind the string of crimes we've had lately."

Flannery gesticulated wildly. "You're too late! We cracked it like a walnut, Washington! We recovered the goods. A lot of it is a bunch of sorry looking shit if you ask me, but we found it. Busted a guy too, You'll hear about it on tomorrow's news."

Jeremy paused, his eyes shifting left for a moment while his brain processed this new information. "So you solved the museum robbery?"

"That's what I'm trying to get across to your thick skull!"

"What about the murders?"

Flannery licked his lips rapidly, like a lizard. "One thing at a time, Washington. We've made good progress on the museum case. Now we can focus on the murders."

"So you don't think they're related?"

"No reason to think that."

"I've got reason to think it. If you don't want to hear it, though, I guess I could take it to someone else."

"Like who?" He leaned forward, supporting himself with a finger on his desk.

"I don't know. The mayor?"

"The may—alright, just fucking tell me, Washington. Damn, you piss me off. You always did, you know that? But fuck that. What do you got?"

"Here's what I got: Matt Knox helped to rob that museum and he killed Josey and Sal."

Flannery snorted once and threw his head back a little.

Jeremy added, "I don't know why, and I don't know how he got involved in the first place, but I know he did it."

This seemed to set Flannery off on peals of additional snorting and more pronounced head movements.

"Is Knox the guy you arrested in connection with the museum?"

When Flannery stabilized he said, "I'm not at liberty to discuss details with a civilian, but in this case, because it's so ridiculous, I'll make an exception. No! We arrested one of Sal's known gang members. You'll see his ugly-ass mug all over the news tomorrow."

"Well congratulations on the museum case. But simply speaking as a concerned *citizen*, may I humbly suggest that you have a murderer running loose around Sandy Cove in the height of the summer tourist season."

"You mean Matt the fucking *saint* Knox? The boat dealer guy on TV? He's your big murder suspect?"

Jeremy nodded.

"The same guy who walks a half block extra to reach a crosswalk even when there's no cars coming?"

Another nod.

Flannery raised his eyebrows and stared at him like he was looking at a critical piece of equipment that was about to fail. A true look of concern.

"Look, Jeremy. If you need help we have people—counselors—who will talk to you—"

"I'm not crazy, Flannery. Look at the damn card."

Flannery gave a sigh of irritation and snatched up the lab results. He glared once at Jeremy over the heavy weight paper before allowing his eyes to take in the information before him.

"Do you see the name, Matthew Knox?" Jeremy queried.

Flannery shook the card between his thumb and forefinger. "How the fuck did you get this forensics report, Washington?"

Jeremy stared him down for a beat. "I'd rather not say."

Flannery rolled his eyes. "Shit on a stick." He paced around in a tight little circle behind his desk before leaning on his desk again to face Jeremy. "Washington, let me paint a picture for your apparently dumb ass. You just got let go for blatantly disregarding established procedures, did you not?"

"A temporary lapse in judgment."

"It's not looking so temporary, though, is it? Waltz into my office even though you no longer work here, giving me lab results that you can't say where you got 'em? What'd you do, fucking bribe somebody for 'em?"

Jeremy looked down at the floor for a second and then addressed Flannery. "No. I got 'em From Tommy."

Flannery scratched his head but said nothing. Jeremy went on.

"Tommy was helping me to find out who robbed the museum."

"And now Tommy's *dead*? You're just a big Bag O' Trouble, aren't you, Washington?"

"Matt the Saint Knox is the shitbag to which you refer, sir. He killed Tommy and his whole family by deliberately causing that boat explosion. He was scared Tommy knew about his involvement in the robbery and then the murders of Sal and Josey. The same prints on Josey's workboat that match Knox's were also found in Sal's apartment."

Flannery rolled his neck around on his shoulders as if relieving stress. When his head came level again he stopped the exercise and locked eyes with Jeremy.

"So let me get this straight. It's your contention that Mr. Matt Knox— a longtime local businessman and all-around do-gooder—has recently murdered..." He ticked off on his fingers. "...five people, all without anyone seeing him do it? Really?"

After Jeremy said nothing, Flannery continued. "Are you sure? No way you could be even a little bit off on this?"

Jeremy directed his gaze to the card. "Prints don't lie."

"But we can't even use those prints, even if we wanted to, since this—*evidence*, if I may be so bold—was illegally obtained. It cannot be presented in court."

Jeremy nodded. "I'm well aware of that, sir, but now we *know* it was him. We just have to prove it."

Flannery exhaled heavily, a flurry of ash swirling out of a plastic tray on his desk. "We don't know jack shit. What's his motive? Maybe he visited the museum as a guest with his family a few days before it was robbed and that's how his prints got there."

"What about Joe's workboat—how'd they get there?"

"He's a yacht dealer, for Christ's sake. Josey could have been doing some work for his store, and he would have had occasion to be on his boat."

Then Flannery seemed to have an itch that caused him to jump a little until he ran his fingers across his arm. "You know what? Forget it. This is preposterous. The museum case is cracked, there's no more reward to fantasize about earning. Suck it up and go get a damn job. Here, take this..."

He held out the card. Jeremy took it. "...and I don't give a fuck if the door hits your ass on the way out. Let us handle the investigating. Stay out of our way, Washington. That's a serious fucking warning."

-72-

ACT OF REDEMPTION

Matt Knox was taking the long way home in his Boston Whaler. He was so hopped up on adrenaline that he couldn't even imagine sitting down to dinner with Summer and the kids right now. He took his boat back over to Davey Jones' Locker, passing it by into the dead end waterways at the terminus of that channel, then turning around and passing it again, accelerating once he saw that no one was there, speeding down the residential waterway.

Reaching the main channel, he made a U-turn and returned toward Dave Jones' house. Passed Dallas' yacht (no signs of life on it, nor in his home), then reached Dave's again. No one there, either. Matt got to the end and turned around yet again, back toward the main channel. Instead of turning right, he made another U-turn and headed back into the waterfront enclave, rocking the docked vessels with his wake.

Back and forth, up and down he motored. If someone noticed, fuck them. One time he pulled his boat up to the dock with Davey Jone's Locker, but he didn't tie up. Just glided up, had a look at the dock box, and shoved off.

Up. Down. Back. Forth. For an hour. A kid kayaking waved at him once but he didn't even notice him, so completely lost in thought was he as he paced the channel. He circled the neighborhood like a mechanical shark, watching for anyone who might approach his bait–the dock box.

No one came. He exited the terminus one more time and pointed the boat's prow at the main harbor channel down the waterway. Time to head home for dinner. But as he motored by Dave Jones' dockbox, his eyes were drawn to it and he slowed the boat. He tied the boat to the dock and hopped onto the pier.

He removed the skeleton key from his pocket and walked up to the dockbox. He didn't bother looking around, just unlocked it and then began grabbing armfuls of loot and heaving it into his whaler until it was all piled about on his deck in great heaps like his was one of the theatrical boats in the Pirates of the Caribbean theme park ride. When he was done he stood back and admired his little runabout, laden with swords, guns, otter pelts, pearls, rare seashells, and more. A boat-load of valuable goods.

Matt glanced both ways, up and down the house-lined canal. If any-body asked him about it he'd say it was fake, for his kids' school play or some shit. No one would take this stuff away from him. Hell, he'd already taken some of it—the two pistols—and nobody did anything about it.

He was the one who had earned this stuff, right? Sal had wanted him to help them get it, and now here it was. Sal's dead but Matt was still here. *He* was the real pirate now. He had the boat. He had the loot. Hell, Sal would probably *want* him to have this stuff! He was just completing their mission, the one that Sal himself had personally enlisted him for. He wished he could find that other motherfucker in Sal's gang, but it was just a matter of time. They would all pay. They wanted him to rob the museum, well they got their wish. And he would get his.

Not only that, Matt thought, strolling across the private dock to his treasure-filled watercraft, but wasn't there a chance that doing this might even reveal whose stuff it is? Because someone would report it missing, right? Someone would notice and say, Hey my stuff got stolen out of my dockbox! Even though it was stolen in the first place, people were arrogant like that.

If no one did come forward after he took the stuff, what then? He'd have the loot. Some of it was pretty cool, Matt thought, stooping to untie the Whaler's dock lines. He'd have some awesome paperweights and living room conversation pieces, some spectacular decorations for his office at the dealership. He'd have–

Matt stepped into the boat as a thought differentiated itself from the others with such force as to be tangible. The idea was so galvanizing it seemed to *knock* his brain into a higher plane of operation, sort of like hitting the outside of a piece of electronic equipment to get it working again.

He'd have the chance to turn the loot in for the reward money. Fifty grand. And it would save him the trouble of finding somewhere to put it all (Hey Summer, move your shoes outta the closet, I need to put this 18th century anchor in there!). He could say he found it (could just make up somewhere he found it, didn't have to tell the truth) and turn it in to the stupid cops to collect the reward.

And after today, he could use something to raise his reputation in Sandy Cove. Nobody could pin that boat explosion on him, but it still occurred on the yacht shop's property, with one of their boats, to one of their customers. He was the manager of the yacht dealership. Not very saintly of him, he had to admit. He was clearly responsible at least on a managerial level. So turning in the stolen museum goods should go some distance toward redeeming himself in the eyes of the town, and make him a nice cash bonus in the process.

He eased out into the canal, the vacant dockbox receding behind him. He looked closely at the houses—the windows—but saw nobody observing him, no curtains fluttering back into place. He shrugged off this veil of caution with a twist of the throttle as he increased his speed.

If someone did hassle him about the museum stuff, well...he'd fuck their shit up. He was Matt the motherfuckin' Saint, this was his territory. The whole fucking town was his. If there were bums on the beach, he'd clean that crap up. If there was stolen loot in somebody's dock box, he'd clean that up, too. He was in charge here. He could do what he wanted. He could give a shit less what anybody thought. He'd earned it. Nobody could stop him. Why would anyone even want to stop him?

Matt turned right into the main channel toward home, his foot atop a pile of authentic gold doubloons.

-73-

ALL THAT GLITTERS

Breakfast in the Robinson household had become a depressing ritual for Jeremy. His daughter had even started asking if he found a job yet. This morning though, the tone was especially bleak with Alisa's little kitchen TV tuned into the local news, where they replayed the footage from yesterday of the burnt sailboat being hoisted from the marina. While Alisa tried to keep their daughter from watching the morbid piece, Jeremy had to pretend to find something of interest in the job classifieds.

He wasn't fooling anyone, though, and his mind soon drifted off between the rows of tiny font that advertised for day laborers, part-time admin assistants and long distance truck drivers to his meeting yesterday with Flannery.

Fuckin' A Flannery. He pondered his next move now that he knew Sandy Cove PD's senior detective wasn't receptive to even considering his leads. And what about the break in the case he'd alluded to? But thoughts of Tommy kept him from concentrating. He pictured his face across the years, grinning over at him from his seat behind the wheel of the squad car, telling one of his offensively hilarious jokes, or throwing a football with his kid on the beach. He thought of the letter he sent—most likely his last to anyone.

He had to nail that bastard for this. Tommy and his whole family had been extinguished by that scum. He could not allow this to go unanswered. If Flannery wouldn't do anything, then—

"Honey...Honey! Look, look!" His wife rapped on the counter to divert his attention and pointed at the television when he looked up. She reached for the volume knob.

A "breaking news" banner blinked across the screen while Jeremy caught the newscaster say, "...news for fans of the Sandy Cove Maritime Museum. As reported by this station, the local landmark was recently the victim of a robbery that gutted the longtime local establishment of its most treasured nautical antiques."

The screen filled with a live shot of the police station, where a trio of Sandy Cove police officers stood on the concrete steps outside their headquarters in front of a long folding table covered with a drop-cloth. But while Jeremy was preoccupied with identifying his former coworkers (Fuckin' A Flannery not among them), the camera zoomed in on the blonde reporter.

"Carol Tepper here, reporting some interesting developments in light of the recent crime wave and what seems like a general run of bad luck here in Sandy Cove. Behind me are three of Sandy Cove's finest, and by their side is Mayor Gina Adams."

Carol turned slightly from the camera to face the cops and the mayor. A sign hanging below the table read, SANDY COVE POLICE DEPARTMENT EVIDENCE.

"Mayor Adams, I understand that you have a major announcement to make regarding the robbery of the Sandy Cove Maritime Museum?"

Gina Adams nodded confidently and leaned in on a small thicket of microphones. "That's right, Carol. There has been a break made in the museum robbery case, though I'm afraid that the news is not all good."

Carol leaned in closer with her microphone, motioning behind her back to her cameraman for a close-up of the mayor, who continued.

"Take a look at the objects on this table."

Next to her, one of the cops nodded, his mirrored aviator style sunglasses gleaming in the morning sun. He leaned over the table and removed the drop-cloth to reveal stacks of seafaring items and piles of treasures. The crowd surrounding the staging area was surprisingly quiet.

"We can confirm at this time that these articles were located in a storage unit just outside of Sandy Cove. On first glance, they appear to be the items stolen from the Sandy Cove Maritime Museum. However, on closer inspection our consultants advise us that all of these items are decent quality fakes. Take a look." The mayor beckoned Carol and her cameraman to follow her over to the table. She leaned over and selected a string of black pearls, holding them out for the camera.

"Beautiful pearls, right? 157 of them altogether. And wouldn't you know it, that's the *exact* number of black pearls on a necklace stolen from the museum. Let me draw your attention to this luxurious fur—a sea otter pelt from long-ago days when that trade was still legal off our coast." The mayor stroked the fur lovingly for a moment before addressing the camera with a serious expression.

"It's fake." She let that sink in during a beat of silence. "The pearls, too, fake. All this stuff," she said waving a hand in a sweeping gesture across the table—"Bogus. Counterfeit. Phony."

Carol Tepper put on her best quizzical expression—a practiced visage of equal parts concern and mild amusement. "You mean to say, Ms. Mayor, that none of these things are genuine? The items stolen from the museum are fakes?"

The mayor shook her head. "All we know at this time is that these articles were located after our detectives pursued investigative leads in the case, but that laboratory analysis and subsequent corroboration from independent experts confirms that they are not in fact genuine. Insurance records tell us that the museum's articles are authentic. What all this means, dear citizens, is that the real museum pieces are still out there somewhere, perhaps being sold on eBay and Craigslist, or maybe even at black market art auctions, online or off."

"And I understand that's not all. An arrest has been made in connection with the case?"

"That's affirmative, Carol. Based on evidence collected at the crime scene, we were able to positively identify a suspect from a local crime gang in connection with the burglary, and that suspect is in custody now in the Sandy Cove Men's Jail."

"Can you tell us the suspect's name?" This from Carol Tepper, who thrust her own microphone in the mayor's direction, who in turn nodded to one of her policemen who stepped forward.

"The suspect is one Pablo Martinez, a known gang member with a well recorded criminal history in Sandy Cove."

Jeremy recoiled as a recent mugshot of Pablo was splashed across the screen. In the shot he sported a freshly split lip and a black eye.

"I would like to add," Mayor Adams said, "that we will catch those responsible for the recent killings in our community. Make no mistake. I know our tourist season is important for our hardworking business owners. We are working day and night to identify and apprehend these killers. If you have any leads or information at all—no matter how insignificant it may seem—*please* call our hotline: 800-SC-CRIME. Together as a community we will stand strong!"

Mayor Adams shook each of the police officers' hands in turn and walked off camera where she was soon flanked by two bodyguards who escorted her out of view. The hotline number flashed on screen.

Jeremy was reeling, lightheaded. He barely felt his wife's hand grip his wrist. The voice of Carol Tepper came to him thin and disembodied, as if carried on a wispy fog dissipating as it rolled in from the sea.

"So, dear viewers, that begs the question: where lies the real treasure of Sandy Cove?"

OUT OF THE FRYING PAN...

Matt Knox flipped the sign on the door to Sandy Cove yachts around to OPEN, though he doubted it would be business as usual today. The owners were understandably on his case about the explosion, calling his cell and home phones with badgering regularity over the last day, making sure he understood how to run damage control. They'd decided it was best if he opened shop today, the day following "the incident," as they consistently referred to it, so as not to make it seem like they were at fault and had to close down.

So far as he could tell they'd bought his story about John being to blame. Typical case of blindly trusting the more senior person. Why should they believe some kid who'd boat-bummed his way down the California coast, selling yachts here and there along the way, and been here less than a year?

He eyed John's empty desk in the center of the main floor. No surprise there. But hey, he needed a scapegoat, and that's what underlings were for, right? He was the manager, John was the worker. Of course it was John who'd screwed up. And by not coming in today, Matt thought, tossing his briefcase on John's desk, it made him look even more guilty. He hadn't actually fired him, after all. But it meant that he would have to man John's station until somebody new could be hired. *Hey I should give that ex-cop guy a call, we're definitely hiring now!* He chuckled to himself at his own silent joke as he got situated behind John's desk.

Matt the Saint would be alright. He found John's appointment system in the computer and was checking the schedule for today when he heard the door chime ring. He looked up from the computer in time to see a pair of Sandy Cove cops stride into the dealership. They headed straight for Matt but looked around as they walked, ever wary, an instinct bred into them from even a short time on the job. Matt recognized one of them as being one of the officers asking him questions on the dock yesterday.

"Morning, Mr. Knox," one of them led off. He did not extend a hand in greeting. Matt rose from the desk.

"Officers."

"Detective Ramsey, this is my partner Detective Jones. We'd like to ask a few more questions about the boat explosion yesterday. Do you mind?"

"Of course not." *Detectives.*

The two detectives stared at him for what to Matt seemed like a long time.

"If you were busy we could come back." One of the cops glanced about the establishment while his partner addressed their interview subject.

"No, no, it's fine. I'm sorry, I'm still reeling from what happened. Physically I'm here, but my mind's not exactly on the job, if you know what I mean."

The cop talking to him nodded while the other seemed to be staring into Matt's office.

Should have left my door closed.

"Basically we're just here to follow up on some simple things. It would help us out a lot if you could provide us with certain information."

"Anything."

"Yesterday you said you could give us name and contact information for the person you purchased the sailboat from. Do you have that now?"

The cops proceeded to ask questions that avoided seeming accusatory but focused on cold, hard facts, like who did you buy the boat from and when, how long ago was first contact made, who approached who first, did he mention any problems with the boat when he sold it to you, how often do you purchase boats? Who normally handles the actual transaction? The transportation? Who were Matt's bosses? How long has John been an employee? How are potential buyers for a particular boat typically identified? How were they identified in this instance?

And so it went for the better part of an hour, with Matt answering truthfully to everything that could be easily verified, but without elaboration. Finally the two detectives seemed to have exhausted their battery of queries and when they looked at each other to see if they had anything else they wanted to ask, Matt took the opportunity to go fishing.

"I'm sorry you guys have to deal with this when I know there's so much going on around here right now, like the murders. Oh hey, I saw the museum stuff was recovered though, and you got a guy in custody for that. That's great news!" Matt recognized the gang member from the "Job," as he thought of it now. Stupid little fucker. *Pablo Martinez.*

"Yeah well as it turns out, as soon as they found out the stuff was fake, they had to let the guy go. Can't charge him for stealing the museum stuff if he doesn't have the museum stuff. He had weird fake replicas that look good but ain't worth jack shit. So the suspect—he's still a suspect—made bail and will be released tomorrow. Not exactly the kind of guy anyone expects to stick around town waiting for court, but that's up to the judge. She'll learn." His partner laughed quietly.

"Gets out tomorrow, huh?"

"That's right. Anyway, Mr. Knox, we're sorry to take up so much of your time. Thank you for your cooperation. If we need to clarify anything, do you mind if we give you a call back?"

"Not at all."

The detectives nodded and made their way out while Matt pretended to busy himself with work, but only one thing ran through his head.

Pablo Martinez. Gets out tomorrow.

-75-

AMATEUR SOCIOPATH, MEET THE PROFESSIONAL

At lunchtime Matt closed the dealership (no appointments set for the afternoon and he wasn't going to knock himself out setting them up) and got into his SUV. He glanced in back at the tarp that covered the mound of goods and smiled.

Time to cash this stuff in.

He pulled out of the harbor lot onto the road and headed across town for City Hall. Traffic was light and he made good progress until he had stop for a light. Glancing back at the loot under his tarp, he saw that the wind had blown a corner off of the stuff. He wished he'd gotten that rear window tint job he argued with Summer about a few months back, (it just wouldn't do to have an 17th century cutlass laying around in plain sight, now would it?), and so he reached back to fix the tarp as best he could from his seat. He'd just tugged it mostly back into place when the horn from the car behind him blared, the driver cursing maniacally at Matt's SUV.

Matt looked in his rear view and caught the driver flapping his arms up and down and mouthing some soundless tirade. He didn't know who the guy was and didn't recognize him from anywhere, but he wore a suit and tie and had one of those phone pieces over his ear and drove a new Mercedes, so Matt pretty much didn't like him from the get-go. But couple that with the fact that he was hurling invectives at him from behind his rolled up windows (tinted, Matt couldn't help but notice through the windshield), and he felt like it would be wrong not to let this entitled, impatient asshole not see the error of his ways.

The car's high beams flashed in time with the horn, an automotive concert of light and sound for an audience of one. The traffic light was full green, but there was only Matt's SUV and the car behind him. Matt started to roll through the light but looked back to see the guy flipping him the bird in synch with his horn honks. F...U...C...K...Y...O...U...

He can't wait five extra seconds to get through a light? Let's see how he does with a couple minutes. Matt braked without warning, forcing the guy to come to halt fast. It occurred to Matt too late that if the guy were to actually rear-end him he risked damaging the loot, having it seen by crash site investigators, or both. But he didn't care. The loot was his to do with as he pleased. If he wanted to risk it to put this motherfucker in his place, then so fucking be it.

He put his gearshift in park. He consulted his mirror. The guy looked surprised now, a little worried, no longer having fun with his creative theater routine. The light was green and now another car was pulled up to the red on one of the perpendicular streets.

Matt opened the door and clicked out of his seatbelt. He put one leg outside the vehicle with a slapping sound as his shoe smacked the pavement. The guy behind him stopped honking and flashing.

Matt got out and walked deliberately back to the other car, fast, with great confidence, taking his chances with the odds that the guy didn't carry a firearm. His two bare hands were free of weapons but at the same time transformed into weapons by the neural signals emanating from his brain. The driver's face morphed into a mask of fright as Matt reached the front of his car. Apparently he was not expecting this at all. His was a keep-your-distance form of road rage where aggressive posturing never translated into physical action.

Matt the Saint brought both fists down as hard as he could on the Mercedes' hood, like twin hammers of aggression, visibly denting the thin metal.

"Hey!" The guy shouted through the little sliver of open window he'd allowed himself, but remained inside his car. Like a camper at

Yosemite confronted with a bear on his vehicle, he found it at once it fascinating and terrifying, the net result of his reaction being to make sure the windows were up and the doors were locked.

Matt leaned over the hood from the side of the car (no need to get run over) and wrenched off the hood ornament. He hucked it at the windshield where it glanced off with a loud *clack* that caused the driver to involuntarily shield his face with his arms. Matt still had no idea what he was going to do, but when he glanced around and saw another car pull up to the cross street red light, he decided he'd made his point. He stood there just a moment longer, enjoying the sight of this pompous asshole cowering in fear inside his little transportation bubble that took him to his overpaid, useless job. He spit on the windshield and watched his saliva slide down the glass right in front of the guy's petrified, uncomprehending face and then retreated back in the direction of his SUV. The driver of the Mercedes just sat there, not moving except to turn on his windshield wipers.

Matt got behind the wheel and proceeded to drive normally to City Hall. He felt good, refreshed, somehow whole. He looked at himself in the rear view mirror, adjusted his collar a bit, smoothed out his hair and checked his teeth to make sure there was no food stuck there from lunch. Satisfied with his appearance, he exited his SUV and fed the parking meter, one of those fancy new digital jobs that accepted credit cards, with far more time than he thought he'd need (didn't need to get towed with his precious cargo). He physically pulled on all four of his doors and the tailgate to make certain they were locked, and then proceeded to walk into the mayor's office.

76

OPPORTUNITY KNOCKS

Jeremy didn't see how he could get any lower, feel any more demoralized. No job within sight, his ex-partner dead along with his entire family, his friend in jail, and Fuckin' A Flannery unwilling to consider his leads in the murder cases. The only bright spot was the fact that Flannery's "loot" had turned out to be fake. He knew that was embarrassing, but he understood how it could happen. The Sandy Cove PD was under a lot of pressure to solve that case—reward money out, people dying, not to mention that the stuff looked real enough. He would have paid good money—money he didn't have—to have been a fly on the wall when Flannery found out the stuff was phony.

But for Jeremy, the road had come to an end. Pablo must know something, judging by that black eye, but he was still in the joint. He would have bailed him out (using some piece of Alisa's jewelry as collateral, he guessed, since he didn't have any cash) but there was no need since the charges were dropped. He'd be spit back out onto the street in a few hours. Probably a good thing, both for his and Pablo's sake, he thought, climbing into his Bronco and starting the engine. Pablo was probably safer in there, and he didn't need that kind of trouble with Alisa.

He'd talk with Pablo when he got out, see if he knew where the real loot was, but he wasn't holding his breath. He wasn't even sure Pablo would tell him even if he did know. For now, it was back to the job hunt. The Harbormaster's office was still advertising for security guards. Couldn't be too bad, driving a little electric golf cart around the harbor, picking up a radio now and then. He'd see if they'd take him. He had to move on at this point. Had to do something the least bit constructive.

When he got to the harbor he parked in the same lot as before when he had visited the fish place. The Harbormaster's office was out on the end of the main harbor channel by the jetty. To get to it he had to walk across the footbridge to the little business district with the shops and the museum. Walking across the bridge he could see a small group of people filtering out of the museum, talking amongst themselves, heads down, trudging along until they reached the outdoor foyer where they stood in a huddle. Reaching the other side of the bridge, Jeremy looked past them to the museum's entrance, but there was no one working in the ticket booth as there was when it was open for business. No surprise there.

Turning right onto the sidewalk fronting the museum, Jeremy slowed his walk a bit as he passed. He was close enough to hear a few words at this point, and to see the people. He recognized Dallas Draper, now shaking his head and saying "..don't know..." He also remembered the insurance rep, who now wore another aloha shirt, and wouldn't you know it, there was one of the junior detectives from Jeremy's alma mater, the Sandy Cove PD. *What was his name...Jacobson.* He was a decent guy from what he could tell, never had to really work with him, though. Right now he seemed a little irritated, throwing his hands up in the air. There were two others—a man and a woman—that Jeremy had never seen before. They didn't give off the aura of law enforcement to him. He supposed they could be lawyers or maybe more insurance types.

Whoever they were, he could tell what this little pow-wow was about just by ambling by on the sidewalk. Fallout from the fake loot discovery. It made sense the insurance guy would be there for that, because if they truly thought the stuff had been recovered he'd have been called. The detective, too. And of course Dallas, the owner. They were still in their huddle by the time Jeremy was no longer in earshot.

When he reached the end of the walkway that led out to the jetty, he walked up to an old wooden structure partially supported by pier pilings extending out over the water. The front of the place had a weathered corkboard plastered with flyers—boats for sale, fishing regulations, help wanted ads (he looked briefly but saw nothing promising), weather and tide info, etc. Stepping inside, he heard the floorboards creak, and looking down between the cracks of the boards he could see water moving below.

"Mr. Washington? That you?" Jeremy turned and saw an old white-haired man craning his neck to see out the doorway of his office.

"Yes, Mr. Solomon?"

"Hi there. Come on in, please."

Jeremy walked into his office. He expected to be politely turned down for the job in about five minutes. He gazed fleetingly at some taxidermy mounted fishes on the walls as he walked into the Harbormaster's office, which itself was decorated with more fish, and posters of local marine life, as well as a collection of tall sailing ship models. The place just had the look of belonging to someone who'd devoted his life to the sea. For all the potential conversation pieces, however, the old man got right to the point.

"Most of the stuff you're likely to encounter on this job is pretty small time, especially coming from the police force—people fishing where they're not supposed to, leaving fish guts where they're not supposed to, parking their cars and their boats where they're not supposed to, that kind of thing. But we do occasionally get our fair share of real crime."

Jeremy nodded and recounted his experience thwarting an attempted burglary at the Fresh Catch. The old man smiled jovially. "Ayuh, heard about that one. Excellent work! I'll get right to the point, son, because I respect you even though I know your story, and I don't want to waste your time. And I certainly don't want to waste my time, as old as I am."

Normally Jeremy would take offense to being called "son" by another man not his father, but this guy had to be at least eighty-five if he was a day, plus he was trying to get a job.

"Sounds good, sir."

"I'm ready to offer you the security guard position we have, if you're interested after hearing the two conditions."

The old man had Jeremy's full attention. *Did he just say 'ready to offer you the position'?*

"Okay."

"First of all this is a *night* watchman position. I don't think that came across in the ad."

Jeremy slumped a little. It certainly didn't. Alisa worked in the day. If he worked at night that meant they'd see each other now and then on the weekends when she wasn't working. He took a deep breath. A job was a job, though. Alisa would tell him to take it until something better showed up. So he smiled and nodded and acted like he wanted it.

"You don't have to pretend it's the greatest job in the world, son. I know it's the pits. But that's what we got open, at least until I kick the bucket. Like I said, if you want it, I'd rather give it to you—a guy with some real experience and who's helped us out around here before—than some immigrant can't speak a lick of English. You with me?"

"Yes sir. Thank you."

"There's one other condition."

"What's that?"

"You need to start tonight."

77

WILL THE REAL HERO PLEASE STEP FORWARD

Jeremy was in a good mood for the first time he could remember in quite some time while he drove home. It was funny, because he never thought that getting a security guard job would be something to be happy about. But it was. When you were down and out anything that was a step up, even a small one, was worth being happy about.

He punched off his police scanner. Time to let it go. He was not a cop. Listening in on his former work wasn't helping him. He flipped on his AM radio to a local news station. *Just let it go.* Tonight marked a new beginning. For the first time since he could remember he actually looked forward to seeing his wife at dinner time so he could break the good news to her.

He took his time on the drive home, taking a longer, more scenic route with less traffic. It was good to get out of the city for a bit, and easy to forget that just outside of Sandy Cove lay some wild coastline that he didn't get to see that often. Passing by the sand dunes with the ocean playing peek-a-boo between the tall ones as he passed, Jeremy turned up his radio when the on air personality announced they had a breaking news bulletin.

"Let us take you now to City Hall, where apparently there's been a new development related to the robbery of Sandy Cove's beloved maritime museum. Mayor Adams is outside City Hall in the courtyard after having called a press conference—the second one today. Let's listen in."

Jeremy reached for the volume knob as he made a left turn onto a road that led inland from the beach.

"Good afternoon, folks. As you probably know, this morning we thought we had recovered the treasures from our local maritime museum, but unfortunately that turned out not to be true. Now, however, it seems fortune has favored our little town and I'm pleased to announce a serious bright spot amidst the recent wave of darkness that has plagued our little slice of paradise."

Jeremy pulled off the side of the road up to a stand of eucalyptus trees so that he could concentrate on the report.

The mayor's voice continued through his tinny speakers.

"With me here is one of the fine citizens of Sandy Cove that make this such a vibrant and rewarding community. By my side is Mr. Matt Knox, who unfortunately we saw on the news yesterday because of the tragic boating accident in our harbor. Today, though, I'm pleased to announce that he's on the air for a much more positive note."

Jeremy heard some shouted questions that sounded as though they came from far away, or at least not properly mic'ed.

"Don't worry, we'll take your questions after the announcement," she promised, and then went on. "It is with great pleasure that I inform you Mr. Knox has turned almost the entire missing inventory of the Sandy Cove Maritime Museum in to us. Only two items are unaccounted for, and the museum's owner assures us that they are not among the more valuable pieces. Mr. Knox found the rare goods stashed in a suspicious looking boat hidden deep in a drainpipe outlet in the harbor. And this time—let me assure you that we had the items lab tested *before* making the announcement."

A trickle of laughter emanated from the gathered assemblage. When it died the mayor continued.

"It's the real McCoy, folks! The items have been verified as authentic and as we speak are in the process of being returned to their rightful owner at the Sandy Cove Maritime Museum, where all of us will soon be able to enjoy them once again."

A round of light clapping was heard, like one might hear at a golf match.

"And now to show our appreciation for this act of concerned citizenry, I'm pleased to present this check for fifty thousand dollars to Matt Knox, the man who gave a town back its treasure. On behalf of all of Sandy Cove, thank you so much, Mr. Knox!"

Jeremy felt the hairs on his arms stand up as he heard Matt's voice invade his car.

"The pleasure is all mine, Mayor Adams. I'm grateful for this reward, thank you so much."

"Once again, it's you that we have to thank. This check will have to do, but believe me when I say that if we could I'd give you the keys to the city!"

Jeremy Washington felt physically ill while the sounds of an enthusiastic crowd applauded their approval through his car speakers. He turned his engine off, killing the broadcast, and leaned his head on the steering wheel.

-78-

...INTO THE FIRE

An hour or so later Matt Knox was back at work, bidding a pleasant goodbye to a customer who'd come in to match paint colors for his speedboat where he scraped it against another vessel. Matt agreed with him that there was no way it was his fault. Turning the museum treasure in to City Hall had clearly gone a long way to restoring his good name, he could tell already from the reception he'd received from City Hall back to the yacht dealership. His bosses had even called to congratulate him, no doubt relieved at the positive publicity so soon after their catastrophe.

The Sandy Cove Yacht Brokerage still had customers, Matt thought. Accidents happen, people understood that. When it came to his own accident, the one that claimed the life of an entire family, it would take some time but he'd regain their trust. In the meantime, business was slow today, even being the only one there having to pick up John's slack.

He opened the web browser on what used to be John's computer and went to the site for the local Sandy Cove news network. He quickly scanned the stories on the boat explosion for updates–nothing new (*great*)–and there he was on the front page accepting the oversized check–(*fantastic!*)–and then scrolled down the page looking for anything about the museum robbery.

A little ways down he found it:

MARITIME MUSEUM ROBBERY SUSPECT TO BE RELEASED

He took in the mugshot of Pablo Martinez. Yep–that's him! He had a hell of a shiner over his left eye that he didn't recall being there before, but it was definitely him. He remembered him in the dim confines of the display room, efficiently bagging the relics handed to him, pointing out objects his associates had missed. He skimmed the article: *Items in Martinez' possession determined to be exact replicas of stolen museum pieces...charges dropped...to be released today at 3:00 P.M.*

Matt glanced at the computer's clock: 2:23. He scrutinized Pablo's mugshot once more. He was part of the group who had enlisted him against his will to help them break the law. Receiving the reward money did nothing to mitigate that. It meant nothing compared to what they'd done to him. Pablo, who had tried to use Matt's character for his own gain, was still standing. But in the process they'd transformed that character and now it was but a shadow of its former self, like a picture is a two dimensional representation of a person.

He closed his eyes and envisioned Pablo's mugshot as a printed picture dropped on a gaudy grave adorned with flowers and Jesus candles the way his people would honor him. He mentally pictured the *In Memoriam* stickers in Old English style font that would be plastered on the rear windows of the cars of his friends and family.

Matt could make that happen. He had the power to manifest those stickers and those candles and those flowers. Because that was the situation that Pablo had brought upon himself. What comes around, and all that. He had wanted what Matt's character could do for him. He would get it, what it would do *to* him, at any rate.

A few minutes later Matt was on the road in his SUV headed for the Sandy Cove Men's Detention Center. He closed the shop for now, but he'd routed the main office line that John formerly handled to his cellphone, so if the powers that be called they wouldn't have to know he wasn't there.

He'd never been to the jail before and was surprised at just how far out of the way it was—set up on a hillside overlooking the outskirts of Sandy Cove, a two lane blacktop the only way in or out. He checked the clock in his dash: 2:54. Took him a little longer to get here than he'd anticipated. He still didn't know exactly what his plan was but he sensed–in that way predators intuited rather than reasoned how to stalk their prey–that he should park as far as he could from the jail entrance and watch for Pablo to emerge. He thought no further ahead than that. He reached a fork in the road where signs read, INMATE RECEIVING and VISITORS. He took the latter road and slowed as he entered the parking lot.

He was taken aback at the lot's ambling sprawl. The jail, a low-set concrete and steel affair, lay almost a football field away. As his clock ticked over to 3:00, Matt pulled his vehicle into a designated parking spot about halfway to the building entrance. He put the engine in park but let it idle.

Glancing around, he didn't see any obvious signs of surveillance. If they were watching him somehow, though, he wasn't doing anything wrong. Just waiting for someone to come out. Looking about the lot, he did see a couple of other cars with people in them as well.

The news report said Pablo would be released at 3:00, but as 3:07 rolled over he realized that with any kind of bureaucratic institution, they couldn't be held to any specific time. He only hoped that they hadn't let him out early. His mind wandered as he waited. He thought about Summer's happy squeal when he showed her the reward check. He'd told her they should use it to pay down the mortgage, she wanted a new car. In the end he'd said what the hell, what color you want? Keep her happy. He had other things to focus on...

...such as Pablo Martinez walking straight out of the jail in civilian clothes, alone, a plastic bag of his jail-processed belongings dangling from one hand. He looked around a little as he crossed onto the black-top, perhaps for a ride? For whomever had done that to his eye? Or maybe the media, but Matt saw no sign of them. He'd overshadowed Pablo's own case by turning in the real treasure. And now he was about to overshadow him in a different way. He wondered if Pablo had seen the news while he was in jail. It must have come as a shock to be released because the valuable loot he thought he had was fake, Matt thought, chuckling to himself.

He edged a little lower in his seat as Pablo began to cross the parking lot. He walked at a normal pace, not too fast nor slow, with a deliberate sense of purpose toward the lot exit. Matt wondered if he had a cell-phone in that bag, and if so, why wasn't he calling someone for a ride? Maybe he didn't have a phone. Maybe he just didn't have anyone to call, fucking loser.

Matt was only sure about one thing. Pablo never looked in his direction as we walked past his SUV. He had been somewhat vigilant as he left the jail building, but now that he had come this far across the parking lot, he seemed to relax.

As Pablo stepped out of sight onto the exit road, Matt Knox put his vehicle into gear.

-79-

HITCHHIKERS MAY BE ESCAPING INMATES

Matt Knox flushed with adrenaline as a police car pulled into the parking lot from the road Pablo had just started down on foot. The back of the squad car was empty, so they hadn't picked up Pablo. He wondered how they knew if a person walking down that road might be escaping the jail or not, but he supposed if you carried the plastic bag of stuff, casually walking like Pablo was, that they knew. He supposed as well that a radio alert would be expected with any jailbreak attempt.

The cops paid Matt no mind as they drove past into the lot, and Matt proceeded down the winding two-lane blacktop that connected the hilltop jail with the flatlands of the city outskirts below. The trees had been cut back some distance from either side of the road, but the woods were thick beyond that.

Driving slowly, Matt craned his neck to observe the twisty little thoroughfare for signs of surveillance cameras, but he saw nothing obvious. He could see no other traffic, but knew that cars could come around the bend at any time. All jail personnel, inmate buses and visitors came in or out via this access road, so he couldn't count on it being empty for long.

He took a hairpin curve to the right at very low speed and sighted Pablo Martinez ambling along the right shoulder toward the next curve below. Whatever he was going to do, he would have to do it fast. Police could pass by at any time. The area was sheltered from sight, though, and once his quarry reached the bottom he'd have many options for escape.

He tested his foot's position on the gas pedal, making sure it was firmly in position, he guessed, but deep down he knew he was just buying time. Was he having second thoughts? Not about killing Pablo, that much was certain. A little voice whispered in his ear that Matt the Saint—Matt the Angel—had lost one of his wings already and could not afford another mistake like the boat explosion. He could simply follow Pablo all the way to the bottom and hopefully to his destination, probably some seedy apartment on the crappy side of town. His SUV accelerated down the hill toward Pablo's ambling form.

It wouldn't be that hard to run Pablo down, to barrel the SUV into him and keep driving. But aside from the risk that presented, Matt just didn't feel like doing that. Instead his right foot sank into the brake pedal. If Pablo heard his vehicle approaching, he showed no fear whatsoever. He did not alter his course the slightest bit. Matt reached into his center console and pulled out a baseball hat and put it on. Then he accelerated, passing Pablo by a few feet before pulling over. He fingered the switch that lowered his passenger side window and called out to Pablo, who by now had stopped walking to look at the vehicle. Matt did his best to make his voice sound casual.

"Need a lift? Happy to drop you at the bottom of the road!" Pablo looked around in all directions and then right at Matt, who wore cap and shades. Matt held his breath until Pablo said, "Sure, thanks."

Clearly he did not recognize his former hostage-accomplice.

Pablo got into the passenger seat. Matt eased back onto the road seconds before an unmarked police car, given away by an assemblage of antennae, came around the turn, heading up. Both men relaxed once it had rounded the curve out of sight. Matt looked over at Pablo.

It's him, right? Make sure it's him!

He saw the black eye, the cursive writing tattooed on the bottom of his neck. Recognized the face, too, from the museum. It was Pablo. He felt the now familiar sense of heightened awareness envelope him as everything clicked into place. *Might as well fuck with this guy's head a little bit. He's dead soon anyway, what the hell.* This thought caused Matt to laugh a little bit. Pablo looked over at him, but Matt contained himself and his passenger continued to stare straight ahead at the road.

"So you work at the jail?" Pablo asked. Just making enough idle conversation to last down to the bottom of the hill. But Matt had some conversation of his own to interject. He turned onto to a relatively straight section of road and looked over at his passenger.

"Pablo, it's me, man. It's *me*!"

This was risky, playing with his head like that, but at least this was about the only time one could reasonably conclude that Pablo Martinez would be unarmed.

Pablo bristled at the mention of his name. He looked over at Matt and said nothing, his face screwed into a mask of concentration. "Sorry, uh, where do I know you from? You one of the guards?"

Matt looked down the road and into his rearview mirror. Then he tore off his baseball cap and glasses, tossing them both onto the back seat while staring at Pablo eye to eye.

"Pablo, it's me, man—Matt. From the *museum*!"

"Say what?" Pablo leaned closer to study his face. Then a glimmer of recognition lighted in his eyes. "What are doing here?"

Matt paused for a second as he rounded a turn. Then he said, "Sal asked me to keep everybody together if things got heavy."

Pablo made a spitting sound. "Look man, I don't know what you've been smoking, but Sal's dead. He was using you to help us get into the museum. You were never one of us."

"Right, that's how it started, but I went to Sal and talked to him about how it was such a rush helping you guys get that stuff, and I wanted to do more things like that! You've got to understand, my life was pretty boring. Same routine every day, same wife, kids, up at six, in to work by eight, come home at around four, wash rinse repeat. This was different, man! So I went back to Sal to ask how I could help and he told me if anything ever happened to him, to keep you guys together."

"Wait a minute. I saw on TV in the jail that you turned in the loot for the reward. You got fifty large, dude!"

Matt grinned like a hyena. "I did, and I plan to give you what's coming to you from that, give you your due."

"No way?"

"Way."

Pablo shifted in his seat. "Yo man, it was you in that storage unit wasn't it? The one with no loot. I saw you drive up to it, man. I thought it might be you but I wasn't sure, and I'm like, *Nah, Matt the Saint? No way.*" Pablo met Matt's turning head with an icy stare, challenging him to lie.

Matt slowed past another police car on the way up to the jail before answering. "Yeah I've been working on it ever since it all went down. You guys lost the loot."

"Did you take it?" Pablo's eyes looked menacing now, dangerous. Matt cautioned himself to get things under control. He couldn't let Pablo become too emotional. He flashed on the flower covered grave, almost like a meditation, and it allowed him to go on.

"I didn't take it from you. You guys were sold out by someone. You know where I found the loot?"

"Where?"

Matt thought fast for a second. Why not just tell him the truth? What were the consequences? None that he could think of, and it would provide some closure for this loser before he extinguished him. Fuck it. Tell him everything. It'll be the last major realization he has in this life.

"In the harbor residential section, in a dock locker belonging to a neighbor of the guy who owns the museum."

Pablo's mouth dropped open. He turned to face Matt. "No *shit?*"

"No shit."

"Not in the owner's locker, but his neighbor's?"

"Yep."

"How'd you know it was in there?"

Matt shrugged. "Been tracking the situation, man, like Sal asked me to. Cruising by in my boat all the time. I kept tabs."

Pablo shook his head as if bewildered. "So the fifty grand. You're going to split it with me?"

"You're the last guy left I can find. Is there anyone else to split it with besides you?"

"No."

"What about the guy who drove the getaway van?"

"He's the one who did this to my face." Pablo touched his left eye.

"What about Bobby, the other guy in there with you?"

"Ran like a scared bitch back to North Carolina or some shit. Said we can keep his share, he's out."

"Well that makes it nice and easy, then."

Pablo looked around the SUV. "You have it, now? In here?"

Matt chuckled. "I have the check. Still have to cash it."

"How much is my share?"

"All of it."

"Say what?"

"I'm just going to give all of it to you. If you want it, that is." He cackled again.

Pablo began to stammer, unsure of what to say. Matt spoke again.

"There's only one condition."

"What's that?"

"You just have to tell me what you're going to do with the money."

Pablo looked out the window for a second then back at Matt. "What am I gonna do with it? Fifty grand?"

"Yeah!"

Pablo laughed. "Man. I'm not sure. Never had that much cash all at once. I guess..." He stared ahead at the road while he thought. "I guess I'd use it to start my own shop. My own mechanic shop. I know you said the money is from Sal to keep the gang together, though, but..."

"No that's okay. I want to know what you would really do with it, no strings attached."

Pablo nodded. "Yeah, well I think that's it. I might pay down a couple of debts, you know, but they're no big deal. Then I'd open my own shop somewhere around town, stop the gang shit, chill out with my woman and just work on cars. That's what I'd do."

Matt slowed the SUV and pulled to the shoulder as he approached the last turn before the final straightaway that would take them into town.

"Cool. Well I hope you get to do that where you're going."

"Well right now I'm just going to work."

"No you're not." While Pablo had been talking Matt had lifted one of his pirate pistols from his door compartment. He pulled the SUV to a stop on the shoulder. He pointed the blunderbuss at Pablo's head.

"Whoa, no way—is that one of the ones from the museum? I thought you turned 'em in?"

Why wasn't he scared, Matt wondered. Pablo's face was relaxed—he appeared genuinely interested in the gun only as it related to their heist, and not as a real weapon that could do him harm.

"Kept this one as a souvenir."

"That's right, they said on the news that all of the stuff except for a couple of items were returned. So it's the guns!"

"Yep. Bye Pablo."

Matt pulled the trigger.

Click.

The sound of the hammer striking flint without igniting gunpowder echoed hollowly in the confined space.

"Shit! Okay, man! I know it's two hundred years old and all but it still makes me nervous with it pointed at me like that." Pablo reached his arm out halfway to Matt, without touching the gun, and panto-mimed moving it off to the side.

Matt withdrew the weapon and looked down at the muzzle, taken aback. He examined the weapon closely. It was the authentic firearm and not the replica.

"I get it. That thing must be worth a lot to collectors. *That's* your share, right?"

Matt leveled the gun at Pablo's head again.

"It's your share too."

He swiped his free hand over the hammer, not bothering to pull the trigger this time.

"I said don't point—"

-80-

NOT AGAIN

"That's fantastic, honey. Congratulations!"

Jeremy's wife set a bottle of champagne in front of him. They were in their own ratty kitchen, not a fancy restaurant, but the scale of the celebration fit the occasion.

She looked so happy that it worried him sick to think a menial job like being a night watchman could be the cause of so much joy. But it was money coming in. It was a step toward making himself look employable again. It was a start.

"We're not going to see each other as much for a while with me working nights."

"We can do it for a while, until you find something even better. Right now this is the best thing for us." She raised a glass and he did the same.

"To getting back on our feet."

They clinked glasses. "You ready for some lunch? Just relax, I'll do everything." She picked up the remote for the little countertop television and clicked it to life before busying herself in the kitchen. For a few moments Jeremy was lost in his thoughts, thinking about which of his "every day carry" gear he would bring to his job tonight, since he trusted his own equipment—flashlights, multitool, etc.— more than whatever they were going to give him on the watchman job—when Alisa's voice brought him back to the present.

"Not again! What is going on in this town?"

Jeremy looked up from has glass of bubbly to see his wife directing a concerned look to the TV. He followed suit and immediately recognized yet another breaking news banner. She'd been watching a reality show, though, which meant the news must be big for the network to run it over a regular show. The banner read, MUSEUM ROBBERY SUSPECT FOUND SLAIN NEAR SANDY COVE JAIL. By the time he'd finished reading it, a voiceover was apologizing for interrupting the program. Jeremy reached for the remote and increased the volume.

He recognized the same woman who'd reported from City Hall on Fuckin' A Flannery's press conference, but now she stood on the side of a road, a bevy of ambulances and other official vehicles clustered at the shoulder.

"Carol Tepper here for Cove 6 News. And just where is here?" She waved her arm at the outdoor surroundings, a few trees visible behind the road, and not much as else besides the emergency workers. "I'm standing at close to the bottom of what's officially known as Highway 14, but more commonly referred to as the 'jail road' because it's the main road connecting the city jail to town. About an hour ago the body of a man was discovered here, face mangled almost beyond recognition. His identification–carried in a plastic bag like those given to released inmates when their belongings are returned to them— allowed his identity to be confirmed as one Pablo Martinez, a thirty-six year old Sandy Cove resident."

Pablo's booking photo went up on screen and Jeremy's mouth dropped open while Tepper continued to report.

"Jail officials confirmed that Martinez had been released only a couple of hours ago, and probably not more than a half an hour before he was murdered, most likely right here on this road." The camera panned and zoomed on a patch of fresh blood on the edge of the pavement.

"Pablo!" Jeremy said, rising from his stool to stand at the counter.

"Oh, Jer..." Alisa started, dropping a plate on the floor. She didn't know what to say. What could she say when the people in her husband's life were dropping dead like flies? It didn't seem possible in their little beachside community during the height of the summer tourist season. But here it was, right on the TV, right here on their streets, right here in Sandy Cove. There was no denying it.

Jeremy pounded his fist on the counter, staring at Tepper's concerned face through his watery eyes.

"That's it," he said, snatching his keys from the counter.

"What's it?"

"I told Flannery who's doing this. He wouldn't listen." He headed for the door.

"Where are you going?"

IF AT FIRST YOU DON'T SUCCEED

"I'm here to see the mayor."

Jeremy stood in the foyer of the City Hall building, facing down a receptionist, or admin assistant or clerk or secretary or whatever the hell they called the lady who sat behind the desk in the public area of the seat of Sandy Cove's government.

She asked him for his name and if he had an appointment.

"Jeremy Washington. No."

She pursed her lips and went back to clacking away at her computer keyboard. "I'm sorry, but an appointment is required to see the mayor. Today of all days."

Jeremy nodded. "I can help her. I have urgent information concerning the murders in our town that the mayor needs to know."

That seemed to get her attention for a couple of seconds but she gave in to one of the calls lighting up her desk phone. She paid no attention to Jeremy while she yapped about some problem she was having with the new calendaring system. Jeremy eyed the closed set of French doors that led to the inner workings of Sandy Cove's center of power.

Jeremy walked toward his seat in order to let the gatekeeper's guard down, but then he ambled over to the doors and tried the handle. It turned and just as he heard, "Excuse me, sir," Jeremy was pushing his way beyond the door into the long hallway that lay beyond.

He'd been in here on a couple of occasions, to attend those rare planning meetings where the opinion of real beat cops was given precedence over that of the department brass. Closed office doors lined either side, potted ficus trees studding the walls every twenty feet. Behind him he heard the *clack-clack-clack* of heels on wood flooring and then the French doors opening, followed by the woman's voice. "Sir! If you don't come back to the lobby I'll have to call security. *Sir!*"

Jeremy ran.

Ahead of him a door opened on his right and he nearly collided with a man carrying a tray of Starbucks. He apologized on the run. He knew that the office of the mayor herself was all the way at the end of the hallway. When he got there, he turned right only to be met with another set of closed double doors. He paused for a second to catch his breath, hearing the foyer lady's voice somewhere behind him in the hallway saying, "He's down there."

He opened the doors and walked into a large outer room with a male receptionist seated at a desk.

"Sir, security has been called." The guy definitely sounded gay to Jeremy, not that it mattered one way or the other. Jeremy was going to do what he had to do no matter who was in his way.

"It's okay, I have critical information the mayor needs to hear immediately." He strode past the guy up to a frosted glass door etched with the mayor's name. At the same time as he opened the door a contingent of security guards came running into the outer office, the foyer lady jogging cautiously behind them.

"Sir, don't do that!" The secretary jumped up from his desk and ran to the mayor's office, saying, "I'm sorry, he just ran in! Security's here. I told him he needed an appointment."

Jeremy stood a few steps past the threshold in the mayor's office. Gina Adams was seated at a small round conference table, facing the door, with two men in suits who looked highly annoyed at the interruption.

"Mayor Adams, I've got information on the murders! I need to talk to you." As he spoke a pair of security officers gripped him by either arm. "Wait! Just hear me out, it'll only take a minute!" Jeremy pleaded.

The mayor narrowed her eyes in an expression of irritation. "In case you hadn't noticed I was trying to run a meeting here. What is your name? You look familiar."

"Jeremy Washington, ma'am."

The mayor wagged a finger at him and smiled a bit. "You were one of our police officers. A damned good one too, if I recall, until you got mixed up in that unfortunate business. But you're not on the force anymore, correct, Mr. Washington?"

"That's correct. Nevertheless, I have information that proves who the murderer is that's running amok in our town."

One of the men in suits smiled as if greatly entertained. The other looked less enthusiastic, saying, "What is this, some kind of reality show? We're trying to conduct business here, mayor." He made a show of looking at his Rolex. "Should we take our proposal to another city?"

The mayor shot him a withering stare. "Why don't we take a break. Come back in a half hour, gentlemen, and we'll conclude our discussion."

"Shall we escort him out, Mayor?" one of the security guards asked.

"No, let him go, but please remain in the room with me. Everyone else can go." The secretary, the foyer greeter and other assorted staff shrunk reluctantly through the door, followed by the two business-men who left their briefcases and computers open on the table.

When it was just Jeremy, two security guards and the mayor, the door was closed and the mayor got up from the conference table to move to her desk. Once seated she indicated for Jeremy to do the same in one of the chairs fronting her desk. He sat while the two guards remained standing on either side of him.

"Okay, Mr. Washington. You've piqued my interest. I hope you're not just wasting everybody's time. What have you got?"

"First off let me state, Mayor Adams, that before coming here I pre-sented the same information I'm about to give you to Detective Flan-nery, but he dismissed it."

"Noted," the mayor said, interlacing her fingers and resting them on the desk. "Just tell me what you know, please. This has to be quick. I can't have it getting around that anyone can simply barge in here without an appointment and get a meeting, or it'd be hell around here all the time instead of only most of the time."

The guards laughed quietly.

"I have laboratory proof that Mr. Matt Knox—the yacht dealer–is the Sandy Cove Killer."

The mayor reared her head back. "The Sandy Cove Killer? We have our very own *killer* now? I haven't heard that term used before in the media, did you make that up?"

Jeremy shrugged sheepishly. "I suppose I may have. He kills people in Sandy Cove, and nowhere else that I know of, so…"

She waved a hand. "I get it, I get it. But let's keep that phrase in this room, please. I'm trying to salvage what's left of our peak season."

Jeremy nodded and the mayor continued.

"I'd be lying, Mr. Robinson, if I said that I believe you regarding the killer's identity, if there is in fact only one killer and not just a bunch of gang-bangers offing each other. Mr. Knox is very well respected in our town–for many years. Why, everyone says the man is a saint! He sold me my boat, for Christ's sake." Then she looked at the guards and added, "Got me a helluva deal, too, on a Hatteras. Helluva deal. I should go out on that thing more often."

Both guards nodded. The mayor turned back to Jeremy.

"So what proof do you have to back up this accusation?"

Jeremy looked up at the guards. "I have to pull something out of my pocket."

"Just do it slow," one of them said. The mayor looked on with interest, apparently unafraid.

Jeremy proceeded to extract the lab report that he'd shown Flannery from his front jeans pocket. He handed it to one of the guards, who examined it briefly before walking it over to the mayor's desk and leaving it there.

"What am I looking at?" she asked as she picked up the card.

"It's a forensics report showing that three of Matt Knox's fingerprints—the pointer, middle and thumb—are exact matches with prints lifted from both the museum just after it was robbed and the murder scene on Josey Jiminez work boat." Jeremy paused to let the mayor digest this. She looked at the prints on the card and furrowed her brow in concentration.

"How did you obtain these lab results? The date on the report shows it was done well after you were terminated from the force."

Jeremy took a deep breath. This was the awkward part. There was nothing he could do now but tell the truth, so he pressed on. "My ex-partner, Tommy..." He choked up for a moment at the thought of his friend.

"The one who just died in the sailboat accident?"

"It was no accident!" Jeremy yelled, louder than he meant to. The mayor's expression registered that she was taken aback by his outburst.

'I'm sorry, I didn't mean to yell. It's just...I know that it wasn't an accident. Matt Knox deliberately rigged that boat to explode so that it would kill Tommy, because he knew that Tommy and I were onto him."

"So you're saying Tommy helped you to get access to the forensics lab?"

"Yes. He also obtained Mr. Knox's fingerprints from his office, because Mr. Knox has no prints on file since he has no existing criminal record."

"No existing criminal record," the mayor repeated. Maybe there's a reason for that, Mr. Washington?"

Jeremy shook his head and looked at the floor. "I know it seems weird, ma'am. And it is. In all my years of law enforcement I've never encountered someone with a perfect record who all of a sudden snaps and goes on a major murder spree. But it's happening with Matt the Saint Knox. I know it is."

The mayor exhaled heavily as she looked at the card. "Unfortunately, Mr. Washington, I cannot act on this...information. I can't even call it evidence since it was illegally obtained, right?"

"Well..." Jeremy began.

"How did Tommy get Matt's prints if they weren't already on file?"

"He went into his office posing as a boat buyer and took a framed photograph home with him that Matt had just touched."

One of the guards made a grunting sound, but no one said anything. Jeremy continued.

"That's why Matt wanted Tommy dead! He messed with the propane tank on the sailboat to make it look like an accident, and then blamed it on his employee, John Samson."

The mayor stood. "I've heard quite enough, Mr. Washington. Those are very forceful allegations. I'm afraid that what you have is either circumstantial or illegally obtained. We cannot arrest someone based on illegally obtained evidence. I appreciate your concern, but I'm going to ask you to leave now. I'm very sorry for the loss of your friend—he was a fine officer—but I cannot condone your tactics. We have a police force in Sandy Cove, Mr. Washington, and you're not on it."

The guards started to lean in on him, but he said, "And now Pablo Martinez is dead—did you see the news today? Matt the Saint is killing off all of the gang members who forced him to help them rob the museum, and anyone else who gets in his way."

"He helped them rob the museum?"

"Yes. I think that's what started this whole thing. Notice that the crime wave in Sandy Cove began with the museum robbery."

The mayor appeared to think about this for several seconds, but said, "Perhaps with more convincing evidence that was obtained *legally*, Mr. Washington, I could do something. But as it is my hands are tied. I have to get back to my meetings." She waved the guards down. "Can I trust you to find your own way out?"

Jeremy nodded and stood. "Thank you for your time, Mayor Adams."

-82-

HAPPY WIFE, HAPPY LIFE

Matt watched from the doorway as Summer tucked their kids into bed. A movie was starting on HBO and he was hoping to resurrect the "date nights" they used to commit to once per week. He knew he'd been preoccupied lately and could feel her retreating a little. The reward money warmed her to him somewhat, but he needed to solidify that by spending some quality time with her. He watched her walk toward him holding a finger up to her lips. *Shhh.* Kids asleep now.

He waved a hand, beckoning her to follow him downstairs.

He sat on the couch and pointed to the opening credits on a low budget slasher movie.

"Want me to make some popcorn?" he asked.

Summer glanced at her watch, the jeweled piece he'd gotten her for one of their anniversaries, he could no longer recall which one. "Babe, I need to pick something up from the store." She looked up from her watch at the television, where an axe blade swung in super slow-mo across the screen.

Matt looked at her. "What do you need?"

"I just remembered that I said I would make cupcakes for Gavin's team tomorrow—for the game. I gotta get the stuff."

"Can't you do it in the morning, early?"

"I need them with me when I drop him off at eight. Just enjoy the movie, babe, I know you've been working a lot lately. You deserve to relax. I'll be back for the second half, and tomorrow we can make it a *full* night."

Even her seductive emphasis on "full" wasn't enough to quell Matt's disappointment as Summer strode from the living room. He heard the door to the garage open and shut while he thought about the cupcakes. Definitely a little odd. She was a planner, and usually if she knows she has to do something on a certain date, she has everything ready. Not the last minute type.

Nobody's perfect, though, Matt thought as he heard the garage door roll up. *Forgot the stuff to make cupcakes and have to go out on a weeknight after dinner to get it. Could happen to anyone.* He clicked off the TV as a jogger was about to run past an axe-wielding assailant hidden in some trees. He could clean his pirate pistols. His latest acquisition, especially, seemed like it could use some maintenance.

Matt rose from the couch. He walked though the kitchen toward his office but when he reached the door to the garage he found himself opening it. He snagged his keys off the rack of hooks (fake fishhooks to keep up the nautical theme of the house) that Summer habitually refused to use, and stepped into the garage.

He cocked his head and listened carefully into the house. Kids had to be sleeping to do this. He couldn't hear anything. He pulled the door shut softly and went to his SUV. He started the engine and waited for the garage door to open again, this time for him.

He drove out into the night, following the route Summer would take to the market she shopped. She was probably getting stuff to make cupcakes. Maybe she even ordered them custom made from the bakery and tried to pass them off as her own from scratch and she didn't want anyone to know. That could be it.

Right? He should go back inside.

Right?

-83-

UNDEREMPLOYED AND OVERJOYED

The headlights from the golf cart Jeremy drove cut a swath through the foggy harbor night. He had cringed upon first seeing the cart, so small and comical looking, a sad substitute of a vehicle for his old squad car. But after a few minutes behind the wheel he had to admit that it was fun and easy to drive, and the silence afforded by the electric motor was a tactical advantage of sorts. At this point he'd take what he could get.

The old man had given him a hearty welcome, handed him the "keys to the kingdom," as he put it, meaning the golf cart and the admin office. It was nice to feel trusted again, even at so basic a level, Jeremy thought, traversing the largest harbor parking lot. All he had to do was patrol the harbor perimeter for any signs of wrongdoing or trouble. If he found any, he was to call 911 for crimes in progress, or, for the simple things, try to assist lost people with directions, maybe provide an escort to a woman walking alone at night, things like that.

Easy enough. So far he'd made the entire circuit once, uneventfully, following along the harbor's rough U-shape and then tracing it back. He'd received a wave from the guy driving the Harbor Patrol boat, and one from a guy walking a dog along the water. He doubted anything serious would ever happen while he was on duty, but then again he supposed that was a good thing. No reason to be overly willing to risk his neck for pay that was about three times less than what a police officer made.

He reached the far end of the parking lot, devoid of vehicles at this late hour with the exception of two empty boat trailers, and parked under the cover of a stand of Eucalyptus trees that kept the glow from the streetlamps off of his cart.

Drive the U again?

He supposed that was pretty much his job, unless he was radioed to be somewhere specifically. During the day there were three guards on duty, but for the night shift he was it. The old man told him he might receive a call from time to time from a business owner asking him to check in on an alarm triggered on their building, but that for the most part things were pretty quiet on the graveyard shift.

He glanced at the handheld radio in a holder on the cart's dash. A private business channel with limited range, it couldn't be used to listen in or communicate with the Sandy Cove PD. He supposed that was a good thing. The last thing he needed was to be mentally holding onto his old job. Time to embrace the new, he thought, putting the cart into gear and rolling slowly back across the lot.

Next time he'd have to bring his coffee mug, he thought, eying the empty cup holder in his cart. He was about to turn out on to the road fronting the lot when a pair of headlights—the newer xenon style with a bluish cast to them—came around the curve off to Jeremy's left. He braked his cart and watched as a two-door BMW slid to a stop on the road fronting the main harbor's shopping section. Everything was closed now, though, so there was no good reason to stop here.

Lost, just programming the GPS or maybe pulling over to use the cell? Jeremy wondered. But he noted with concern that the car's lights blinked off and, to his dismay, the driver's door opened.

Here we go. My first traffic stop. After being a cop for so long, there was no way he could think of it as anything else, although he was well aware that now he had none of his former authority. He was going to have to confront this driver and inform them that no way on God's green Earth was anybody allowed to park there. There was even a NO PARKING TOW AWAY ZONE sign posted just a few feet from where the BMW sat.

Jeremy decided he'd rather ride up to them than walk, as if his little cart with its city logo gave him so much more power of intimidation than his uniform alone. But again, it was a matter of working with what you had. He started to put his foot down on the accelerator but stopped just as the sole of his shoe made contact.

The driver was getting out. He saw a shapely calf in a brand name running shoe hit the pavement. Then a head of blond locks came into view, and the door closed. Jeremy was about to call out to the driver—("Hey, can't park there!" or would perhaps a more diplomatic approach be best: "Excuse me, please!"). But none of that mattered because he recognized the vehicle's operator.

I'll be damned if that isn't Matt Knox's wife.

He tried to think of her name, but couldn't. He'd seen her before around town—was hard to forget her, too, with those looks—but she was definitely married to the Saint. With her husband working in a harbor business, you'd think she would know the parking rules, Jeremy thought. Or maybe it was just the opposite—she knew the rules but felt entitled to break them.

He watched her hike through a thin strip of landscaping plants to access a manicured footpath that led to the rear, street-facing facades of the Fisherman's Wharf section of the harbor. The entrances to these buildings was on the waterfront side along the Fisherman's Wharf walkway, which made it even more unusual for anyone to walk up to the back door of one of the places at night.

But that's what Knox's wife did.

Just as he was about to lean on the pathetic excuse for a horn that the cart had, she walked up to the rear door of one of the buildings, looked left, then right, and knocked.

Jeremy sucked his breath in a little when he looked at the sign above the business she had walked up to.

SANDY COVE MARITIME MUSEUM

What the–?

He could see her tapping her foot impatiently, then palming her cell and pecking at its glowing screen. Then the door opened and she looked up, smiled, put the phone back in her designer purse and stepped inside. He couldn't see who had let her in. He heard the sound of the door closing.

Jeremy exhaled deeply as he gripped the wheel of his still parked cart. As far as his paid duties were concerned, the fact that someone had entered the museum after being let inside was not by itself an issue. That that someone happened to be Mrs. Matt the Saint Knox, and that the museum happened to have been robbed with some involvement by her husband, however...

And Matt Knox had just collected the reward for finding and returning the stolen items!

Jeremy stepped from the cart and walked toward the museum. He was less noticeable on foot. Whatever was happening inside that museum was not his business as far as his new job was concerned, but the illegally parked BMW in back of the establishment was. That was his ticket, his excuse to go in there and check things out. He had to know what the Saint's wife was doing in there. Perhaps he could find a way inside without being heard. And if he was detected, he'd claim he just wanted to locate the owner of the beamer because a tow truck was on the way.

He considered the front entrance but decided against it. First of all it was actually more visible than the back, even though it wasn't on an actual road, because it faced the harbor. Some people lived on their boats and they would be able to see him there, not to mention the Harbor Patrol boat making the rounds. Also, the front doors were the obvious point of entry and more likely to be fortified. No, if he was going to make entry, it would have to be on this side. He checked for windows but saw none on this side, anyway.

He reached the back entrance and proceeded to walk around the BMW, pretending to inspect it for a parking violation. He couldn't write parking tickets himself, but he could have a vehicle towed. After putting on a sufficient show of security guard awareness, he walked up to the rear door. He put his ear to it but heard nothing. Gently, he tried the handle.

Locked.

Jeremy scratched his head while turning around to glance up and down the street. Still clear, but now what? The lock didn't concern him. Only the line that it represented. The line he was preparing to cross. A veteran cop knew a thing or two about urban preparedness. Jeremy removed his wallet and extracted a slim credit-card shaped container. He slid its top off and removed a couple of stainless steel tools—part of his lock-picking set.

He'd learned long ago as a policeman that it was best to be prepared for anything. Prepare for the worst, hope for the best. If he had a motto, that was probably it, he thought as he worked first one, and then the other of his implements into the lock.

The faint *click* produced in him a flash of satisfaction, one that was quickly eclipsed by the choice that now confronted him. His "just-trying-to-keep-you-from-getting-towed" cover story was thin at best, he realized. Anyone who worked in this building would know that the security guards don't have keys to the business establishments, and therefore that he must have gained entry illegally. He could say it was open, but anyone who was careful about security—such as a place that had been robbed not too long ago—would know that was horseshit.

But the situation was just too tempting. What was Knox's wife doing in there? Was Matt Knox in there, too? He had to find out. He owed it to Pablo. He owed it to Tommy. He owed it to himself.

With a last look around outside, harbor security guard Jeremy Washington slipped inside the Sandy Cove Maritime Museum.

-84-

TWO'S COMPANY

Jeremy stood stock still just inside the museum's rear entrance. The interior was very dimly lit, so much so that he considered using his tactical flashlight—small yet powerful—but decided against it. Instead he waited, allowing his eyesight to acclimate while listening. He wasn't sure what he expected to find in here, besides Matt Knox's wife and at least one other person, but silent emptiness was not it. He had considered that perhaps she was volunteering for a fundraiser to help the museum in its time of need or something like that, but there were no volunteer workers here busily endeavoring to raise money.

There seemed to be no one here at all. He peered down the short hallway out onto what used to be one of the main exhibit floors. He took a couple of tentative steps forward. He was not familiar with this part of the building. When he'd been here before with the insurance adjuster, he'd come in through the front entrance and barely saw the main entrance before being ushered out.

He took two more steps. He worried the old wood might creak but so far he tread silently. So quiet was the place that he was beginning to wonder if the wife and whoever let her in had already exited out the front entrance.

That's when he heard a noise—a *thud*—come from *above* him. He looked up but saw only the hallway ceiling. Then he heard a woman's voice. Talking loudly, not quite shouting, by the sound of it, but raising her voice. He couldn't make out the words.

Creeping to the end of the hallway, Jeremy looked around the main museum exhibit space. He saw only empty and broken display cases, some trash strewn about the floor. It didn't appear that any strides had been made toward reopening the museum. But from this vantage point he could clearly hear people from above.

He looked around the corner and saw a stairway that led to the museum's second floor. He'd been here before once or twice with his family and didn't recall any public areas up there. Conjuring a mental image of the building as it appeared across the way from the Fresh Catch, however, reminded him that there was indeed a second floor. Must be just office or storage.

A velvet rope attached to a pole stand was knocked over near the base of the stairs. Jeremy looked around at the main floor again—was there anybody down here? Seeing no one, he approached the bottom of the stairs. He could hear two voices now—the wife and also a male voice, coming from the second level. He slipped out of his shoes, carrying them in one hand, and slid silently across the floor in his socks until he reached the stairs.

He made out the first words: "...don't care if that's what you want!" This from the woman. He took advantage of the volume raise by taking the first couple of steps up. Would these old stairs creak? One did, very softly, but he doubted it could be heard. "..not what I wanted," he heard the male say as he ascended a few more steps. He didn't think it sounded like Knox, but couldn't yet be certain. He could see now that there was a landing about halfway up and then the stairway continued at a right angle.

"What else can I do?" the man said. Jeremy didn't know what the layout of the second floor was like, but judging from the sound of the voices the people were at the opposite end of the building from the top of the stairway. He made the landing and paused, looking up. He couldn't see over the top stair from here. What the hell would he do if they saw him? He actually feared for his safety a little, knowing that many people would shoot first and ask questions later were they to find someone in their building late at night.

But between the barest modicum of authority his security position gave him and the sense of duty to uncover the truth for his fallen friends, his desire to find out what was going on here outweighed his better judgment. He started up the second flight of stairs, hugging the left wall as he went. He removed his flashlight, thinking it made him look more security guard like, but kept it turned off. He could also hit someone with it if it came to that, he mused, taking another step.

When he reached the last two steps he got down on his hands and knees and crawled the rest of the way up until he could just see over the top step.

He held his breath as he scanned the scene stretching out before him. The area was much smaller than he'd expected—not a mirror of the first floor, but just a contained space suspended below the ceiling. He was looking at a simple yet nicely appointed office area. Oriental rugs on the old wooden floor, a roll-top wooden desk in the far corner, an antique brass telescope in a small alcove window on the far side of the space. A black canon mounted on wheels sat in front of a fireplace. Built-in bookshelves were lined with dusty tomes. A chandelier produced a dim glow from above, illuminating a wall lined with filing cabinets and chests of drawers on the right. Two crossed cutlasses, their blades etched with intricate engravings, were mounted on the wall over the fireplace.

Beneath these weapons stood Matt Knox's wife, her face etched with intricate expressions of concern. She pointed a finger at none other than Dallas Draper, who Jeremy recognized as the museum's owner. The two were by now engaged in heated conversation, staring each other down. Jeremy backed ever so slowly down the stairs so that his head was below their view. He didn't need to see any more at this point, just hear.

Jeremy heard Dallas' footfalls across the wooden floor and shrank back, tensing as he wondered if he'd make a turn toward the stairs. But the conversation continued and he remained safe for the time being.

"Dallas. Look at me. We had our moment, but it's over. I'm happy with Matt."

"I bet you are, now that he's got the fifty thousand reward, half of which came from me."

"Dallas! This has nothing to do with money. We're not rich but we have everything we need."

"You sure? Did you have everything you needed that weekend on my boat?"

"How dare you! Just forget about me and take a break down in Costa Rica like you've been planning."

Jeremy risked poking his head above the stairs. He caught a glimpse of Dallas standing in the middle of the office throwing both hands in the air, heard raised at the ceiling.

"What I've been planning is for *us* to go to Costa Rica, permanently. Move there. You and me. I thought we had something together, something real. I've gone to great lengths to provide for us down there. Come with me and you'll never need to work a day again if you don't want to, and neither will I. Just you, me, and paradise."

"What are you talking about, gone to great lengths? You said you inherited a rain forest bungalow from your father when he died, and that's where you've always planned to retire after the museum closes down."

A beat of silence ensued during which Jeremy held his breath. When Dallas spoke again it was in a softer voice.

"Well, the museum has closed down, hasn't it?"

"You're not going to reopen it? Matt turned in the stuff, you'll get it back!"

"Yeah, about that, Summer. I think it best if I make my way down there now, before things change too much for me here."

"What do you mean, right now?"

"Yeah. You see, I got a little greedy and things didn't go exactly the way I planned, partly due to your so-called saint of a husband."

"Greedy how?"

Jeremy heard Dallas make an audible inhalation. "I've had this museum for twenty-seven years. For a while it made a modest profit, then it broke even, but for the last five or six years it's been a real money pit. I beefed up the insurance policy on the place a few years back, in case anything ever happened to it. Since it's so old."

"Like what?"

"You know–fire, flood, theft. Earthquake."

"And you had a theft."

"Right, but it wasn't really a theft."

"Dallas, this doesn't sound good. Why are you telling me this?"

Jeremy heard Dallas' heavy footsteps cross the floor in Summer's direction. "Because I'm trying to explain how much you mean to me. I have gone to great lengths. I wanted to be able to take you with me to my Dad's old place in Costa Rica, not just on vacation but to live there, and to do that I'd need money."

Summer made some kind of snorting sound. "Dallas, that's outrageous! I never gave you any kind of signals like that. We had a little fling, I never said I wanted to move in with you, much less repatriate to Costa Rica. What about my kids, you never took that into consideration!"

"They could come with! Plenty of room on the homestead. Think of the one-of-a-kind cultural experience they'll have growing up! Spanish. Rain forest ecology. Pristine beaches. What else do they need?"

"They need their father."

"I'm not so sure they do."

"What the hell's that supposed to mean?"

"I was trying to tell you—I don't think you know your husband as well as you think you do."

"Never mind him. I'm starting to think I don't know *you* as well as I thought I did. What happened with your insurance?"

Jeremy wished he'd had the foresight to bring a voice recorder along. This was getting interesting.

"I wanted out from under this place now so that I could retire to the hacienda, and hopefully take you with me. Tried for a while but couldn't find a buyer who'd give me anywhere near what the place is worth. So I started thinking about the insurance money and how to get it—an accidental fire, maybe. But then this guy Sal, a gang-banger from around town—"

"The one I saw dead the other day on the news?"

"Yeah, I had nothing to do with that but that's him. Anyway, he did some work for one of my fishing buddy's boats and we got to talking. I told him if he'd rob the place, he could have the stuff, I just wanted the insurance money."

"And he went for that."

"Yeah, except he did something I wasn't expecting, which was to bring your husband into it."

"Matt?"

"Yes, you mean you don't know? Matt never told you Sal forced him to rob the museum?"

"Nooooo. No way. I don't believe that for one second! Anyway, if the stuff was returned I guess the gang didn't make any money? And what about the fake stuff that the police thought was real?"

Silence.

"Dallas?"

"I got greedy and figured, hey, if I'm bugging out to Central America, I'll never be back here again so why not go for broke. So the night before Sal was supposed to rob the place I switched out all the museum goods with high quality fakes."

"So Sal—and Matt—stole fake stuff?"

"That's right."

"So you planned to collect the insurance money for your stolen stuff, *and* you still had the real stuff?"

"That was the plan. But somehow your saintly husband found the real stuff and turned it in for the reward. Still not sure exactly how he did that."

"Dallas, that's terrible! Tricking everyone like that with fakes, how could you?"

"I did it for you. For *us*. I still care about you even if you don't want to be with me, Summer. You've got to listen to me. Matt has *four* guns: two that look antique but are as reliable as modern firearms—those are the fakes I switched out that he ended up with. But then he has the other two that'll randomly explode almost as often as they work. Those are the real deal that he also must have ended up with because they're the only articles that weren't turned in along with the rest of the stuff! So he has four of them. I'm concerned, Summer."

"About what, your scheme backfiring on you?"

"About you. About being alone with him."

"What? Why?"

"Summer, sit down. I don't want to scare you. But I saw the picture of Sal's face when he was found dead. I also saw Pablo's. They look like they could have been shot with a musket. That means—"

"Oh, please. He's a saint! Don't say something you can't take back."

"If I'm wrong I'll apologize later. If I'm not wrong I may not get the chance."

"It's over between us, Dallas."

Jeremy heard the staccato rhythm of her heels stalk across the floor. He tensed, ready to move.

Dallas called after her. "If you change your mind you can always join me in Costa Rica. Come stay for a while. Promise me you'll do it if you don't feel safe?"

"I won't be going to Costa Rica, Dallas."

And that was when Jeremy heard the front door of the museum open.

-85-

THREE'S A CROWD

Jeremy didn't hear a key turning. Just the door handle clicking, then the door being pushed back into its frame. Perhaps the front door had been unlocked? Whatever the case, the conversation between Dallas and Knox's wife carried on so it didn't seem like they noticed anyone had entered.

And then a voice called out from the first floor.

"Summer?"

The conversation above him quickly devolved into a flurry of indecipherable whispering and then ceased. Jeremy heard footsteps quickening below. Approaching the stairs. He recognized the voice as it called out a second time.

"Summer! You okay?"

It was Matt Knox.

Jeremy raised his head for a look over the stairs. Dallas and Summer stood face to face, Summer shaking her hands free of his grasp. "I will not hide! Obviously he knows I'm here.

"How the hell did he know that?"

"I don't know. He must have followed me."

"Shit." Dallas scratched his head, then repeated his oath.

"Matt, I'm fine," Summer yelled. "Up here, second floor."

Jeremy could hear Matt's feet pounding up the first half of the stairway. A few more steps and he'd be to the landing dividing the top half from the bottom. Jeremy's policeman sense told him that caught in the middle of a lover's triangle—especially when two of the three had been committing serious criminal acts, was not a safe place to be. He'd rather take his chances up there with Dallas and Summer than surprise Matt the Saint and be on the receiving end of whatever *that* reaction might be.

Jeremy flashed on his mental image of the second floor layout. *Ottoman or something a few feet in, left side.* It might conceal him for a little while. He wormed his way over the top stair (sneaked a quick glance at the lovelorn couple who thankfully faced mostly the other way and were still arguing in hushed tones) onto the floor and belly crawled to the low-lying furniture piece. Jeremy slithered underneath it— he was grateful that it had solid wooden end pieces which were oriented such that his body would be concealed as one came over the stairs.

"I think it's time you made a choice, Summer!" Dallas said, as Jeremy ensconced himself beneath the furniture. His was a ridiculous position to be in, but here he was. There was nothing he could do at this point but to go on. The lovers' quarrel shaping up seemed to be distracting them from noticing him.

But Matt Knox was stepping into the room.

"Summ—*Dallas*? What's going on here?"

Jeremy slowly drew one of his feet further inside the outline of the furniture piece.

"I said what the fuck is going on, damn it!"

Dallas and Summer both spoke at once and it was unintelligible.

"I came to—" Summer started, but was overrode by Dallas.

"She's having an affair. With me."

The words stunned even Matt, who stopped moving and talking. Jeremy held his breath on the floor.

"No he's *not*!" Summer shouted.

"What else would you call our time together then? You're just afraid of him, afraid of what he might do to you if he finds out. But I'm not. I won't let him hurt you." Dallas said. He took a step away from the fireplace, where he had been standing beneath the wall-mounted head of a massive narwhal, its unicorn-like tusk protruding just over his head.

"What time together?" Matt Knox walked deeper into the room as he said this, stepping into Jeremy's field of vision from the waist down. Jeremy felt his skin grow taut as he saw Matt hitch up the sweatshirt he'd been wearing to reveal a two gun leather holster worn around the waist, like those seen in old western movies. Jeremy could see the handle of one of the pirate pistols protruding from the side he had a view of, and he could only assume that its twin occupied the opposite holster.

"The time on my boat, the time in my house the—*hey are those my guns?* Summer, call 911. Now!"

Jeremy was shocked at how fast the situation was escalating beyond all semblance of control. Even armed with his service pistol, he'd have been nervous. As it was all he had was the flashlight and a miniscule keychain folding knife, which at the moment was awkwardly placed in his front left pocket. He forced himself to stay calm and breathe deeply but silently.

"Dallas, it's okay. Matt, honey, let's go home. I'll explain everything to you there. And who's watching the kids?! Did you get a sitter?"

"God's watching the kids. Why don't you just explain it to me now?" Matt stopped walking and stood in the middle of the room.

Jeremy saw Dallas' legs in motion as he crossed the room to his desk. "You're scaring me, Matt," Summer said.

"Summer, the kids are fine. Dallas, don't move!" Matt commanded.

"Fuck you, I'm calling the police." Dallas took another step toward his desk and then Matt drew one of his guns and pointed it at him.

"I said, *stop*. Don't move."

Dallas halted.

"Matt, what are you doing? Is that real?"

"It's real," Dallas said. "He found it with the museum things but obviously didn't turn it in with the rest of the stuff."

"Put that down, Matt," Summer said to her husband. To Jeremy it seemed like she was completely underestimating the reality of the situation. She had the same tone of voice a wife might use for nagging her husband not to leave the toilet seat up or for leaving the TV remote in a weird place.

"Did you have sex with this fat schlub, Summer?"

Then Jeremy heard the scrape of a flint. He thought Matt had fired his weapon but the spark that blossomed in Dallas' hand told him otherwise. It was only a Bic lighter. But as Dallas stooped low with the wavering flame, Jeremy's vantage point was the best in the room.

The iron cannon on wheels that was the room's informal centerpiece began to crackle with light as Dallas touched the open flame to a short wick. It seemed unbelievable, but it looked to Jeremy as though Dallas had already had the cannon pre-loaded with ball and powder. *What kind of guy keeps a loaded cannon sitting in his office, just in case*, Jeremy started to think but he never completed his reflection.

A concussive blast rocked the museum's second floor as the cannon detonated. The sharp tang of cordite spread through the room along with a puff of smoke. Being low to the ground, Jeremy's view was smoke free. He heard Summer whimpering—she'd been hit in the shins by the cannon's wheeled base when its recoil sent it reeling backwards.

But it was Matt Knox who commanded his attention. He'd been hit by the cannon ball—or grazed, Jeremy thought, since his leg was still there—but part of his upper thigh had been sheared away, leaving a bloody hole in his jeans that resembled a marbled steak. He stood stock still, one of his pistols still leveled at Dallas while he used his other hand to tenderly trace the contours and depths of his wound.

"I don't think Tylenol's going to fix that, you stupid fuck," Dallas said, now out of sight somewhere behind the desk.

"You a medical doctor now, Dallas?" Matt said, taking a step forward. He winced with the effort, but took one more step.

Outside they could hear loud voices.

"You shot a hole in your own precious museum, Dallas," Matt said. "Cannon ball went clean through the wall of this old place and landed out there somewhere. You could have just killed somebody–how's that make you feel, buddy? Will that satisfy your little midlife crisis or thirst for adventure or whatever the fuck you're looking for enough to stay the hell away from my wife?"

They heard more shouting coming from outside, no distinct words.

"Because if it didn't..." Matt raised his pistol even though he couldn't see Dallas. "...this might."

"Matt, honey, you need to get to the hospital. I'll drive you. Put the gun down."

"I had no idea you had thing with Dallas, babe. How long's that been going on for?"

"I'm not talking to you, Matt, until you put down the gun. Please."

Matt squeezed the trigger and Summer let out a yelp. The corner of the desk Dallas hid behind exploded in a spray of particle board.

"Matt stop! Stop it, please!"

Jeremy tensed, wondering if now was the time to make a move. He could try to tackle Knox and at least disarm him before more shots were fired–but he didn't see how Matt wouldn't notice him when he sidled out from under the ottoman. He felt helpless just laying here, and compounding that was the fact that with a cannon ball being shot through the wall down into the harbor somewhere, unless it had plopped harmlessly into the water, there was a good chance that people would be looking for Security right about now.

Great, I'm gonna be shit-canned from this job, too.

"Lookout, Summer. Out of my way." Matt crossed the room with his pistol extended, giving the desk a wide berth. After the canon stunt, who knows what other tricks Dallas might have up his sleeve? Summer grabbed his arm but he sidestepped away from her, never taking his eyes off the desk.

Without warning he tried to kick the desk backwards, catching the wooden lip and titling it up on two legs, but his wounded leg couldn't support the move. Gravity pulled the desk back to the floor and they heard Dallas grunt. Believing his cover about to be upended, the museum curator crab-walked away from the desk. He turned and broke into a run, making a grab for some kind of tropical islander spear, decorated with exotic feathers, hanging on the wall.

He had just wrapped his fingers around the weapon when Matt the Saint Knox shot him in the side of the head with his pistol.

Summer's shrieking rent the air as what remained of Dallas Draper's face slid from his head. The big man was still alive, though, trying to stand while sputtering, "What happened? Can't see. What happened?" Due to his injuries his words weren't that clear, but that only made what he said that much more terrifying.

"Aw duh ights ood? Rummer? Heeee, Ruuuuuumm-"

Matt Knox clubbed him about his sopping head, raining down four or five quick but hard-hitting blows that found their way through the goop into whatever part of Dallas' brain was still sending out signals to the rest of his body. He said nothing while he did it, just went about his business like a man with a job to do. An unpleasant job, but a job nonetheless.

Summer collapsed to her knees on the floor, clawing at the old boards in sobbing hysterics, while Matt released his hold on Dallas' body and took a step back as the bloody corpse slumped to the floor.

Neither Matt nor Summer noticed a figure slowly rise behind them.

-86-
DO KNOW HARM

Jeremy Washington. The policeman. The citizen. The husband. The father. The security guard. The hidden one.

He stood. There was no hiding from this. He would neutralize the monstrosity the Saint had become or else he would be in hiding the rest of his life from the knowledge that he had done nothing.

He had no weapon. Didn't need one. He was the weapon. He saw the Saint rise from Dallas' bloody carcass and he flung himself over the desk and into Matt the Saint's torso, tucking his head as he did so in a move reminiscent of his high school football days— long ago days when he had yet to truly know the human capacity for harm.

Matt reflexively jerked an elbow backwards, catching Jeremy hard in the ribs, cracking one. The blow knocked him backwards and he tried to grab Matt's forearm to take him down with him but it was slick with blood and he couldn't hold on.

"Run Summer!" Jeremy yelled. "Get out, call 911!"

But she only lay on the floor in a sobbing heap.

"Don't you do it if you want to keep those good looks, Summer," Matt Knox called to her.

Jeremy got a hand on the spear Dallas had knocked to the floor and snatched it up, but as he did so Matt shoved him into the desk. Jeremy maintained his grip on the spear. He lashed out with the butt end of it—the only way he could from his position on the floor—but Matt dodged it and the stick jammed into the wall.

Jeremy's eyes caught on one of Matt's blunderbusses lying on the floor within arm's reach but he saw the blood on the butt end and knew it was the one Matt had used to first shoot and then bludgeon Dallas to death with. The good thing for Jeremy about Matt's firearms of choice was that they could only be fired once before reloading. With one gun already spent, it meant that Matt only had one shot remaining.

That gun rode in the holster on Matt's side that was farthest from Jeremy. He assumed it to be primed and ready but had no way to tell for sure. Judging by the way Matt kept reaching for it, though, between attempts at stiff-arming Jeremy—it was likely ready to fire.

A fresh volley of kicking and hitting ensued between the two men. Jeremy felt warm blood trickle form his nose and a sharp pain between two of the knuckles on his right hand where he'd connected with Matt's teeth, but he kept his eye on Matt's remaining gun and kept fighting. Dimly registering in his consciousness was Summer still crying on the floor. She was no help. Then Matt's voice brought an extra dimension to the battle.

"You're a—" he struggled for breath as his hand slid from Jeremy's shoulder. "Security guard! Should have told me, might have had a job for you at the shop after all." He laughed while he pushed Jeremy into the desk, sliding it along the floor with a scraping noise. Jeremy kicked him in his thigh wound. Matt spun around, a sucking sound issuing from his lips. As he did Jeremy saw the loaded blunderbuss come within reach on Matt's hip and he made a grab for it.

Jeremy's right hand snaked out and snatched the antique weapon by the handle. The catch was already undone and it slid easily from it holster. Just as it came free, however, Matt recovered enough to bring an arm up in a karate chop slicing motion into the underside of Jeremy's wrist bone that caused the gun to fly upwards.

Both men tried to push the other away from the airborne weapon but neither succeeded. The gun landed between them trapped between their chests and arms. Matt twisted and writhed and Jeremy felt the gun slip from his fingers. He knew he'd made a mistake as Matt wrested the gun from him and reached back with it pointed at his assailant's face. Jeremy gave a guttural yell as he stared down the barrel that was just out of reach.

As if in a dream, he registered voices coming upstairs now, feet pounding their way up to the second floor. But they would be too late to help him.

There was only the black hole of the barrel. And Matt's hand, sliding through the air in what seemed like slow motion on a collision course with the blunderbusses' hammer. Matt's other hand had Jeremy pinned against the desk by his neck. Jeremy wagged his head back and forth violently but couldn't shake free of the pistol's sights.

This is it, Jeremy thought. And then he had time for no more thoughts. Matt's open palm brushed over the tip of the blunderbusses' hammer.

Click.

The whole room seemed to be swallowed whole by that hollow sound. Even Matt Knox froze, and Summer stopped crying. Jeremy could read the surprise in Matt's eyes plain as day, though. That gun was loaded, it just hadn't fired.

Before Jeremy could register what happened, Matt had replaced the gun in his hand with the spear. Matt jammed one foot into Jeremy's chest, pinning him to the floor while he raised the spear in a two-handed grip reminiscent of one of the tribal ceremonies it was once intended for.

Jeremy stared at the sharpened wooden tip that was poised to rip apart his face and shatter his skull. He felt Matt's shoe press even harder into his chest. His hand flailed about on the floor, seeking something, anything that might help him—perhaps a leg of the desk he could use as leverage to pull out from under his assailant. He caught a splinter deep in a finger as his hand slid across the wooden floor just before it came into contact with something heavy that moved.

"Should have minded your own damn business, Washington."

Jeremy's bloody fingers wrapped around what he instantly recognized as the handle of Matt's blunderbuss. The one that didn't fire—the original historical piece. Jeremy raised it from the floor while he tried to block out Matt's words in order to focus.

"That's the trouble with you cops—even though you're off the force you're still a fucking pig, you can't fool me. Once one of them, always one of them."

"That's right."

Matt narrowed his eyes as Jeremy's reply seemed to have caught him off guard. But not for long.

"Off to the slaughterhouse, pig." Matt the Saint inhaled deeply and raised the spear an inch higher while flexing his good leg.

And then Jeremy raised the blunderbuss and pointed it at Matt Knox's chest. Matt started his downward swing with the spear. For a fraction of a second Jeremy's brain registered the sound of people reaching the top of the stairs, but instantly dismissed it as being unimportant if he was to live. Jeremy reacted the only way he knew how. He pulled the trigger of the old pirate pistol.

And this time it went off.

-EPILOGUE-

3 MONTHS LATER

Jeremy Washington pulled his patrol car off the side of the road into the cover of some bushes that were even more overgrown than he remembered them. He waited. From his partially concealed vantage point he had a commanding view of the intersection ahead. He aimed his radar gun at the four-way and clocked vehicles as they drove through.

Speed limit...Five mph under the speed limit...Five over, not worth the trouble... Jeremy cracked a smile as he eased into the rhythm of his old job again. He hadn't yet been assigned a partner—he suspected they knew how difficult it would be for him to work with a anyone besides Tommy—but that would come. Two weeks after being reinstated and it was just beginning to seem real again.

He hadn't applied on his own volition. A letter had just appeared in his mailbox one day, from the City of Sandy Cove and signed by the mayor and the Chief of Police, thanking him for his good deeds as a citizen in uncovering the crimes of Matt Knox and for going through the "trying ordeal" that ended the threat of what some were calling the beach town's first ever serial killer. The letter had closed by inviting Jeremy to apply for reinstatement to his former position with the police department.

Jeremy set his speed gun down as the light turned red. *Back on the force with a ten percent raise.* He pictured Alisa's face when he'd told her the news. The happiest he'd seen her in a long time. He felt like he was home again...

He watched a car pull up to the intersection and stop. The driver, white male—late twenties/early thirties, Jeremy automatically registered—looked around and then accelerated through the red light.

Jeremy sighed. *That was no biggie—the driver came to a stop first and looked both ways and saw there was nobody coming before he ran it.* There was no way to tell if he's really a good guy at heart doing a random bad thing, or if he's a bad guy just adding another link to his bad guy chain.

Jeremy flipped on his siren and flashers and put his car into gear. The truth was it didn't matter, because the law is clear. You can't do what he just did. And Jeremy's job was to uphold the law. His world was as black and white as the squad car he drove. There were lawbreakers and there were law abiders. At any given moment you were either one or you were the other.

Jeremy caught up with the driver, pulled him over and wrote him a ticket. He watched the guy drive off, like a fish caught and released to swim the waters again until its dumb animal instinct caused it to be netted once more.

And then even though there was no emergency, Jeremy himself proceeded to make a U-turn and drive through the same red light he just ticketed the guy for. After a while he veered off the road and took a more circuitous route through Sandy Cove. His shift was nearly over and it was time to head home. As he drove past rows of upscale houses, he tried to look into them, through them, wondering at all the laws being broken right now behind those very walls, all of the evil plots being hatched--some of them out of cruelty or greed or momentary lapses of judgment—others borne of unadulterated desperation, but all of them winding their way inexorably, inescapably, inevitably right to him.

Jeremy Washington forged on toward the harbor as if he could drag the town's every illicit scheme, every conniving design, every unsavory strategy and sleazy contrivance with him to the water's edge where the blood red sun would dissolve along with them into the still liquid. That wouldn't happen, though, and he knew it.

But tomorrow was another day on the job.

Photo credit: Tabbatha Chesler

RICK CHESLER holds a Bachelor of Science in marine biology and has had a life-long interest in the ocean, its creatures, and the people that call it their home. He currently lives in the Florida Keys with his wife and son. Visit him at rickchesler.com.

Also by Rick Chesler:

Tara Shores Thriller Series
Wired Kingdom
kiDNApped
Solar Island

www.ingramcontent.com/pod-product-compliance
Lightning Source LLC
Chambersburg PA
CBHW021409110726
47901CB00008B/2123